Jessica Sorensen lives in Wyoming with her husband and three children. She is the author of numerous romance novels. All of her New Adult novels have been *New York Times* and ebook bestsellers.

Keep in contact with Jessica:

jessicasorensensblog.blogspot.co.uk
Facebook/Jessica Sorensen
@jessFallenStar

Praise for
Jessica Sorensen

Breaking Nova

'*Breaking Nova* touches the heart and squeezes the most powerful emotions from your body . . . one of those books that pushes you to the limits and makes you feel things you never thought you would feel for characters'
UndertheCoversBookBlog.com

'*Breaking Nova* is one of those books that just sticks with you. I was thinking about it when I wasn't reading it, wondering what was going to happen with Nova . . . an all-consuming, heartbreaking story'
BooksLiveForever.com

'Heartbreaking, soul-shattering, touching, and unforgettable
. . . Jessica Sorenson is an amazingly talented author'
ABookishEscape.com

Nova and Quinton: No Regrets

'Totally consumed me . . . heart-wrenching . . . [Sorensen]
is masterful when it comes to dealing with the hard
issues life throws your way'
LiteratiBookReviews.com

'Torn, twisted, and beautiful are the best words I can use
to describe this story. Jessica Sorensen has taken her talent
on a new level with this one'
LittleReadRidingHood.com

'It just dug into my heart . . . This book was more
than entertainment for me; it was a lesson in life . . . Five
stars and highly recommended!'
TheBoyfriendBookmark.com

'This series goes down as one of my all-time favorites . . . It
was definitely heartbreaking to read some parts, but oh so
worth it . . . I can't recommend this enough'
TheBookHookup.com

Saving Quinton

'This story pulls at so many emotions and is written so
well . . . I would recommend this to anyone looking for
a gut-wrenching yet very realistic book full of hope
and second chances'
DarkFaerieTales.com

The Secret of Ella and Micha

'Heart-breaking, heart-stopping and heart-warming, I couldn't put it down once I started reading'
onemorepage.co.uk

'The steamy hot relationship is something you won't forget . . . intriguing and unforgettable'
neverjudgeabookbyitscover.co.uk

'The sultry, tense atmosphere is supported by interesting characters . . . I loved their chemistry and I was championing them from the start'
solittletimeforbooks.co.uk

'A beautiful love story . . . complicated yet gorgeous characters . . . I am excited to read more of her books'
SerendipityReviews.co.uk

'A really great love story. There is something epic about it . . . If you haven't jumped on this new adult bandwagon, then you need to get with the program. I can see every bit of why this story has swept the nation'
TheSweetBookShelf.com

Breaking Nova

JESSICA SORENSEN

SPHERE

First published in Great Britain in 2014 by Sphere

Copyright © 2014 Jessica Sorensen

A CIP catalogue record for this book
is available from the British Library.

ISBN 978-0-7515-5533-2

Printed and bound in Great Britain by Clays Ltd, St Ives plc

Papers used by Sphere are from well-managed forests
and other responsible sources.

MIX
Paper from
responsible sources
FSC® C104740

Sphere
An imprint of
Little, Brown Book Group
100 Victoria Embankment
London EC4Y 0DY

An Hachette UK Company
www.hachette.co.uk

www.littlebrown.co.uk

*For anyone who's ever felt lost and struggled
to find their way back.*

Acknowledgments

A huge thanks to my agent, Erica Silverman, and my editor, Amy Pierpont. I'm forever grateful for all your help and input.

To my family, thank you for supporting me and my dream. You guys have been wonderful. And to everyone who reads this book, an endless amount of thank yous.

Breaking Nova

Prologue

Nova

Sometimes I wonder if there are some memories the mind doesn't want to deal with and that if it really wants to, it can block out the images, shut down, numb the pain connected to what we saw—what we didn't want to see. If we allow it to, the numbness can drown out everything, even the spark of life inside us. And eventually the person we once were is nothing but a vanishing memory.

I didn't always used to think this way. I used to have hope. I used to believe in things. Like when my father told me if I wanted something bad enough that I could make it happen.

"No one else in the world can make things happen for you, Nova," he'd said while we were lying on our backs on the hill in our backyard, staring up at the stars. I was six and happy and a little naïve, eating his words up like handfuls of sugar. "But if you want something bad enough and are willing to work hard at it, then anything's possible."

1

"Anything?" I'd said, turning my head toward him. "Even if I want to be a princess?"

He smiled, looking genuinely happy. "Even a princess."

I grinned, looking up at the sky, thinking how wonderful it would be to wear a diamond tiara on my head and a sparkly pink dress and matching heels. I would spin around in circles and laugh as my dress spun with me. Never once did I think about what it truly meant to be a princess and how impossible it was for me to actually become one.

"Earth to Nova." My boyfriend, Landon Evans, waves his hand in front of my face.

I blink my gaze away from the stars and angle my head sideways along the bottom of the grassy hill in his backyard, looking him in the eyes. "What's up?"

He laughs at me, but his smile looks unnatural, like it doesn't belong there. But that's normal for Landon. He's an artist, and he tells me that in order to portray pain in his portraits he has to carry it within him all the time. "You were totally spacing off on me there." The front porch light is on, and the fluorescent glow makes his honey-brown eyes look like the charcoal he uses for his sketchings.

I roll on my side and tuck my hands underneath my head, so I can really look at him. "Sorry, I was just thinking."

"You have that look on your face, like you're thinking deep." He rotates on his hip and props his elbow up on the ground, resting his head against his palm. Wisps of his inky-black hair fall into his eyes. "Want to talk about it?"

I shake my head. "No, I don't really feel like talking."

He offers me a trivial but genuine smile, and the sadness in my mind fleetingly dissolves. It's one of the things that I love about Landon. He's the only person on this planet who can make me smile—except for my dad, but he's no longer alive anymore, so smiles are rare in my book.

Landon and I were best friends up until about six months ago, and maybe that's why he can make me happy. We got to bond on a deeper level and understand each other before all the kissing and hormones came along. I know we're only eighteen and haven't even graduated high school yet, but sometimes, when I'm alone in my room, I can picture him and me together years ahead, in love, maybe getting married. It's surprising because for a long time after my dad died, I couldn't picture my future—I didn't want to. But things change. People evolve. Move on. Grow as new people enter their lives.

"I saw the picture you drew for the art project," I say, brushing some of the hair out of his eyes. "It was hanging up on Mr. Felmon's wall."

He frowns, which he always does whenever we're talking about his art. "Yeah, it didn't turn out how I planned."

"It seemed like you were sad when you were drawing it," I tell him, lowering my hand to my hip. "But all your drawings do."

Any happiness in his expression withers as he rolls onto his back and pinpoints his attention to the star-cut sky. He's silent for a while and I turn onto my back, letting him be, knowing

3

that he's stuck in his own head. Landon is one of the saddest people I've met, and it's part of what drew me to him.

I was thirteen, and he'd just moved in across the street from me. He was sitting against the tree in his front yard, scribbling in a sketchbook, when I first saw him and decided to go over and introduce myself. It was right after my dad had died, and I'd pretty much kept my distance from people. But with Landon, I don't know, there was just something about him.

I'd crossed the street, very curious about what he was drawing. When I stopped in front of him, he glanced up at me, and I was taken aback by how much anguish was in his honey-brown eyes—the torture and internal suffering. I'd never seen so much of it in anyone my age before, and even though I didn't know what was causing it, I guessed we were going to be friends. He looked how I felt inside, like I'd been broken apart and the pieces hadn't healed correctly. Just like I guessed, we did become best friends—more than best friends, actually. We're almost inseparable, addicted to each other, and I absolutely hate being away from him because I feel lost and misplaced in the world whenever he's gone.

"Do you ever get the feeling that we're all just lost?" Landon utters, jerking me away from my thoughts again. "Just roaming around the earth, waiting around to die."

I bite on my lip, considering what he said as I find Cassiopeia in the sky. "Is that what you really think?"

"I'm not sure," he answers, and I turn my head, analyzing

4

his perfect profile. "I sometimes wonder, though, what the point of life is." He stops, and it feels like he's waiting for me to say something.

"I'm not sure." I rack my brain for something else to add. But I can't think of a single coherent, reasonable response to his dark thoughts on the meaning of life, so I add, "I love you."

"I love you too, Nova," he promises without looking at me, then he reaches across the grass and grabs my hand, twining his fingers through mine. "And I mean that, Nova, no matter what. I love you."

We get lost in the stillness of the night while we watch the stars glimmer and fade. It's peaceful but unsettling at the same time, because I can't turn my thoughts off. I worry about him when he gets depressed like this. It's like he goes into his own little world that's carved of gloomy thoughts and a blackened future, and I can't reach him no matter how hard I try.

We lie quietly, watching the stars and holding on to each other. Eventually, I drift to sleep with my face pressed against the cool grass, the spring breeze chilly against my skin, and Landon's fingers soothingly stroking the inside of my wrist. When I wake up again, all the stars have blended in with the grayness of morning, the moon is tucked away in the glow of daybreak, and the grass is damp with dew. The first thing I notice is that Landon's hand is missing from mine, and it makes me feel empty, like one of my arms has been detached from my body.

I sit up, rubbing my eyes then stretching my arms above

my head as I glance around the backyard, searching for Landon. The only thing I can think of is that he got up to go to the bathroom, because he would never leave me sleeping on the hill alone in his backyard.

I push to my feet and brush the grass off the back of my legs before hiking up the hill toward his two-story house at the top of the backyard. It seems like a really long walk, because I'm tired—it's too early in the morning to be up. When I reach the back porch, I take my phone from my pocket to text Landon and see what he's doing. But I notice the back door is cracked, and I find myself walking inside, which is a little out of character for me. It's not like I'm used to walking into his house without being let in. I always knock, even when he texts me and tells me to come straight up to his room.

But this time, something begs my feet to step over the threshold. It's cold inside the kitchen, and I wonder how long the back door has been open. Shivering, I wrap my arms around myself and cross the entryway to the kitchen. Landon's parents are asleep upstairs, so I make sure to walk quietly, heading downstairs to Landon's room, which is in the basement. The stairs creak underneath my shoes, and I hold my breath the entire way down, not sure what will happen if his parents wake up and catch me sneaking down to his room.

"Landon," I whisper as I walk toward his bedroom. It's dark, except for the spark of the sunlight through the windows. "Are you down here?"

Silence is the only answer, and I almost turn around and

go back upstairs. But then I hear the lyrics of an unknown song playing softly from somewhere in the house. I head for his bedroom door, and the music gets louder.

"Landon," I say as I approach his closed door, my nerves bubbling inside me. I don't know why I feel nervous. Or maybe I do. Maybe I've known for a long time, but I never wanted to accept it.

My hand trembles as I turn the knob. When I push the door open, every single word Landon's ever said to me suddenly makes sense to me. As the powerful lyrics playing from the stereo wrap around me, so does an undying chill. My hand falls lifeless to my side and I stand in the doorway, unblinking. I keep wishing for what I'm seeing to go away, to disappear from my mind, to erase the memories. I wish and wish—*will* it to happen—telling myself that if I want it badly enough, it'll happen. I start to count backward, focusing on the pattern and rhythm of the numbers, and after a few minutes, numbness swallows my heart. Just like I wanted, my surroundings fade and I can't feel anything.

I fall to the floor, hitting it hard, but I can't feel the pain . . .

Quinton

I'm driving way too fast. I know that and I know I should slow down, but everyone's complaining for me to hurry up and get them home. They're worried we're going to miss our curfew. Sometimes I wonder how I get myself into these kinds of messes. It's not like it's a big deal, but I'd probably be having a lot more fun if I was wasted with the rest of them, because it's spring break and I should be having fun. I'm not a fan of being the designated driver, but I usually end up offering to be one, and now I'm stuck driving around a bunch of drunken idiots.

"Stop smoking in here." I roll down the window as smoke begins to fill up the car. "My mom will smell it from a mile away, and then she's not going to let me drive her car anymore."

"Oh come on, Quinton," my girlfriend, Lexi, pouts as she takes a deep drag off her cigarette, then extends her arm out the open window. "We'll air it out."

Shaking my head, I reach over with my free hand and snatch the cigarette from her. "No more smoking." I hold the cigarette out my cracked window until the cherry falls off, then release the rest out into the night. It's late, the road we're driving on is windy and curves around a lake, and we haven't seen a car in ages. It's good, though, since everyone else in the car is underage and drunk out of their minds.

Lexi sticks out her lip and crosses her arms over her chest, slumping back in her seat. "You're so boring when you're sober."

I press back a grin. We've been dating for a couple of years now, and she's the only girl I've ever been with and can ever see myself being with. I know it sounds superlame and cheesy because we're only eighteen, but I'm seriously going to end up marrying her.

Still pouting, she slides her hand up my thigh until she

reaches my cock, then she gives it a good rub. "Does that feel good? Because I'll keep doing it if you just let me smoke."

I try not to laugh at her, because she's wasted and it'll probably piss her off, but it's funny how annoyed she's getting by my soberness. "And you're feisty and pouty when you're drunk." I squirm as she hits the right spot and fight not to shut my eyelids. "But I'm still not going to let you smoke in the car."

She rolls her eyes, draws her hand away from me, and glances in the backseat, where my cousin Ryder is making out with some guy she met at the party. Their hands are all over each other. I'm not a fan of hanging out with her, but she comes out to Seattle sometimes and stays with my grandma. Lexi and Ryder became best friends during one of her visits when they were about twelve, and they've been inseparable ever since, which is pretty much how I met Lexi.

When Lexi looks away, her nose is scrunched. "So gross."

I decelerate the car for a sharp corner in the road. "Oh, don't pretend like you don't wish it was you and me back there." I wink at her and she rolls her eyes. "You know you do."

She sighs and lets her arms fall to her lap. "Yeah, right. If we were back there and I was trying to stick my tongue down your throat, you'd totally be like"—she makes air quotes—" 'Lexi, please, there are people in the front seat who can see us.' "

"You're making me sound like an old man." I flash a playful grin at her as I downshift the car and the engine roars. The road is getting windier, and I have to slow down.

"You kind of are."

"Bullshit. I'm fucking fun as hell."

"No, you're nice as hell, Quinton Carter. You're seriously like the nicest guy I know, but the most fun? I'm not sure…" A conniving look crosses her face as she taps her finger against her lip. "How about we find out?" Without taking her eyes off me, she rolls the window down the rest of the way. The wind howls inside and blows her hair into her face.

"What the hell?" Ryder says from the backseat, jerking her lips away from the guy's, and plucks strands of her hair out of her mouth. "Lexi, roll up the damn window. I'm eating my own hair here."

"So Mr. Fucking Fun as Hell," Lexi says, with her eyes on me as she arches her back and moves her head toward the window. "Let's find out just how fun you are."

I don't like where she's going with this. She's too drunk, and even sober she's always been a daredevil, impulsive and a little bit reckless. "Lexi, what are you doing? Get in here. I don't want you to get hurt."

A lazy smile spreads across her lips as she sticks her head farther out the window. The pale glow of the moon hits her chest and makes her skin look ghostly against the darkness. "I want to see just how fun you are, Quinton." She extends her arms above her head as she slides up onto the windowsill. "I want to see how much you love me."

"Quinton, make her stop," Ryder says, scooting forward in the seat. "She's going to hurt herself."

"Lexi, stop it," I warn, gripping onto the steering wheel

with one hand and reaching for her with my other. "I love you and that's why I need you to get down. *Right now.*"

She shakes her head. I can't see her face or if she's not holding onto anything. I have no idea what the hell she's doing or thinking, and I'm pretty sure she doesn't, either, and it's fucking terrifying.

"If you're so fun, then just let me be free," she calls out. Her dress is blowing up over her legs and her feet are tucked down between the seat and the door.

Ryder lifts her leg to climb over into the front seat, but smacks her head on the roof and falls back. Shaking my head, I gently tap on the brakes as I lean over in the seat to grab Lexi. My fingers snag the bottom of Lexi's dress and that's when I hear the scream. Seconds later, the car is spinning out of control, and I don't know what's up or what's down. Shards of glass fly everywhere and cut at my arms and face as I try to hold onto Lexi's dress. But I feel the fabric leave my fingers as I'm jarred to the side. Everyone is screaming and crying as metal crunches and bends. I see bright lights, feel the warmth of blood as something slashes through my chest.

"Quinton...," I hear someone whisper, but I can't see who it is. I try to open my eyes, but it feels like they're already open, yet all I see is darkness.

But maybe that's better than seeing what's actually there...

Chapter One

Fifteen months later...

May 19, Day 1 of Summer Break

Nova

I have the web camera set up perfectly angled straight at my face. The green light on the screen is flickering insanely, like it can't wait for me to start recording. But I'm not sure what I'll say or what the point of all this is, other than my film professor suggested it.

He'd actually suggested to the entire class—and probably all of his classes—telling us that if we really wanted to get into filming, we should practice over the summer, even if we weren't enrolled in any summer classes. He said, "A true videographer loves looking at the world through an alternative eye, and he loves to record how he sees things in a different light." He was quoting straight out of a textbook, like most of my professors do, but for some reason something about what he said struck a nerve.

Maybe it was because of the video Landon made right before the last seconds of his life. I've never actually watched his video, though. I never really wanted to and I can't, anyway. I'm too afraid of what I'll see or what I won't see. Or maybe it's because seeing him like that means finally accepting that he's gone. Forever.

I originally signed up for the film class because I waited too long to enroll for classes and I needed one more elective. I'm a general major and don't really have a determined interest path, and the only classes that weren't full were Intro to Video Design or Intro to Theater. At least with the video class I'd be behind a lens instead of standing up in front of everyone where they could strip me down and evaluate me. With video, I get to do the evaluating. Turns out, though, that I liked the class, and I found out that there's something fascinating about seeing the world through a lens, like I could be looking at it from anyone's point of view and maybe see things at a different angle, like Landon did during his last few moments alive. So I decided that I would try to make some videos this summer, to get some insight on myself, Landon, and maybe life.

I turn on "Jesus Christ" by Brand New and let it play in the background. I shove the stack of psychology books off the computer chair and onto the floor, clearing off a place for me to sit. I've been collecting the books for the last year, trying to learn about the human psyche—Landon's psyche—but books hold just words on pages, not thoughts in *his* head.

I sit down on the swivel chair and clear my throat. I have no makeup on. The sun is descending behind the mountains, but I refuse to turn the bedroom light on. Without the light the screen is dark, and I look like a shadow on a backdrop. But it's perfect. Just how I want it. I tap the cursor and the green light shifts to red. I open my mouth, ready to speak, but then I freeze up. I've never been one for being on camera or in pictures. I'd liked being behind the scenes, and now I'm purposely throwing myself into the spotlight.

"People say that time heals all wounds, and maybe they're right." I keep my eyes on the computer screen, watching my lips move. "But what if the wounds don't heal correctly, like when cuts leave behind nasty scars, or when broken bones mend together, but aren't as smooth anymore?" I glance at my arm, my brows furrowing as I touch a scar with my fingertip. "Does it mean they're really healed? Or is it that the body did what it could to fix what broke...," I trail off, counting backward from ten, gathering my thoughts. "But what exactly broke...with me...with him...I'm not sure, but it feels like I need to find out...somehow...about him...about myself...but how the fuck do I find out about him when the only person that truly knew what was real is...gone?" I blink and then click the screen off, and it goes black.

&

May 27, Day 7 of Summer Break

I started this ritual when I got to college. I wake up and count the seconds it takes for the sun to rise over the hill. It's my way of preparing for another day I don't want to prepare for, knowing that it's another day to add to my list of days I've lived without Landon.

This morning worked a little differently, though. I'm home for my first summer break of college, and instead of the hills that surround Idaho, the sun advances over the immense Wyoming mountains that enclose Maple Grove, the small town I grew up in. The change makes it difficult to get out of bed, because it's unfamiliar and breaks the routine I set up over the last eight months. And that routine was what kept me intact. Before it, I was a mess, unstable, out of control. I had no control. And I need control, otherwise I end up on the bathroom floor with a razor in my hand with the need to understand why he did it—what pushed him to that point. But the only way to do that is to make my veins run dry, and it turned out that I didn't have it in me. I was too weak, or maybe it was too strong. I honestly don't know anymore, what's considered weak and what's considered strong. What's right and what's wrong. Who I was and who I should be.

I've been home for a week, and my mom and stepfather are watching me like hawks, like they expect me to break down again, after almost a year. But I'm in control now. *In control.*

After I get out of bed and take a shower, I sit for exactly five minutes in front of my computer, staring at the file folder that holds the video clip Landon made before he died. I always give myself five minutes to look at it, not because I'm planning on opening it, but because it recorded his last few minutes, captured him, his thoughts, his words, his face. It feels like the last piece of him that I have left. I wonder if one day, somehow, I'll finally be able to open it. But at this moment, in the state of mind I'm stuck in, it just doesn't seem possible. Not much does.

Once the five minutes are over, I put on my swimsuit, then pull on a floral sundress over it and strap some leather bands onto my wrists. Then I pull the curtains shut, so Landon's house will be out of sight and out of mind, before heading back to my computer desk to record a short clip.

I click Record and stare at the screen as I take a few collected breaths. "So I was thinking about my last recording— my first—and I was trying to figure out what the point of this is—or if there even had to be a point." I rest my arms on the desk and lean closer to the screen, assessing my blue eyes. "I guess if there is a point, it would be for me to discover something. About myself or maybe about...him, because it feels like there's still so much stuff I'm missing...so many unanswered questions and all the lack of answers leaves me feeling lost, not just about why the hell he did it, but about what kind of person I am that he could leave so easily...Who was I then? Who am I now? I really don't know..,But maybe when I look back and watch these one day far, far down the road, I'll realize what I really think about life and I'll finally get some answers to what leaves me confused every single day, because right now I'm about as lost as a damn bottle floating in gross, murky water."

I pause, contemplating as I tap my fingers on the desk. "Or maybe I'll be able to backtrack through my thoughts and figure out why he did it." I inhale and then exhale loudly as my pulse begins to thrash. "And if you're not me and you're watching these, then you're probably wondering who *he* is, but I'm not sure if I'm ready to say his name yet. Hopefully I'll get there. One day—someday, but who knows...maybe I'll always be as clueless and as lost as I am now."

I leave it at that and turn the computer off, wondering how long I'm going to continue this pointless charade, this time filler, because right now that's how it feels. I shove the chair away and head out of my room. It takes fifteen steps to reach the end of the hall, then another ten to get me to the table. They're each taken at a consistent pace and with even lengths. If I were filming right now, my steps would be smooth and perfect, steady as a rock.

"Good morning, my beautiful girl," my mother singsongs as she whisks around the kitchen, moving from the stove to the fridge, then to the cupboard. She's making cookies, and the air smells like cinnamon and nutmeg, and it reminds me of my childhood when my dad and I would sit at the table, waiting to stuff our mouths with sugar. But he's not here anymore and instead Daniel, my stepfather, is sitting at the table. He's not waiting for the cookies. In fact he hates sugar and loves healthy food, mostly eating stuff that looks like rabbit food.

"Good morning, Nova. It's so good to have you back." He has on a suit and tie, and he's drinking grapefruit juice and eating dry toast. They've been married for three years, and he's not a bad guy. He's always taken care of my mom and me, but he's very plain, orderly, and somewhat boring. He could never replace my dad's spontaneous, adventurous, down-to-earth personality.

I plop down in the chair and rest my arms on the kitchen table. "Good morning."

My mom takes a bowl out of the cupboard and turns to me with a worried look on her face. "Nova, sweetie, I want to make sure you're okay...with being home. We can get you into therapy here, if you need it, and you're still taking your medication, right?"

"Yes, Mom, I'm still taking my medication," I reply with a sigh and lower my head onto my arms and shut my eyes. I've been on antianxiety medication for a while now. I'm not sure if it really does anything or not, but the therapist prescribed it to me so I take it. "I take them every morning, but I stopped going to therapy back in December, because it doesn't do anything but waste time." Because no matter what, they always want me to talk about what I saw that morning—what I did and why I did it—and I can't even think about it, let alone talk about it.

"Yeah, I know, honey, but things are different when you're here," she says quietly.

I remember the hell I put her through before I left. The lack of sleep, the crying...cutting my wrist open. But that's in the past now. I don't cry as much, and my wrist has healed.

"I'm fine, Mom." I open my eyes, sit back up, and overlap my fingers in front of me. "So please, pretty please, with a cherry on top and icing and candy corn, would you please stop asking?"

"You sound just like your father…everything had to be referenced to sugar," she remarks with a frown as she sets the bowl down on the counter. In a lot of ways she looks like me: long brown hair, a thin frame, and a sprinkle of freckles on her nose. But her blue eyes are a lot brighter than mine, to the point where they almost sparkle. "Honey, I know you keep saying that you're fine, but you look so sad…and I know you were doing okay at school, but you're back here now, and everything that happened is right across the street." She opens a drawer and selects a large wooden spoon, before bumping the drawer shut with her hip. "I just don't want the memories to get to you now that you're home and so close to… everything."

I stare at my reflection in the stainless-steel microwave. It's not the clearest. In fact, my face looks a little distorted and warped, like I'm looking into a funhouse mirror, my own face nearly a stranger. But if I tilt sideways just a little, I almost look normal, like my old self. "I'm fine," I repeat, observing how blank my expression looks when I say it. "Memories are just memories." Really, it doesn't matter what they are, because I can't see the parts that I know will rip my heart back open: the last few steps leading up to Landon's finality and the soundless moments afterward, before I cracked apart. I worked hard to stitch my heart back up after it was torn open, even if I didn't do it neatly.

"Nova." She sighs as she starts mixing the cookie batter. "You can't just try to forget without dealing with it first. It's unhealthy."

"Forgetting *is* dealing with it." I grab an apple from a basket on the table, no longer wanting to talk about it because it's in the past, where it belongs.

"Nova, honey," she says sadly. She's always tried to get me to talk about that day. But what she doesn't get is that I can't remember, even if I really tried, which I never will. It's like my brain's developed its own brain and it won't allow those thoughts out, because once they're out, they're real. And I don't want them to be real—I don't want to remember *him* like that. Or me.

I push up from the chair, cutting her off. "I think I'm going to hang out next to the pool today, and Delilah will probably be over in a bit."

"If that's what you want." My mom smiles halfheartedly at me, wanting to say more, but fearing what it'll do to me. I don't blame her, either. She's the one who found me on the bathroom floor, but she thinks it's more than it was. I was just trying to find out what he felt like—what was going on inside of him when he decided to go through with it.

I nod, grab a can of soda out of the fridge, and give her a hug before I head for the sliding glass door. "That's what I want."

She swallows hard, looking like she might cry because she thinks she's lost her daughter. "Well, if you need me, I'm here." She turns back to her bowl.

She's been saying that to me since I was thirteen, ever since I watched my dad die. I've never taken her up on the offer, even though we've always had a good relationship. Talking about death with her—at all—doesn't work for me. At this point in my life, I couldn't talk to her about it even if I wanted to. I have my silence now, which is my healing, my escape, my sanctuary. Without it, I'd hear the noises of that morning, see the bleeding images, and feel the crushing pain connected to them. If I saw them, then I'd finally have to accept that Landon's gone.

❧

I don't like unknown places. They make me anxious and I have trouble thinking—breathing. One of the first therapists I saw diagnosed me with obsessive-compulsive disorder. I'm not sure if he was right, though, because he moved out of town not too long after. I was left with a therapist in training, so to speak, and he decided that I was just depressed and had anxiety, hence the antianxiety medication for the last year and three months.

The unfamiliarity of the backyard disrupts my counting, and it takes me forever to get to the pool. By the time I arrive at the lawn chair, I know how many steps it took me to get here, how many seconds it took me to sit down, and how many more seconds it took for Delilah to arrive and then for her to take a seat beside me. I know how many rocks are on the path leading to the porch—twenty-two—how many branches are on the tree shielding the sunlight from us—seventy-eight. The only thing I don't know is how many seconds, hours, years, decades, it will take before I can let go of the goddamn self-induced numbness. Until then I'll count, focus on numbers instead of the feelings always floating inside me, the ones linked to images immersed just beneath the surface.

Delilah and I lie in lawn chairs in the middle of my back-yard with the pool behind us and the sun bearing down on us as we tan in our swimsuits. She's been my best friend for the past year or so. Our sudden friendship was strange, because we'd gone to high school together but never really talked. She and I were in different social circles and I had Landon. But after it happened...after he died...I had no one, and the last few weeks of high school were torture. Then I met her, and she was nice and she didn't look at me like I was about to shatter. We hit it off, and honestly, I have no idea what I'd do without her now. She's been there for me, she shows me how to have fun, and she reminds me that life still exists in the world, even if it's brief.

"Good God, has it always been this hot here?" Delilah fans her face with her hand as she yawns. "I remember it being colder."

"I think so." I pick up a cup of iced tea on the table between us and prop up on my elbow to take a sip. "We could go in," I suggest, setting my glass down. I turn it in a circle until it's perfectly in place on the condensation ring it left behind, and then I wipe the moisture from my lips with the back of my hand and rest my head back against the chair. "We do have air-conditioning."

Delilah laughs sardonically as she reaches for the sparkly pink flask in her bag. "Yeah, right. Are you kidding me?" She pauses, examining her fiery red nails, then unscrews the lid off the flask. "No offense. I didn't mean for that to sound rude, but your mom and dad are a little overwhelming." She takes a swig from the flask and holds it out in my direction.

"Stepdad," I correct absentmindedly. I wrap my lips around the top of the flask and take a tiny swallow, then hand it back to her and close my eyes. "And they're just lonely. I'm the only child and I've been gone for almost a year."

She laughs again, but it's breezier than before. "They're seriously the most overbearing parents I know. They call you every day at school and text you a thousand times." She puts the flask back into her bag.

"They just worry about me." They didn't used to. My mom was really carefree before my dad died, and then she got concerned about how his death and seeing it affected me. Then Landon died, and now all she does is constantly worry.

"*I* worry about you, too," Delilah mumbles. She waits for me to say something, but I don't—I can't. Delilah knows about what happened with Landon, but we never *really* talk about what I saw. And that's one of the things I like about her—that she doesn't ask questions.

24

One... two... three... four... five... breathe... six... seven... eight... breathe... Balling my hands into fists, I fight to calm myself down, but the darkness is ascending inside me, and it will take me over if I let it and drag me down into the memory I won't remember; my last memory of Landon.

"I have a brilliant idea," she interrupts my counting. "We could go check out Dylan and Tristan's new place."

My eyes open and I slant my head to the side. My hands are on my stomach, and I can feel my pulse beating through my fingertips, inconsistent. Tracking the beats is difficult, but I try anyway. "You want to go see your ex-boyfriend's place. *Seriously?*"

Swinging her legs over the edge of the chair, Delilah sits up and slips her sunglasses up to the top of her head. "What? I'm totally curious what he ended up like." She presses her fingertips to the corners of her eyes, plucking out gobs of kohl eyeliner.

"Yeah, but isn't it kind of weird to show up randomly after not talking to him in like forever, especially after how bad your guys' breakup was," I say. "I mean, if Tristan hadn't stepped in, you would have probably hit Dylan."

"Yeah, probably, but that's all in the past." She chews on her thumbnail and gives me a guilt-ridden look as she smears the tanning-spray grease off her bare stomach. "Besides, that's not technically accurate. We kind of talked yesterday."

Frowning, I sit up and refasten the elastic around my long, wavy brown hair, securing it in a ponytail. "Are you serious?"

I ask, and when she doesn't respond, I add, "Nine months ago, when he cheated on you, you swore up and down that you'd never talk to that"—I make air quotes—"'fucking, lying, cheating bastard' again. In fact, if I remember right, it was the main reason you decided to go to college with me—because you needed a break."

"Did I say that really?" She feigns forgetfulness as she taps her finger on her chin. "Well, like everything else in my life, I've decided to have a change of heart." She reaches for the tanning spray on the table between us. "And besides, I did need a break, not just from him, but from my mom and this town, but now we're back and I figure I might as well have some fun while I'm here. College wore me out."

Delilah is the most indecisive person I've ever met. During our freshman year, she changed majors three times, dyed her hair from red, to black, then back to red again, and went through about a half a dozen boyfriends. I secretly love it, despite how much I pretend that I don't. It was what kind of drew me to her; her uncaring, nonchalant attitude, and the way she could forget things in the snap of a finger. I wish I could be the same way sometimes, and if I hang around her a lot, there are a few moments when I can get my mind on the same carefree level as hers.

"What have you two been talking about?" I wonder, plucking a piece of grass off my leg. "And please don't tell me it's getting back together, because I don't want to see you get crushed like that again."

Her smile shines as she tucks strands of her red hair behind her heavily studded ears, then she removes the lid from the tanning spray. "What is with you and Dylan? He's always put you on edge."

"Because he's sketchy. *And* he cheated on you."

"He's not sketchy...he's mysterious. And he was drunk when he cheated."

"Delilah, you deserve better than that."

She narrows her eyes at me as she spritzes her legs with tanning spray. "I'm not better than him, Nova. I've done supercrappy things, hurt people. I've made mistakes—we all have."

I stab my nails into the palms of my hands, thinking of all the mistakes I made and their consequences. "Yes, you are better. All he's ever done is cheat on you and deal drugs."

She slaps her hand on her knee. "Hey, he doesn't deal anymore. He stopped dealing a year ago." She clicks the cap back onto the tanning spray and tosses it into her bag.

I sigh, push my sunglasses up over my head, and massage my temples. "So what has he been up to for a year?" I lower my hands and blink against the sunlight.

She shrugs, and then her lips expand to a grin as she grabs my hand and stands, tugging me to my feet. "How about we go change out of our swimsuits, head over to his place, and find out?" When I open my mouth to protest, she adds, "It'd be a good distraction for the day."

"I'm not really looking for a distraction, though."

"Well, then you could go over and see Tristan." She bites back an amused smirk. "Maybe reheat things."

I glare at her. "We hooked up one time and that's because I was drunk and..." *Vulnerable.* I'd actually been really drunk, and my thoughts had been all over the place because of an unexpected visit from Landon's parents that morning. They'd wanted to give me some of his sketchings, which they'd found in a trunk upstairs—sketchings of me. I'd barely been able to take them without crying, and then I'd run off, looking to get drunk and forget about the drawings, Landon, and the pain of him leaving. Tristan, Dylan's best friend—and roommate—was the first guy I came across after way, way too many Coronas and shots. I started making out with him without even saying hello.

He was the first guy I'd made out with since Landon, and I spent the entire night afterward crying and rocking on the bathroom floor, counting the cracks in the tile and trying to get myself to calm down and stop feeling guilty for kissing someone else, because Landon was gone and he took a part of me with him—at least that was what it feels like. What's left of me is a hollow shell full of denial and tangled with confusion. I have no idea who I am anymore. I really don't. And I'm not sure if I want to know or not.

"Oh come on, Nova." She releases my hand and claps her hands in front of her. "Please, can we just go and try to have some fun?"

I sigh, defeated, and nod, knowing that the true feelings of why I don't want to go over there lie more in the fact that I hate new places than anything else. Unfamiliar situations put me on edge, because I hate the unknown. It reminds me just how much the unknown controls everything, and my counting can sometimes get a little out of hand. But I don't want to argue anymore with Delilah, either, because then my anxiety will get me worked up and the counting will, too. Either way, I know I'm going to have a head full of numbers. At least if I go with Delilah, then I can keep an eye on her and maybe she'll end up happy. And really, that's all I can ask for. For everyone to be happy. But as I all too painfully know, you can't force someone to be happy, no matter how much you wish you could.

Chapter Two

Quinton

I ask myself the same question every day: *Why me? Why did I survive?* And every day I get the same response: *I don't know.* Deep down, I know there really isn't an answer, yet I keep asking the same question, hoping that maybe one day someone will give me a hand and give me a clear answer. But my head is always foggy, and answers always come to me in harsh, jagged responses: regardless of why I survived, it was my fault, and I should be the one buried under the ground, locked in a box, below a marked stone. Two people died because of me that day. Two people I cared about. And even though the guy I barely know miraculously lived, he could have very easily died, and his death would have been my fault, too.

All my fault.

"Thanks for letting me stay here, man," I say for the thousandth time. I can tell my cousin Tristan is getting a little irritated by how many times I've said it, but I can't seem to stop. I'm sure it wasn't easy for him to help out the most hated member of our family. The one who destroyed lives and split apart a family. But I needed to leave, despite how much I didn't want to; something that became clear when my dad finally spoke to me after over a year of near silence.

"I think it's time for you to move out," he'd said, eyeing my lazy ass sprawled out on the bed as music played in the background. I was sketching something that looked like an owl in a tree, but my vision was a little blurred, so I couldn't quite tell for sure. "You're nineteen years old and getting too old to live at home."

I was high out of my mind, and I had a hard time focusing on anything except how slow his lips were moving. "Okay."

He studied me from the doorway and I could tell he was disappointed in what he saw. I was no longer his son, but a washed-up druggie who lay around all day wasting his life, ruining everything he'd worked so hard to achieve. All that time spent in high school, getting good grades, winning art fairs, working hard to get scholarships, was exchanged for a new goal: getting high. He didn't try to understand why I needed drugs—that without them, I'd be worse off—and I never wanted him to. It wasn't like we'd had a good relationship before the accident. My mom had died in childbirth, and even though he never said it, I sometimes wonder if he blamed me for killing her when she brought me into this world.

Finally, he'd left, and the conversation was over. The next morning, when my head had cleared a little, I realized I actually had to find a place to live in order to move out. I didn't have a job at the moment, due to the fact I failed a random drug test at the last job, and I had a bad track record of getting fired. Not knowing what else to do, I'd called up Tristan. We used to be friends when we were younger... before everything happened... before I killed Ryder, his sister. I felt like a dick for calling him, but I remembered him being nice, and he even talked to me after the funeral, even though his parents no longer would. He seemed reluctant, but he agreed, and a couple of days later I packed up my shit, bought a ticket, and headed for my temporary new home.

"Dude, for the millionth time, you're good, so stop thanking me." Tristan picks up the last box out of the trunk of his car.

"Are you sure, though?" I ask again, because it never really seems like I can ask enough. "I mean, with me staying here, especially after... everything."

"I told you on the phone that I was." He shifts his weight, moving the box to his free arm, and then scratches the back of his neck uncomfortably. "Look, I'm good, okay? You can stay here until you can get your feet on the ground or whatever... I'm not going to just let you live out on the streets. Ryder wouldn't have wanted that, either." He almost chokes on her name and then clears his throat a thousand times.

I'm not sure I agree with him. Ryder and I were never that close, but I'm not going to bring that up, considering things have already gotten really awkward and I've only been here for like five minutes.

"Yeah, but what about your parents?" I ask. His parents insist that the accident was my fault and that I should have been driving more safely. They told me that I ruined their family, killed their daughter.

"What about them?" His voice is a little tight.

"Won't they be pissed when they find out I'm living with you?"

He slams the trunk down. "How are they going to find out? They never talk to me. In fact they've pretty much disowned me and my lifestyle." I start to protest, but he cuts me off. "Look, you're good. They never stop by. I barely talk to them. So can you please just chill out and enjoy your new home?" He heads for the gate and I follow. "I do have to say, though, that it probably would have been better if you drove out here. Now you're stranded if you want to go anywhere."

"It's better that way." I adjust the handle of the bag over my shoulder and we walk toward a single-wide trailer. The siding is falling off, one of the windows is covered with a piece of plywood, and the lawn is nonexistent; instead there's a layer of gravel, then a fence, followed by more gravel. It's a total crack house, but that's okay. This is the kind of place where I belong, in a place no one wants to admit exists, just like they don't want to admit I exist.

"You know there's no bus here, right?" He steps onto the stairway, and it wobbles underneath his feet. "It's a freaking small-ass town."

"That's okay." I follow him with my thumb hitched under the handle of my bag. "I'll just walk everywhere."

He laughs, shifting the box to one arm so he can open the screen door. "Okay, if you say so." He steps inside the house, and I catch the screen door with my foot, grab the handle, and hold the door open as I maneuver my way inside.

The first thing I notice is the smell; smoky but with a seasoned kick to it that burns the back of my throat. It's familiar, and suddenly I feel right at home. My eyes sweep the room and I spot the joint burning in the ashtray on a cracked coffee table.

Tristan drops the box on the floor, steps over it and strides up to the ashtray. "You good with this?" He picks up the joint and pinches it in between his fingers. "I can't remember if you're cool or not."

It's not really a question. It's more of a warning that I have to be cool with it if I'm going to live here. I let the handle of the bag slide down my arm and it falls to the floor. "I used to not be." I used to care about things—I used to think that doing the right thing would make me a good person. "But now I'm good."

His eyebrows knit at my vague answer and I reach for the joint. As soon as it's in my hand and the poisonous yet intoxicating smoke starts to snake up to my face, I instantly feel at ease again. The calm only amplifies as I put it to my lips and take a deep drag. I trap it in my chest, allowing the smoke to burn at the back of my throat, saturate my lungs, and singe my heart away. It's what I want—what I need—because I don't deserve anything more. I part my lips and release the smoke into the already tainted air, feeling lighter than I have since I got on that goddamn plane.

"Holy fucking shit, look what the dog drug in." Dylan, Tristan's roommate, walks out from behind a curtain at the back of the room, laughing, and a blonde girl trails at his heels. I've only met him a couple of times during the few visits my dad and I made to Maple Grove to visit Tristan's parents. He looks different—rougher—a shaved head, multiple tattoos on his arms, and he used to be a lot stockier, but I'm guessing the weight loss is from the drugs.

"Hi, Quinton." The blonde waves her hand, then winds around Dylan and moves toward me. She keeps her arms tight to her side, pressing them against her chest, so her tits nearly pop out of her top. She seems to know me, yet I have no fucking clue who she is. "It's been a long time."

I'm racking my brain for some sort of memory that has her in it, but the weed has totally put a haze in my head, putting me right where I want to be—numb and obliviously stupid.

When she reaches me, she glides her palm up my chest and leans in, pressing her tits against me. "The last time I saw you, you were a scrawny twelve-year-old with braces and glasses, but good God you've changed." She traces a path from my chest to my stomach. "You're totally smoking hot now."

"Oh, it's Nikki, right?" I'm remembering something about her...a time when we were kids and the whole neighborhood decided to play baseball. But it's nothing more than a distant memory I'd rather forget. It reminds me too much of what was and what will never be again. "You've..." I scroll up her body, which I can pretty much see all of. "Changed."

She takes it as a compliment, even though I didn't mean it that way. "Thanks." She smiles and shimmies her hips. "I always try to look my best."

I still have the joint in my hand and I take another hit, trapping it in until my lungs feel like they're going to explode, then I free the smoke from my mouth and ash the joint on the already singed brown carpet. I hand it to Tristan, allowing the numbness to leach into my body. "Where should I put my stuff?" I ask him.

Dylan hitches a finger over at the hallway. "There's a room at the back of the hall. It's a little small, but it's got a bed and shit."

I collect my bag and move around Nikki, heading for the hall. "I'll take whatever's easiest on everyone."

Dylan nods his head at the hallway and then says to Nikki, "Nikki, why don't you show Quinton where the room is?"

"Absolutely." She flashes an exaggerated smile at me and snatches the joint from Tristan's hand. She wraps her lips around the end, inhales, and then lets it out. She hands it back to him and then saunters in front of me so I can watch her ass as she struts down the hallway.

"Are you two dating?" I ask glancing back and forth between Nikki and Dylan.

Nikki rolls her eyes. "Um, no."

Dylan departs for the small, cluttered kitchen in the corner of the house. "I don't really date," he points out with a nonchalant shrug as he stuffs his hands in the pockets of his jeans. "Besides, I have an old girlfriend of mine coming over tonight."

"Delilah?" Tristan asks as he flops down on the couch, and Dylan nods. "Is Nova back, too? Is she coming over with her?"

"Nova?" I question. "Is that like her car?"

Tristan shakes his head and laughs. "No, it's a girl, you dipshit."

"Interesting name," I say, curious what a girl who's named after my favorite car would be like, but it doesn't really matter. None of it does. I'll never date again, never feel for anyone.

"Would you get over her?" Dylan scoops up a plastic cup that's by the kitchen sink and throws it at Tristan, who ducks as it zips above his head. "You made out with her one time, and she was fucking trashed."

"So what?" Tristan retorts as he leans over the arm of the chair to pick up the cup. When he sits up, he throws the cup back at Dylan, but it lands on the floor a few inches away from him. "You're still hung up on Delilah after eight months of her being gone, and I can still have a thing for Nova if I want to. And it's not really even a thing, so much as I'm curious about what she's like now after a year."

"You're such a fucking liar." Dylan kicks the cup across the floor and jerks the fridge door open. "And besides, Nova's got more baggage than you can handle."

"You don't know how much I can handle," he mutters, staring down at the brownish orange carpet. He rubs his hand across his face and then blows out a breath, his gaze flicking up to me. There's a hint of anger transpiring in his eyes, directed toward me and what I represent, but beneath the anger there's also pain. Lots and lots of pain masked over by weed.

It's my cue to leave. I put some of Tristan's baggage there, since I'm the one solely responsible for the death of his sister. I follow Nikki down the hallway, feeling like shit again as my past catches up with me. But I focus on the few steps ahead of me, knowing what's going to happen when I reach the room. It's obvious what Nikki wants, and honestly, I need the distraction. Today's been a rough day, especially after my father dropped me off at the airport. I could tell he didn't want to be there, but I think he felt obligated because I'm his son.

"See you later," was all he said, and then he left me at the entrance doors.

I shouldn't have cared that he didn't give me a hug or anything, but I haven't been hugged in a year and sometimes I miss it, the connection, the contact, knowing that someone loves you.

"So the bed's supersoft." Nikki plops down on the twin bed and gives a little bounce, crossing her legs.

I drop the bag on the floor of the closet-sized room and

stand in front of her, staring down at the filthy mattress. "Oh yeah?"

She seductively grins at me. "Definitely." Then she reaches up and snatches the front of my shirt, tugging me down to her mouth.

Her lips are dry and taste like weed, but I close my eyes and kiss her back, shutting myself down as I lean over her and we collapse against the bed. I know it's wrong. Neither of us really gives a shit about the other. There's no meaning to it. It's as pointless as existing and equally as insignificant. But that's exactly what I deserve, and the moment that I do feel meaning—the moment I feel the slightest bit of contentment and happiness with another woman—is the moment I break my promise to Lexi.

Chapter Three

Nova

There's a strange kind of serenity that comes with silence, but maybe that's because it's nearly impossible to achieve. Not only do I have to shut out the outside noise, but I also have to tune out the noise within me, the thoughts that want to whisper who I am, what I should or shouldn't be feeling, what I did or didn't do—what went wrong. Sometimes, when I'm awake late at night, I try to achieve the blissful serenity of silence, but it's always the part that I didn't do that ruins it for me, the constant whispering in my head. *You should have saved him.* I wonder if Landon ever achieved that silence and if that's why he did it. Maybe he heard nothing at all, and he took that as a sign that it was time to end things.

"How do I look?" Delilah fixes her lipstick in the rearview mirror of the old pickup she used to drive around before we left for college. She blots her lips and then looks at me with a dazzling smile.

"You look perfect." I, on the other hand, didn't even bother to brush my hair, because I'm not here to impress. I'm here because she wants me to be here. Nothing more. Nothing less.

She reaches down the front of her low-cut crimson top and rearranges her boobs so she shows more cleavage. It gets a small smile out of me, but the momentary spark of life is quickly buried as I start to count the stairs leading up to the single-wide trailer home in front of us, and the amount of tires piled on the front lawn. *Four and eight.*

Her gaze slowly skims across my short floral dress and my feather earrings. "You look nice," she says with accusation. "Are you sure you're not wanting to hook up with a certain someone again?"

I shake my head and aim my finger at her. "I already told you that hooking up with Tristan was a onetime thing."

Delilah raises her brows in doubt. "Whatever you say."

I sigh and start to climb out of the truck, but she captures my arm, preventing me from going further. "Wait. You should add this to your little movie thing."

I glance around at the trailer park, the dogs barking behind the neighbor's fence, and the car next door that's rusted, tireless, and balanced on cinder blocks. "This place?"

She smacks my arm, laughing. "No, me right now. I could say what I'm feeling right now or something. I mean, isn't that the point of what you're doing? To figure out how people feel and see life?"

I shrug, my legs hanging out of the car as I prepare to jump out. "I don't know. I was kind of just thinking that it could be like a video diary or something about my life...my thoughts...the way I see things."

"Hey, I'm a huge part of your life, Nova Reed. You better include me in this."

"Did you seriously just last-name me, Delilah *Peirce*?"

She grins, grabbing the keys from the ignition. "Oh, yeah. Now pull out that damn camera so I can tell the world my insightful views on life."

I readjust my legs back into the car and retrieve my phone from my pocket, regretting telling her my summer filming plan. "Okay." I swipe my finger across the screen and click on the video icon.

"We're so going to get you a real camera." She turns sideways in the seat and tousles her auburn hair with her fingers. "That thing's going to make me look all blotchy."

I hold up the phone, positioning it so I can see her in the screen. "You know they cost a shitload of money, right?" I click Record. "Okay, go."

"Wait, what should I say?" she asks, still fussing over her hair. The sun shines brightly behind her and all that's really showing up on the screen is her silhouette. "I'm drawing a blank."

Pressing my lips together, I try to restrain the laughter bubbling up in my throat. "I don't know. You're the one who wanted to do this."

She narrows her eyes at me. "Well, you're the director."

"I am not," I protest. "I'm just a girl with a camera trying to see life through a different eye."

She points a finger at me and gives a clever look. "That should be your title."

I sigh with frustration. "It only records for a few minutes, so if you're going to say something, you better hurry up and do it."

She wavers for a few seconds longer, and then smiles perkily at the camera, flipping her hair off her shoulder. "Okay, so here's the deal. I know what you're all thinking. That I'm just a ditzy redhead wearing slutty clothes that's about to go in and screw her ex-boyfriend who cheated on her." She waves her finger at the camera and clicks her tongue. "But don't be fooled, my friend. What you see on the outside might not be who I am on the inside, and I always have my reasons for the crazy, impulsive things that I do." She strikes a pose, blowing a kiss at the camera, and then rolls her eyes and her shoulders slump. "Okay, Nova, I'm done."

I keep recording for a few seconds longer. She's never said anything like that before, and I find it fascinating that she'll say it to a camera, especially with me behind the lens. I press Stop, and the screen shifts back to the icon. I tuck my phone back in my pocket, and Delilah grabs the door handle.

"Shall we?" she asks.

I nod. "We shall."

We climb out of the truck and meet around the front.

I start counting my steps the moment we head across the gravel. *One... two... three...*

"So I was thinking we should relax tonight," Delilah says, linking arms with me as we walk toward the gate lined with rusty five-gallon paint buckets.

Four... five... six...

"And avoid any kind of drama," she adds as she opens the chain-link gate.

Seven... eight... nine... "Like getting into fights?" I latch the gate shut. *Ten... eleven... twelve...*

When we make it to the front door, she slips her arm from mine. "Hey, I only did that once," she says, squaring her shoulders and sticking out her chest. "And the bitch deserved it."

"You broke her arm," I remind her, as she raps her fist on the door.

"She tried to kiss Dylan," she hisses with a conniving grin, then she pops her knuckles. "She totally deserved more. She's lucky you were there to stop me."

I shake my head and a small smile escapes. Every once in a while, in the rarest of moments, I manage to get it right: to smile without feeling guilty about it. But as quick as it comes, I'm frowning again as I drift back into the numbness.

"Come in!" someone hollers from the other side of the door after Delilah knocks on it again.

She puts her flirting face on, hiking up her denim skirt a little, before shoving the door open and strutting inside. I follow her, walking into a room full of humidified smoke tainted with the stench of weed, dingy plaid sofas, and a cracked coffee table. The wood panel walls have water stains on them, and the once white ceiling is discolored. The kitchen to my side overflows with empty alcohol bottles, cigarette butts, dirty dishes, and garbage. On the far wall is what I'm guessing is a hallway, but a putrid orange curtain hangs over the entrance. A little over a year ago, I'd never be caught in a place like this—it wasn't who I was or who Landon would let me be. But I don't know who I am anymore, and that makes it harder to find reasons not to be here, except for maybe the fact that the unfamiliarity raises the obsessive need to count all the damn photos hanging on the wooden paneling.

"Holy hell. You look even more beautiful than I remember." Dylan rises from the chair he's lounging in and places the cigarette he's holding in the ashtray. He's tall, kind of lanky, and his head is shaved. There are intricate tattoos covering his arms, most in black, but a few are filled in with shades of crimson and indigo.

Delilah lets out a squeal as she jumps up and down, then runs into Dylan's arms. They embrace each other passionately and immediately seal their lips together in a fervent kiss. Tristan, who's playing darts over in the far corner by himself, looks at me then rolls his eyes at Delilah and Dylan, giving me a halfhearted shrug. I don't know Tristan very well, but he's always seemed like a really nice guy. Under normal circumstances kissing him would have probably been enjoyable. He had nice lips, and even though his blond hair is a little scraggly, it's really soft. He has lean arms, is tall with broad shoulders, and has dark blue eyes. In reality, as I look at him, he seems out of place in a home like this, littered with glass bongs and roach clips and ceramic pipes, kind of similar to the ones Landon kept hidden in his room.

Minutes later, Dylan's and Delilah's lips are still attached, and their hands roam all over each other as they wander through the curtain, leaving me in the room with Tristan and his darts.

He watches me for a moment, and then grabs a red plastic cup from the coffee table. "So what have you been up to?" he asks, setting the cup down after he takes a swallow. He turns back to the dartboard, aiming the tip of one while shutting an eye.

"School." I wind around a sofa, reducing the distance between us. There's music playing from an old stereo in the corner, "Emily" by From First to Last. "Other than that, not a whole lot." I step up beside him and stare at the dartboard as he throws the dart, hitting it just outside of the center. "You?"

He shrugs and extends his hand for the cup again. "Work, life, honestly nothing that great." He puts the rim of the cup up to his lips and tips his head back, chugging a mouth full before crushing the cup and tossing it into an overflowing trash can in the corner near a lamp without a lampshade. "You need a drink or something?"

I debate my options. The buzz from the few sips I took from the flask has simmered down, so either I can stand here and count all night until Delilah finishes up with Dylan or I can take Tristan up on his offer and try to find some kind of silence in alcohol. "What do you have?" I ask.

He smiles and motions at me to follow him as he hops over the back of the couch and proceeds for the kitchen. I choose to walk around the sofa, constructing my own path, noting it takes me twelve controlled, steady steps to follow him to the fridge. He opens the door, pokes his head inside, and starts rummaging around through the various brands of beer. He ends up selecting a Corona, and I can't help but briefly smile because after eight months he still remembers my drink. He kicks the fridge door shut with his foot, walks over to the counter, and places the top of the bottle on the edge of the countertop, knocking the cap off.

The golden liquid bubbles as he hands me the opened bottle. "Here ya go."

I let out a breath I didn't realize I'd been holding and move the mouth of the bottle up to my mouth. "Thanks,"

He squeezes between me and the counter and moves back to the living room, rolling up the sleeves of his long-sleeved black shirt. "No problem," he says. "You look a little tense anyway. Maybe that'll relax you."

Nothing will relax me. *Ever.* Nothing will drown out the memories of that day—no matter how much I fight it—everything I missed. *Why did you do it, Landon? Why?* As soon as my mind recollects the faint flicker of his sad laughter, the feeling of that goddamn night start to chip away at the wall

I put around it. I blink and blink again as tears start to sting my eyes. *Shut the hell up. Shut the hell up. Now is not the time. Wait until you're at home, alone.* But they pool in the corners of my eyes, hot liquid about to burn down my cheeks and stain my skin. Panicking, I start to count the lines of the panels that make up the wall. I reach fifteen, and then I tilt my head back, and gulp down half the Corona before I can breathe again.

"You good?" Tristan asks, watching me devour the beer as he holds an assortment of darts in his hand.

I lick the remaining beer off my lips and stride over to the dartboard. "Yeah, I'm great, but can I play? I need a distraction."

A smile curves at his lips as I start to remove the red darts from the board. "Absolutely, but how about we make it fun and play for something?" His gaze skims up my bare legs, to the hem of my dress, and then up to my eyes. I think he's going to propose something sexual, by the fiery look in his eyes, but all he says is, "Winner owes the loser twenty bucks?"

I suck back the remaining tears still wanting to spill and stick out my hand. "You have a deal."

We shake on it and he gives my hand a squeeze before pulling away. "Ladies first," he says and then steps back toward the couch, making room for me to step up.

I weave around him and position myself in front of the board. I count backward before I inhale and hold my breath as I throw the dart. It hits the bull's-eye. I force myself to breathe through the memory of the last time Landon and I played darts and he let me win, even though he denied it.

"Wow, I think I might have just thrown away twenty bucks." Tristan rubs his scruffy jawline and steps up to the dartboard, taking his time targeting the dart. When he shoots it, he starts cursing as the dart bows to the side. It ends up hitting the outer edge of the board and he turns to me, shaking his head.

"Okay, I think I might have had one too many drinks to be playing darts for money," he says, sitting down on the arm of the chair. He looks me over as the light above my head flickers. "Where'd you learn how to play like that? Or was it beginner's luck?"

Without looking at the dartboard, I toss the dart and it almost hits another bull's-eye. "I learned from the best."

"Who?" He slants his head as the corners of his lips quirk. "Was it Dell down at the bar?" he jokes, because Dell's the town drunk and thinks he's the champion of everything. "Because he's always bragging about being a super dart champion."

I swallow hard as vivid memories puncture my brain. "This guy I used to date taught me, actually." I take another long sip, telling my head to shut up. *Don't go there. Please don't go there. Not right now.*

I hear his breath catch as he probably remembers what happened. Everyone in this town heard about it within hours after it happened, and it's been kind of hard for everyone to forget. It wasn't too long after Tristan's sister died, but hers was by accident, a simple wrong place at the wrong time.

After a gap of silence drags by, Tristan blows out a

breath and stands up from the armrest. "You want a shot or something?"

"Yes, please," I say way too quickly and wind the neck of the nearly finished Corona around in my hand, channeling my tension on it.

He walks over to the kitchen area and digs around in the cupboards, hunting for shot glasses. I sit down on the sofa, tip my head back and suck down the last of the Corona, regretting my decision to come back here. Not to Dylan's house, but back home. I'd been okay at college—not great, but okay, or at least focused on something besides my obsessive compulsions and Landon's death.

A giggle floats from the hallway and I gratefully exhale, thinking it's Delilah. I start to get up but when the curtain is drawn back, I sink back down when a leggy blonde steps out, adjusting her top back over her bulging curves.

She takes one look at me and then plasters on a plastic smile. "Hey...it's Nova, right?"

I have no idea who she is, but she looks about my age. "Yeah..."

"Like the car." The sound of his voice is familiar, way too familiar, like the world has decided to play a cruel joke on me. When a guy steps out of the hallway, I just about drop dead on the floor as the similarity intensifies and sends my mind spinning. Everything about him screams Landon, and for a second I really believe it's him.

It's not really the similarities in features as much as

something less visible. He's taller than Landon, with dark brown hair inside of black, and it's shaven short instead of hanging in his eyes. He also has slightly more muscle tone to him, and there's an indistinct scar over his top lip. All these things don't match up, but it's the little details that push an insanity button in my head. Like the charcoal on his hands, or the fact that the laces of his boots are untied, something Landon used to do all the time. The sound of his voice, deep and smooth like melted butter, has a strikingly comparable ring to it. And his eyes. Those goddamn honey-brown eyes with so much sorrow in them it nearly swallows any happiness in the room. I've only seen that much sadness in one person's eyes. *Ever.* And when they lock on me, it's like I'm drowning in his sorrow—Landon's sorrow.

I continue to stare at him, and I can tell it's making him uneasy, but I can't seem to look away. It's like I'm waking up a year ago and he hasn't left me on the hillside, alone, not just on the grass, but in the world.

"Are you okay?" The sound of Tristan's voice slams into my chest and rips me from my daze.

I tear my eyes away from the guy and blink up at Tristan. "Huh?"

He has a small shot glass in his hand that's topped off with a crystal clear liquid. "You look upset." He glances over at the guy and then back at me. "Are you okay, Nova?"

I nod, snatch the shot out of his hand, and slam it back, basking in the burn. Then I set the empty glass down on the table and press my hand to my burning throat. "I'm fine. I'm just tired."

Tristan's not buying it, but he doesn't press. We're not good enough friends for him to press. He takes a seat in the tattered leather recliner that's shredded to pieces. I try to keep my gaze fixed on the popped seams in the armrest, but I can't help but glance over at the guy with honey-brown eyes, even though I don't want to.

He sits down on the sofa to the side of me, and the blonde strategically places her ass onto his lap. She giggles as she runs her fingers over his head, but he only seems mildly interested as he retrieves a pack of cigarettes from the coffee table and pops one into his mouth.

"So did Dylan wander back there?" Tristan asks, sipping on his beer.

The guy shrugs as he cups his hand around the end of the cigarette, flicks a lighter, and the end crinkles and shrivels. "I think they went into his room, but I'm not sure." Smoke snakes out of his lips.

"With that bitch Delilah," the blonde says, shooting me a malicious look.

Okay, so she knows Delilah and obviously hates her, which isn't surprising—most girls do. But why does she seem to hate me?

"Oh shit," Tristan says, smacking his head with the heel of his hand. "I totally fucking forgot introductions."

"We already know who she is," the blonde sneers, glaring at me. "That's Nova Reed."

I have no clue what her name is, and I think Tristan can tell. "Nikki, quit being a bitch," he says.

Nikki. It clicks. She used to go to school with me before she dropped out. She also used to have a crush on Landon right before I started dating him at the beginning of senior year. She's changed a lot, put on some weight in the chest area, and her hair used to be light brown, not bleached blonde.

Nikki huffs, poking her chest out as she crosses her arms, then she reclines against the guy's chest. "Quit being an asshole," she snaps at Tristan, and then bats her eyelashes at the guy.

The guy shifts his weight, throwing her off balance, and she slides off his lap and lands on the couch. "Sorry, but he's my cousin and this is his house. If he says quit being a bitch to Nova"—he glances at me with a quirk at his lips and a furrow at his brows—"then quit being a bitch."

I don't like the way my heart leaps in my chest when he says my name or that he remembers my name when he only heard it a minute ago. I hate how I can't seem to look away from him and find something to count, because if I could, then I could call down the storm building in my chest.

Nikki looks pissed, but she keeps her lips sealed. The guy takes a deep inhale from his cigarette as he reaches for the remote on the coffee table. Tristan gets up from the recliner and heads down the hall. It grows quiet, and the guy whose name I still don't know picks up a remote and flips through the songs on the stereo. Nikki makes it her mission to glare at me, but I barely pay attention. All my focus is on the ghost of a memory sitting next to me. I know he's really not Landon, but he's chillingly comparable, even in the way he moves.

Eventually, looking at him becomes too much, and I get up and walk out of the house. I step into the cool night, place my hands on the railing, and hunch over, battling back the memories as they thrust their way to the surface, counting under my breath, doing everything I can to focus on the numbers instead of the images, but the images conclusively win.

"So if you could only paint one thing over and over again for the rest of your life, what would it be?" I hold on to the stairway railing and watch Landon sit on the bottom step and sketch the old oak tree on the hill in the backyard. *"That tree?"*

"I wouldn't paint anything," he says. *His hand moves perfectly along the white sheet of paper, staining it with shades of gray and black. He pauses, glancing over his shoulder at me, with a ghost smile touching his lips. "You know how much I hate painting."*

I scrunch my nose and sink down on the step beside him. "Okay, then, what would you sketch?"

"If I could only sketch one thing?" he asks, and I nod. He taps the end of his pencil on his chin, leaving black smudges. "Probably you."

I stick out my tongue, but my heart dances. I've often wondered what it would be like if he really did like me, if he kissed me, if he were my boyfriend instead of just my friend. "You so would not. If you were to actually pick a person, which I doubt you would, you'd probably pick someone like Karisa Harris."

He wavers. "I have to admit, she does have a nice rack."

I slap his arm, pretending to be offended, even though I'm used to it. We've been friends for four years, and he's a seventeen-year-old guy. Being a pervert is kind of a given. "That's so gross," I say.

When he rolls his tongue to hold back his laughter, I swat his arm again, and his laughter slips through. Landon rarely laughs, so even though he's irritating me, I let it go and laugh with him, because the sound of it makes it hard to stay angry. Eventually he quiets down and licks his lips, almost licking the charcoal off.

Shaking my head, I reach forward, place my thumb on one of the smudges right by his lips, and rub it away, trying to ignore the intensity in his gaze as he watches me. "You always have this stuff on you, even when you're not sketching," I remark as I pull my hand away. But he stops me with a touch of his fingers. I freeze as he wraps his hand over mine, and my heart starts to flutter inside my chest.

"I've been thinking." He brings my hand back to his mouth. "About trying something," he whispers against my palm.

"Oh yeah." My voice cracks and I can't stop staring at his lips.

He nods, without taking his eyes off me. "I've been thinking about it for a while..." He takes a deep breath and then lets it out, seeming uneasy. "About kissing you."

My pulse quickens as he pauses, like he's waiting for me to say something, but my throat is thick with my nerves and I can't get my lips to form words. I've never kissed a guy before, and Landon isn't just a guy. He's my best friend. Even though I've thought about it many times, I've also thought about what it would be like to lose him. He's the only one who keeps me connected to the world ever since my dad died. Without him, I don't know what I'd be, or if I'd be anything.

I start to protest, but then he shuts his eyes, and my doubts temporarily wash away from the feel of his lips against the palm of my hand. He kisses it gradually, like he's savoring the moment—and knowing Landon, he probably is. He moves his lips down to my wrist and he does the same thing there, only this time he slips out his tongue and I bite down on my lip as I shudder. My eyes *close on their own accord, and I hold my breath in antic-ipation, waiting for him to kiss me. I wait. And wait, but nothing happens.*

"Nova," he says in a low, husky voice. "Open your eyes."

I obey, marginally disappointed because I really thought he was going to kiss me.

His honey-brown eyes are smoldering cinders in the fiery sunlight. His lips part and then he seals them together again, eyeing my mouth before sighing. "I wasn't lying," he says, looking back at the tree as he puts the tip of his pencil back to the paper. "I could spend hours—even days—sketching you. It would be perfect." He del-icately touches the corner of my eye with his fingertips, before pulling back, the uneasiness in his eyes amplifying. "Especially those."

I don't know what to say to him, so I keep my lips fastened, watching him as he tucks his head down and wisps of his hair fall into his eyes. His hand starts moving again, tracing the lines of the massive leafless tree in the distance. The uneasiness quickly erases from his expres-sion as he falls into his peace with his art, and I get lost in my thoughts of why he didn't kiss me and why he looked so sad when he was about to.

I start to dry-heave as the burn of the alcohol forces its way back up my throat. Leaning over the railing, I gag until my stomach is empty, my abdominal muscles are throbbing, and the gravel below is drenched in my vomit. Wiping my mouth off with the back of my hand, I turn around and sink down onto the deck. Hugging my knees to my chest, I recline against the railing and angle my head back, looking up at the stars shining vibrantly against the charcoaled sky. I start counting them, one by one, and my mind and body start to relax.

I remain that way until the front door to the trailer swings open and then slams shut. Tearing my gaze away from the night, I look over at the door, hoping it'll be Delilah and I can get the hell out of here. But it's just Nikki.

She looks livid, her face red as she stomps down the stairs toward the gravel driveway. "Fuck you . . . and fuck your stupid art."

The door opens again and the guy with honey-brown eyes walks out with an unlit cigarette stuck between his lips. Standing at the top of the stairs, he cups his hands around the end of the cigarette, lighting it while Nikki slips off one of her fluorescent pink stilettos.

"You're an asshole, you know that?" she cries and then chucks her shoe at him.

He blows out a breath of smoke as the shoe flies by his head, but he doesn't even flinch. Nikki stomps her bare foot on the ground as the guy steps back and bends down to collect her shoe. He walks to the top of the stairs and extends the stiletto out to her and she snatches it from him.

"I'll never hook up with you again," she spits, wiggling her foot into her shoe as she stumbles to the side in the loose gravel. "You're ridiculous...you're like a..." She gets her foot into the stiletto and she stands upright. "Do you even feel anything at all?" She folds her arms and taps her foot as she waits for him to respond.

He takes a long drag, his chest rising and falling as he releases the smoke out in front of his face. "Not really," he says with a frown, brushing his thumb along the bottom of the cigarette. Ashes scatter all over the ground.

She clenches her fists, lets out a frustrated scream, and then she storms off for her car, her hair whipping across her shoulder as she whirls. He watches her car back away, then he rests his arms on the railing and stares off into the darkness of the trailer park.

The longer he stands there, the more I wonder if he even realizes I'm sitting here. Should I just get up and leave? Stay put until he goes back in? I'm starting to get nervous, my palms beginning to sweat, because I can't make a decision.

"So did your parents really name you after the car?" he unexpectedly says without looking at me.

It takes me a moment to answer. "My dad had one when I was born. He loved it and he loved me, so he thought the name was fitting."

He nods, then turns around and reclines against the railing, slanting his head to look at me. "Does he still have the car?"

I begin to shake my head but then halt, contemplating how to respond. "Well, it's parked in the garage at my mom's house, but it's not his anymore." I summon a breath as he gives me a confused look and even though I don't want to, I add, "He died six years ago. He left the car to me, but I don't know... I'd feel weird driving it." I have no idea why I'm telling him this. I never talk to people about my father, except for Landon and sometimes the camera.

"I get it," he states. This look crosses his face; sadness, mixed with anger, tinted with shame. "Sorry about Nikki. She's just pissed off at me about... well, I honestly can't fucking remember." He gazes off, looking lost, and I notice how red and bloodshot his eyes are. He's probably stoned and by morning he probably won't remember any of this. Or me. Strangely, that thought makes me a little depressed.

"You don't need to apologize for her." I place my feet underneath me and stand up, dusting the dirt off the back of my legs. "It's not your fault. Nikki is always kind of bitchy, if I'm remembering right."

A smile starts to form at his lips, but it dissolves by the time I take my next breath. "Well, that's nice to know. That it's not just me that unleashes it from her."

I relax back against the railing and prop my elbows against the wood. There are only the steps between us, but he seems really far away from me. "How do you know her? You don't live here, right?"

He shakes his head as he puts the cigarette into his mouth and takes a drag. "I'm just here for the summer. Tristan's my cousin, and I need a place to crash. He stepped up." Smoke eases from his lips as he shrugs with a miserable look on his face.

"Tristan's nice," I say, shuffling my toes back and forth in front of me. "I've known him since I was a kid."

"Yeah, he's a good guy." He frowns at the ground, his brow puckered. "He can totally look past stuff, you know." He lets out a faltering exhale, and when he looks up at me I nearly fall down. It's too much. He looks so much like him, and I don't know what to do. My heart feels like it's rupturing open again. I want to run, hide, and not go through this again, but I also want to take the pain away from him, like I couldn't do the first time around.

"What's your name?" I ask, taking a tentative step toward him, knowing that by asking I'm pushing the door open a little.

"Oh, sorry," he apologizes, extending his hand. His palm is covered with smudged charcoal. "It's Quinton."

I half-expected him to say Landon. My fingers tremble as I place my hand into his, but once I come into contact with him, I find myself feeling calm for the first time in a year. "It's nice to meet you, Quinton."

"And it's nice to meet you, Nova-like-the-car." A small trace of a smile appears at his lips again as he wraps his long fingers around mine and his skin is warm. I don't like that it is because the last time I touched Landon's skin it was ice-cold, and it painfully reminds me that Quinton's not him, that he's just someone who looks like him, and not even that.

He's just someone who carries anguish and torture inside, like Landon did.

"So you're going to be here for the whole summer?" I ask, unable to let go of his hand, aware that the calm will leave me the moment I let go—let go of Landon again.

He nods, adjusting his hand, and I think he's going to pull away. But he continues to hold on to mine. "Yeah, at least until I can figure out a plan."

"A plan?"

"Yeah, a life plan, or whatever the hell people call it."

"I don't call it anything," I say with honesty. "I don't really have one."

He assesses me closely with a confounded expression. "Yeah, me either." His forehead creases and he bites at his lip, fleetingly glancing at mine. "Do you want to—"

The screen door swings open and bangs against the side of the house. We swiftly pull our hands away as Delilah and Dylan stroll out with smiles on their faces and contentment in their eyes. Delilah notices Quinton and me pulling away from each other and she shoots me a discreet, quizzical look, but I'm too distracted by the calmness evaporating from my body to return an answer.

"Well, I see you two skipped right past the introductions," Dylan comments like he has some sort of insight into what was going on. But nothing was going on, at least that's what I'm telling myself.

He pulls out a pack of cigarettes from the pocket of his

unbuttoned plaid shirt and starts tapping it on his wrist while Delilah pops the tab of the beer she's holding and smooths down her ruffled auburn hair.

Quinton flicks his cigarette over the railing. "I'm going inside," he mutters, then hurries for the door.

My fingers long to grab on to the back of his shirt so I can drag him back and beg him to tell me why he looks so depressed, but all I do is watch him walk away. When the door slams shut behind him, I feel guiltier than I ever have in my entire life.

"I'm ready to go," I tell Delilah, wrapping my arm around my stomach as nausea sets in.

Usually Delilah argues when I want to bail out early, but she takes one look at me and nods. "Okay, meet me at the truck."

I nod and walk quickly toward the gate, taking even but swift strides, reminding myself to count and *breathe*. I climb in the car and tap the lock, while I mentally bottle up my feelings. Delilah kisses Dylan good-bye on the top of the stairs. By the time she climbs in the truck, I'm somewhat settled down.

"Jesus, Nova, are you okay?" she asks as she slides into the driver's seat and slams the car door. "You looked like you were about to throw up or something."

"I had a shot." I slouch down in the seat and overlap my arms on top of my stomach. "It made me a little sick."

She puts the keys in the ignition and the engine roars to life. "I've seen you slam down like five shots in a row before.

Tell me what's really up. Was it...did something happen with that Quinton guy? Because Dylan says he has major issues, and I think that's probably the last thing you need." She pauses, considering something as she fiddles with the radio station. "Although it'd be nice to see you date someone. All I've ever seen you do is kiss a few random guys when you occasionally get really drunk."

I stare at the trailer's front door as she backs up. "Because that's all I want to do," I say. "And nothing happened between Quinton and me." The sentence feels like the biggest lie I've ever told, because something did happen.

I felt something for the first time in over a year, but what it was I'm not sure.

Quinton

I only came outside to make sure Nikki didn't say any more shit to Nova, and now I'm holding her goddamn hand. I know what I'm doing is wrong, but I can't seem to let go of her hand and I need to let go of it and walk away. *Now. Leave the poor girl alone. You avoid girls like this for a reason. You don't need to ruin more lives or get attached.* No matter how hard I try, though, I can't seem to convince myself to do the right thing and walk away. Nova looks so lonely, sad, and alarmingly unsettled, and I just want to make her feel better. Somehow.

It's not like we're talking about anything important, but I don't like how I'm noticing how beautiful she is or how I start to wonder what it would be like to sketch her. She has these amazingly striking eyes that probably look blue to a lot of people, but when I study them more closely, I notice little specks of green hiding in them. Her lips look soft as hell and there are freckles on her nose, and I can picture myself taking hours sketching each one. I love how her hair falls down on her bare shoulders and the slight crookedness of her nose. It's the little imperfections on her that make her ideal for drawing, and I want to take her back in my room and stare at her for hours.

She also makes me smile twice, and it's been a long time since someone's made me smile. When I realize what kind of emotions are emerging inside me, I panic and my thoughts get jumbled. I almost end up asking her to come inside with me, and that's the last thing I want to do with a girl like her, one that will actually talk to me instead of just fuck me. The ones that have no substance and like to fuck are the ones I'll never care about, and that's what I need—deserve. Plus, it's already been made pretty clear that Tristan has a thing for her, and he's the last person I'd ever want to steal a girl from.

Luckily Dylan walks outside right as I'm about to ask Nova to come into the house, and I take the opportunity to make a quick exit back inside and make a beeline straight for the fridge to get a beer.

Tristan scrutinizes me from the couch with his feet kicked up on the coffee table, as he works to clean the resin out of a glass pipe with a small pocketknife. "What were you doing out there?"

I grab a beer and slam the fridge door shut. "Just talking."

"With Nova." He frowns, obviously not thrilled about the idea.

I pop the cap off the beer and toss it in the trash. "Yeah, but you don't need to worry."

He sets the pipe down on the table by his feet. "Who said I was worried?"

I shrug and cross the living room, ready to lock myself up in my room, so I can singe my brain cells away and draw for hours. "I was just under the impression you had a thing for her."

He doesn't say anything and the tension between us builds. I duck underneath the curtain, wishing that I wasn't here, wishing that it was a year ago and that I would have gotten the car pulled over in time.

After I make it into my room and lock the door, I go to the two things that make me feel content. I grab the pipe and bag of weed Tristan lent me from off the dresser and my sketchpad from out of my duffel bag, then I sink down on the bed. I set the sketchpad aside, take the lighter out of my pocket, and pack the pipe before putting the mouthpiece up to my lips. Flicking the lighter, I suck in a deep breath and inhale the numbness in large, welcoming breaths. Once my lungs are charred and the restlessness in my body has stilled, I lean back against the bed, prop the sketchbook on my knees, and start to trace lines on a drawing I've been working on for a year but have never been able to complete. Because once I finish it, I'll finally have to accept that Lexi's really gone. And that I killed her.

I keep drawing and drawing, smoking bowl after bowl, until I'm so lost in my own head, all that's left to do is pass out. I toss my sketchpad aside and lay down on the filthy mattress, shutting my eyes, hoping I'm high enough that the nightmares don't take over my sleep. But usually, I'm not that lucky.

Blood gushes down my forehead, down my cheeks, so thick I can barely see. My chest is aching, the pain more unbearable than when I accidentally smashed my thumb with a hammer and broke all the bones in it. I feel like I can't move, and I have to work to keep my lungs gasping for air.

I'm upside down, the blood is rushing to my head, and the sky is now the floor of the car. There are rocks and dirt and glass everywhere, and I can see a continuously flashing light out of my peripheral vision.

I cough, and blood streams from my lips. Searching around the dark, I feel around until I find the buckle to the seat belt. I push the button, the buckle slips out, and the strap on my shoulders loosens. I fall down, hitting my head on the mangled roof of the car. I cough up some more blood as I turn on my side and push myself up on my hands and knees, blinking through the pain ringing through my skull, and crawl out of the car. I glance back inside, noting that no one is left in the car. Where did they go? Did they climb out and go to get help? Did they... did they get thrown out? I'm pretty sure I'm the only one who had a seat belt on. Why didn't I make them put theirs on?

It's hard to see anything but the headlights flashing through the trees surrounding the lake, and all I can hear are the waves rushing toward me. Sucking in a breath, I stagger to my feet and stumble across the gravel, broken glass and crunched metal, grunting at the pain that erupts through my chest. My shirt is ripped open and so is my chest, and blood pours out of my skin, soaking the fabric. It hurts more than my brain can register, but the pain doesn't matter. I need to find Lexi.

Hunched over, I stagger up the edge of the road. "Lexi…" I cough, stumbling over my own feet. I fall into the gravel and my palms split open. "Lexi…" My voice is weak, nearly soundless, but I push back to my feet and keep walking up the road. But a few steps up the road my knees give out on me and I crumple to the asphalt. God damn it, this is all my fault. I reach for my phone, but it's not in my back pocket.

My hand shakes as I try to remember what happened. We hit the other car, and then flipped a few times, before settling near the lake. "Shit…" I struggle to breathe, my eyelids growing heavy as I roll onto my back and stare at the sky. I'm about to give in to exhaustion when I hear her voice.

"Quinton…" It's barely audible, but it gives me hope.

I don't know how, but I somehow I manage to get to my feet and run toward the sound of her voice, even as I lose more blood and I grow more light-headed. None of it matters, though. The pain. The injuries. How I feel inside and out. I just need to get to her. As I stumble around one of the trees and trip through the grass, I hear her voice again. I follow the sound, slowing down as the outline of her body comes into view, and suddenly all I want to do is lie down and die beside her.

Chapter Four

Nova

"So how long do I have to lay here like this?" I ask Landon for the thousandth time. I'm lying on his bed with my hands slack to my side and my head tipped back. The dress I'm wearing has ridden up to the tops of my legs and I'm pretty much flashing him. I went to rearrange it, but he told me not to move, that I was perfect the way that I was. I'm actually kind of uncomfortable, but I gave into him, because it's really hard to say no when he looks at me with his puppy-dog eyes. He wins me over every time with them, no matter what. But then again, I'd pretty much do anything for him.

"You are seriously the most impatient person I know." His hand sweeps across the paper, and there's a trace of a smile on his lips. He's not wearing a shirt and I have no idea why—he was bare chested when I showed up early today. He has jeans on, and his hair hangs down on his forehead in traditional Landon style. The room smells *like pot, probably because he was smoking some before I came over. He hates smoking it around me and says I'm too good to be doing it myself. But it makes no sense to me, because if I'm too good for it, then why isn't he?*

"And you're seriously the slowest person I know," I retort, grinning as I stare up at the ceiling. His walls are painted black, which makes his room always seem dark even when it's midday. There are sketches all over his wall of images and people that mean something to him or that have inspired him in one way or another. But there's not one of me. The one he's drawing right now is the first one he's ever done of me. Why, I have no idea. I've known him for a few years, but he's never asked to draw me before. Until this morning.

"Why are you drawing me again?" I ask, wiggling my nose, trying to get the itch to go away.

He shrugs. "It just seemed like it was time."

Music is playing in the background and I start to sing along, giving up on trying to figure out what he's really thinking.

"You know how you get a song stuck in your head?" he says, letting out a quiet breath. "And no matter how hard you try, it just keeps playing over and over again until finally you just have to start singing it aloud."

I smile as I finish the set of lyrics. "Yeah."

"Well, that's why I'm drawing you."

"Because I was stuck in your head?"

"Because I couldn't stop thinking about you," he says, and I pretty much stop breathing. "It's actually been that way for a while now."

I'm wary to ask, but I have to know. "Is that a good thing or a bad thing? Because sometimes when a song gets stuck in my head it can get kind of annoying."

He pauses and I wait for him to start teasing me and make a joke about me being a pain in his ass. But he doesn't say anything, and the sound of the pencil scratching against the paper stops. I want to tip my chin down so I can see what he's doing, but I'm too nervous, so I lie there, singing under my breath.

Seconds later, he's climbing over me with a small, but diffident smile on his face. "It's not annoying at all." He props an arm on each side of my head and positions his body over me. I don't move, don't breathe, and I'm pretty sure my heart stops beating. "You're like my favorite song, Nova. The one that I never want to forget. That I want to play over and over again."

I try not to grin because it sounds like a line. But Landon's never been the kind of guy to feed girls cheesy pickup lines. In fact, he hardly talks to girls except me, and the fact that he's using a music analogy says how much he knows me. "Would you put me on repeat?" I ask like a dork, because he's too close and it's making me nervous and stupid, apparently.

He bites at his bottom lip, confining a smile. "I do...
you're always in my head..." He leans toward me, and
I wonder if this is the moment when he's finally going
to kiss me, instead of almost kiss me. "Always...." Right
before our lips touch, I detect a flash of sadness in his eyes,
heavier than what's normally there, but it vanishes the
instant our lips come into contact.

I suck in a slow, shaky breath as warmth spreads
throughout my body and his tongue slips over mine. He
tastes like spices I've never dared taste before. I know it's
not his first kiss, but he knows it's mine. I wonder what
he thinks about me. Why he's kissing me. I'm thinking a
lot of things.

"Nova," he whispers, and I realize his lips are no
longer touching but hovering over mine, his breath warm
against my skin. "Do you want me to stop?" he asks.

My chest is heaving and every time it rises up, it
brushes against his. "No."

He wets his lips with his tongue, and then runs his
eyes over me, shifting his weight to the side so he can
brush my hair out of my eyes. "Relax," he says, and when
I nod, he reconnects his mouth to mine.

I try to do what he says and relax, but when his
tongue enters my mouth again, I start to panic, wondering if I'm doing everything right. But the longer
his tongue massages mine, the more my muscles start to
unravel. I become a little daring and bite his lip, which

he seems to like, because he shudders. My hands are still lying motionlessly at the side of me, but his are all over me, feeling my sides, my waist, my hips. His fingers start to sneak underneath the bottom of my dress and I tense, deliberating whether I should tell him to stop. But as I search for a reason why, I realize there's not one and that I want him to touch me.

I loosen up and move my hands up to his chest, taking the opportunity to feel the lines of his lean muscles. His fingers graze the bottom of my panties, and for a second the weight of him falls against me. I arch my body into his, knowing that our friendship that once existed is no more, but I don't care. I want this—want him.

Our slow kiss starts to heat up as his tongue explores the inside of my mouth, and then I gasp for air as he slowly slips a finger inside me.

"I should stop, right?" he pants, pulling back for a minute to look me in the eyes.

I blink through the amazing feelings developing inside my body, trying to focus on his beautiful face and the intensity in his eyes, but I'm losing touch with reality. "No...," I manage to get out as my neck curves and my head tips back.

He listens to me, touching me more and making me feel things I only ever imagined. He kisses me all the way through it until my body can no longer take it and he has to stop, otherwise I'd pass out from lack of oxygen. His eyes are glossy as he encircles his arm around my waist, and he pulls me with him as he rolls onto his back. I rest my head on his chest, my eyes wide at the implausibility of what just happened.

I drape my arm over his stomach as he plays with my hair. "So am I still stuck in your head?" I say and then roll my eyes at myself.

His fingers stop combing through my hair and he sketches a line down to my cheek to my jawline, where he hooks a finger underneath my chin and tips my chin up so I meet his eyes. "Yes. In fact, I think it's worse." He says it like he's disappointed, almost as if he was hoping that I wouldn't be, and it makes me sad. I'm about to ask why he looks so upset, but then he dips his mouth to mine and starts kissing me again, and just like that I forget about everything.

Chapter Five

Nova

June 5, Day 17 of Summer Break

The feisty tune of "Last Resort" by Papa Roach plays in the background, but I have it turned down low so it won't drown out my words. The blinds are shut, blocking out the morning sunlight, and my hair hangs to my shoulders, still damp from the shower I just took. The computer has been recording for about five minutes, but I haven't said a word. I've gotten up a few times and paced my floor, trying to get the thoughts in my head to connect and form coherent sentences. I wonder if that's what Landon did before he made his video...I wonder if he planned it out.

Finally, I decide there shouldn't be any preplanning, and plop down in the chair. I'm a little restless as I slant the screen and then tuck my leg under my butt to boost myself up, and then let the first sentence that pops into my head barrel out of my mouth, despite my initial instinct to censor. "Okay, so it's been a little over two weeks since I got home from college and the dreams and memories of . . ." I attempt, but then trail off, knowing I'm going to have to say his name, even if I don't want to. It's strange, though, talking about him, while looking at myself on the screen of the computer. I can see how just the thought of uttering his name aloud makes my eyes go wide and my pupils shrink, like I've suddenly been possessed by a distant memory. I take a deep breath, then another, running my fingers through my hair, and sweeping it out of my face. "Landon . . ." My eyes enlarge. What will people think if they ever watch this? What will they wonder about me and how I saw myself? "The dreams about him are more intense than they've ever been," I say. "Part of me wants to find a way to shut them off, but part of me wants to hold on to them—hold on to him . . . forever."

I cross my arms on the desk, lean closer to the screen, and examine my eyes, noting the vastness in my pupils, circled by a slender blue ring. "When I look at myself, everything inside me pretty much screams to stop thinking about him and to turn off the memories . . . and I try to count through them . . . like it's that simple . . . but it's not." I blow out a breath, gathering my hair behind my head. "I just wish I could figure out a way to know what he was thinking . . . somehow track things back to why he gave up so easily . . . why he left me . . . why I couldn't see where he was headed." I bite at my fingernail. "Or maybe I could and I was just in denial . . . Was that the kind of person that I was? One who denies what's in front of her?"

My voice drops off at the end as the blunt honesty escapes my mouth. I don't want to hear it or think about it anymore, so I shut the computer down, no longer wanting to look at myself.

⌇

Later that day, Delilah and I are hanging out in my room. The blinds are open and the sunlight flows inside, making the air stifling, even though I have a fan on full blast. I'm sifting through some of my video clips, trying to figure out what the hell the purpose is, besides watching me babble about pointless nonsense that doesn't really make sense. Am I trying to understand myself? Who I am? Or am I trying to understand Landon? Life? Death? What he was thinking in his final moments, and why did he decide to sit down and record it?

Why do I always have so many fucking questions in my head?

"We should go to that concert down in Fairfield at the end of July. Wouldn't that be fun? To feed your music addiction," Delilah says as she sifts through a stack of CDs on my shelf and pulls a few out. She's wearing a short red dress that matches her red-stained lips and is only a couple of shades darker than her hair. "And why do you have these still? No one listens to CDs anymore."

I take them from her hand and set them down on my computer desk in an orderly, alphabetized stack: Blink-182 to Taking Back Sunday. "Landon gave them to me," I say and then keep talking to avoid going down that road with her.

I close one of my video files down and try to ignore the file marked "Landon's" as I open another video clip of mine. "And what concert? I don't remember hearing about one."

"That's because you live in your own little crazy Nova Land." She crosses her eyes and circles her finger around her temple, and then she plops down on my bed and tucks her hands underneath her legs. "It's been advertised all over town and I've mentioned it a few times. It's just a bunch of indie bands. But it's going to be like a weeklong event or something."

I mull over the idea of going to a concert. As much as I love music and used to love going to concerts, I don't feel like going to them anymore. There's too much connection to Landon with them, and there'd be a lot of noise and a lot of people and a lot of unfamiliarity, which would make it hard to keep track of everything around me. Plus, if it's a weeklong concert, my morning routine would be wrecked and my anxiety would probably go through the roof, unstable, out of control. "I'm not sure I'm up for a concert, Delilah, or if I'll have time." I move the cursor across the screen to click on another video file. "I think I might enroll in some summer classes . . . maybe a film one or something."

She shakes her head as she shoves to her feet, then she stomps over to the computer and hammers her thumb against the off button on the tower. "No way. We made a pact not to do classes this summer. Besides—" she taps her finger on the computer screen "—you already got your own little film lesson going on here. Although I don't get why. You've never really been into filming before, at least not to the point where you did it for fun."

"I'm still trying to figure out what the point is, too." Sighing, I rotate the chair around to face her and change the subject. "I know we said no classes, but I need a distraction."

She plants her hands on her hips and narrows her eyes at me. "From what?"

I shrug and put my hand over the scar on my wrist. "This town... my own head. Life."

"Isn't that going to be hard, since we're here?" She points out the window at the undersized, nearly identical houses that line the street. "And I don't know what to tell you about escaping your own head or life other than you could get high."

"Are you being serious right now?" I ask. I've never smoked weed myself. Landon did though... always smoking it, all the time... and telling me I shouldn't. I always just let it be, because I was never really the kind of person who wanted to. Now, though... I'm not really sure who I am. And I want to find out just what kind of person I am. Do I really like music anymore, or is my love for it gone? Do I really like making videos? Would I like getting high?

She shrugs, her expression unreadable. "I'm not saying to do it, only that you could do it."

"Do you still do it? Smoke weed, I mean."

She shakes her head. "I told you I stopped when we went to college."

I'm not sure if I believe her. We lived in the same dorm and everything, and I saw her pretty much every day, but she also went out a lot more than I did, mainly because I hate going to new places and the ones she loved to go to were unpredictable, rowdy, loud, head spinning.

She flops down on my bed, which is overflowing with purple and black throw pillows, and the mattress bounces beneath her. "Nova, I love you to death—I really do—but you are the saddest person I've ever met and sometimes...sometimes I think you almost are this way on purpose."

"I'm not sad all the time, am I?" I ask. She doesn't answer but only offers me a sympathetic look. I stretch my legs out and stare down at my feet. I have flip-flops on, and the scar where I cut my foot open the day I found Landon shows. It happened when I fell down on the floor. My foot caught on the bottom of his bookshelf, and it scraped the entire layer of skin off. It probably hurt, but the shock numbed it. I didn't even scream. I just lay there...looking at him...like that until... My head pounds and blood roars in my eardrums as images clip the inside of my skull. *Darkness, the soft sound of music... how pale his skin looked even in daybreak...*

One...two...three... I start counting the dark threads of fabric on the carpet, forcing the thought from my head. *Four...five...six...*

"Nova, what the hell." Delilah waves her hand in front of my face and I flinch, breaking the steady pattern of numbers in my head. "You're totally spacing out on me."

I inhale, then progressively free the breath from my lungs, causing my bangs to drift to the side of my face. "Sorry."

She vacillates, bobbing her head from side to side, and then she seizes my hand and hauls me to my feet. "We are so getting out of here."

She leads me toward my bedroom door, and I rush to keep up with her. "Where are we going?"

She yanks open the door and tugs me out into the hall, pulling me toward the front door. "Anywhere but here."

I don't like that she doesn't have a destination, and my pulse soars as we step outside and head toward her truck. I suddenly wish I had a camera in my hand, because it seems like it would be a lot more calming watching myself wander into the unknown, through the lens, because it wouldn't seem so real.

It's hot and I'm wearing cutoffs and a thin black tank top. My hair is a little tangled, and I only have eyeliner and mascara on, which is melting from the heat. "I'm not dressed to go anywhere," I protest, as she swings open the front gate.

She glances over her shoulder and inspects my outfit and hair. "You look great. You always do." She stops when we arrive at her single-cab truck parked in front of the garage. She lets go of my hand and positions herself in front of me. "Look, when I first met you, you were seriously so sad, and I was kind of terrified of you. But then I got to know you, and you know what? My opinion changed."

"Only because Ms. Kenzingly forced us to work on that final project together." I smile at the memory of our first awkward introduction. She was the pretty, outgoing girl who sometimes got into trouble, and I was the depressed, weird girl who used to date Landon. It had been four weeks since I'd found him in his room, and I was still the one everyone was afraid of, because I saw things no one wants to admit exist. "God, I can only imagine how hard it was trying to get me to even talk to you."

She smiles, too, but it's shadowed by a stern look. "Yeah, and to this day I'm so glad I managed to get you to say something, even though it was 'Yes, I think so,' because it opened the door for our friendship." She pauses, rubbing her lips together as she shields her eyes from the sunlight with her hand. "But it was hard, you know, being your friend, because you never told me the truth about what was going on in that head of yours, but at college you seemed a little better. Not great, but better." She waves her hand in front of me and blows out an exasperated breath. "But we've been back for over a couple of weeks now and you're getting sadder, if that's even possible."

"It's possible," I say, leaning back against the truck door. "It really is."

She's quiet for a while and then she takes my hands in hers. "Can we just go somewhere for a while? Escape or something. Do something crazy and unexpected. We could go hang out at Dylan's tonight and just relax."

Crazy and unexpected? I start counting the rocks under my feet but there are too many. "Are we just escaping from my sadness? Or from your mom?"

"Both," she says simply, giving the top of my hand a pat.

I keep trying to count the rocks, but more and more appear in my vision, and finally it becomes overwhelming and I give up. Throwing my hands in the air, I decide to try and not be sad for the day. *Try to survive.* "Okay."

She jumps up and down, clapping her hands. "Thank you, Nova."

"You're welcome." I open the truck door and hop into the seat, feeling as though I've failed because the rocks remain uncounted. "But you really don't need to be thanking me. I didn't do anything, you crazy woman." I shut the door and she skips around to the other side.

"Yes, you did." She smiles as she climbs into the driver's seat, then turns on the ignition. "You decided to be happy."

I keep quiet and let myself drown in my thoughts, knowing that's not what I'm doing. I'll probably never truly be happy again, no matter how much I want to, because no matter what, Landon will always be gone and I'll still be here.

Alone.

❧

We end up stopping at the local ice cream parlor, because Delilah says that some sugar in my system will cheer me up. It was what my dad used to say all the time: *Eat some candy and you'll feel better.* My mom hated it and would always put something healthy in my hand, like an apple or a carrot, then when she'd turn away, my dad would steal it and wink at me as he handed me a sucker or a candy bar.

I miss him so bad. His life ended way too soon, but unlike Landon's, I couldn't have prevented it. He had a heart condition he didn't know about until it was too late, and there was nothing I could have done to help him. Still, it had been horrible to watch . . . him lying on the ground helpless and afraid, and there was nothing I could do but watch his life leave him. I never thought I'd be the same again, and then Landon came along and it felt like he understood me and he gave me a reason to smile again. But then he left me, too, out of choice, something I still can't figure out, even after a goddamn year. And now I'm here, walking around, half the time feeling like a zombie with no real direction, lost and lonely, and everything I felt when my dad died has multiplied.

God, what the fuck? Why did you do it? Why did you leave me here? You can't leave me here.

I'm sitting in one of the booths, watching a wind chime outside twirl in the light summer breeze as I stir the bowl of cookie dough ice cream in front of me. The chime is made of thin clear strings and shimmering pieces of aqua and teal sea glass that magically reflect the sunlight every time it hits them. There's some cheesy '90s music playing, and I'm totally zoning in my thoughts while Delilah tries to get the cashier guy to give her more maraschino cherries.

I hear the door's bell ding as someone walks inside, and my

gaze instinctively drifts from the chime to my barely touched bowl of ice cream, which is now melted and liquefied. Then I hear Delilah say something really loud, and I reel around in the booth and look toward the front counter. Dylan, Tristan, and Quinton are standing beside her, and she already has her arms and lips fastened on Dylan, who's cupping her ass as he lifts her up. The cashier guy seems really uncomfortable by their public display of affection and walks back to the stocking room.

Tristan starts laughing at something on the order board and then he playfully slaps Quinton in the stomach. Quinton gives him a shove, a smile forming at his lips, but his eyes are still hued with sorrow. Tristan stumbles to the side, nearly crashing into an oblivious Dylan and Delilah, then he regains his balance and leans in to say something to Quinton. When he catches sight of me, he gives me a little smile and wave.

I return the wave and then my hand falls to the table as Quinton looks over at me. Biting his bottom lip, he seems uneasy as he raises his hand and waves at me. I return the wave with a tight smile, then sighing I turn back to my sad little melted bowl of ice cream.

Quinton starts to head over, even though he looks like it's the last thing he wants to be doing. His hands are stuffed in the pockets of his faded jeans, and there's a small hole in the bottom of his black T-shirt. It looks like there's dirt or some kind of shavings in his hair, and he's got black smudges tracking up his arms. The closer he gets, the quicker I count, until the numbers in my head are blurred together and suddenly I can't see a path. My adrenaline surges, and I feel overwhelmed. I need to find a path again, something to concentrate on, something I can control and keep track of.

"Hey," he says when he arrives at my table, and the sound of his voice immediately begins to slow down my pulse.

"Hey," I reply, stirring my melted ice cream as I tip my chin up, my gaze gradually scrolling up his body.

Silence builds between us, but a real, comfortable silence, just like when I spent time with Landon. *But he's not Landon.*

"So rumor has it that you're a music junkie," he finally says, scooting into the seat across from mine. "And that you play the piano and the drums."

I nod, internally cringing at the mention of drums, the instrument I loved most, but can no longer even contemplate playing without it hurting every inch of my mind and soul. "Who told you that? Tristan?"

His glances at Tristan, who's up at the counter, rambling off an order to the cashier guy. "Yeah, he did the other day, after you left our house."

I notice the smell of his cologne, laced with a hint of smoke, and I hate to admit it, but I kind of like it, even though it doesn't remind me of Landon in any way. His eyes are glossy like caramel, and he keeps looking at my melted bowl of gooey ice cream like it's the most fascinating thing in the world. "Okay... why were you guys talking about me?"

He glances up from the ice cream, blinking his bloodshot

eyes. "Because I asked him about you." He bites his lip after he says it, like he wants to retract his statement.

"Well, that doesn't seem fair," I say, trying to keep the conversation effortless. "I don't know anything about you."

He flops back in his seat, putting his hands behind his head with his elbows sticking out as he gazes through the window. "There's not much to know."

I shut my eyes, telling myself to get up and walk away, because it feels wrong. But when I open them again, he's looking directly at me, and I can't help myself. I need to understand him, because in a weird, distorted way I feel like understanding him might help me understand Landon a little better, if I can get deep enough.

"You're an artist," I say straightforwardly as I set the spoon down on the table.

His arms drift to his lap and he looks so mystified that it momentarily eliminates the pain in his eyes. "How did you know?"

I inch my hand across the table, trying to keep my fingers steady as I touch a splotch of charcoal on his forearm. "Because of these."

He glances down at my fingers on his arm, unnerved. "Yeah, but most people would think it was grease or something."

I wonder if he knows—if Tristan told him about Landon. "I'm just that good." I sink back in the booth, fold my arms, and chew on my bottom lip, fighting back a smile.

Curiosity crosses his face. "Well, I guess so." He waits for me to elaborate, but I don't. I'm kind of enjoying mystifying him.

I fiddle with the leather band bracelets on my wrists. "Where did you move from?"

His expression sinks as he looks back to the window. "Seattle."

"Seattle . . . how far is that from here?"

"The plane ride was a little over an hour." He thrums his fingers on the table, his shoulders stiffening as he grows more uncomfortable. "So Dylan said Delilah mentioned a concert, and I guess they want to go." He changes the subject, just like Landon used to do when he'd get uncomfortable with a topic.

"Yeah, she was saying something to me about it earlier," I say, picking up the spoon. I want to ask him more about why he came here, but I can't seem to work up the nerve to press for information. I don't know him, and generally when people don't want to talk about something it's hard to get it out of them. That was always the problem with Landon. He never wanted to talk. And I always let him get away with it. "I'm not a fan of concerts anymore, though."

His head slants to the side as he studies me. "You're a fan of music, you play the drums and piano, but you don't like concerts?"

"I used to," I clarify as I start to stir the ice cream again. "But now . . . I don't know, they're too noisy." *Chaotic, disorganized, sporadic.*

"Music in general is noisy." He's amused by me, and for a moment the craziness inside my head is worth it.

"Yeah, but at concerts the crowd is, too." I know I sound insane, but I can't explain further without explaining all of me. I bring the spoon to my mouth and slurp the ice cream off it, pulling a face when I realize how warm it is.

He laughs at me as I gag, and it makes me smile a little because happiness looks so beautiful on his face. "That bad, huh?" he asks, and I nod. Sliding his hands across the table, his fingers seek the bowl. "Mind if I try it?"

I gesture at the melted bowl of goo. "Be my guest."

He looks way too happy to be receiving my melted, second-hand ice cream as he grabs the bowl, and relaxes back in the booth, scooping up a spoonful. "Bottoms up," he says and elevates the spoon to his lips. I'm fascinated by the way he sucks it off the plastic spoon, deliberately, like he's savoring every taste of it. A little drips from his mouth and trickles down his lip, and his tongue slides out of his mouth to lick it off, and for a second I picture myself behind a camera, recording the movements of his lips and throat.

Then he takes another large bite, nearly devouring it, and I scrunch my nose. I never was a fan of melted ice cream, but he might be because he's stoned. Landon would sometimes get these weird cravings when he was high, like for caramel ice cream topping straight out of the jar or cherries on a peanut butter sandwich. "So how is it?"

He stares up at the ceiling thoughtfully, then takes another bite. "Delicious, but I've always kind of had a thing for melted ice cream."

"I think it's gross," I divulge, crossing my arms on the table. "I like it right out of the freezer when it's so frozen you have to stab the spoon into it."

He puts another spoonful into his mouth and then looks at me with a puzzled, amused expression as he points the plastic spoon at me. "You're an interesting person, Nova, which by the way can I say is my favorite car." His smile is adorable, but he's hitting a sensitive subject. Not just with the mention of the car, but with me. Landon used to call me interesting—or quirky—instead of weird like everyone else.

"You're not weird," Landon had said once when I'd come home from school upset after Nina Ramaldy told me I was a freak who no one would ever want or understand. "You're interesting and . . ." He'd tapped the end of his pencil on his chin. "Entertaining."

"Is that a good thing?" I'd questioned doubtfully.

"It's a beautiful thing, Nova," he'd replied with one of his rare smiles. "It'd suck if you were normal. You'd be no fun."

I shake the memory away and concentrate on Quinton and his honey-brown eyes. "Are you seriously going to eat all that melted ice cream?"

He puts another spoonful into his mouth and some of it drips down the back of his hand. "You know, melted or not, ice cream is just ice cream." He licks the back of his hand, and it makes me laugh.

"No way," I disagree. "Ice cream isn't meant to be warm."

He hesitantly stares down into the bowl as he scrapes the spoon around the edge, then peers up at me. "Here." He moves the spoon toward me, and there's a large chunk of cookie dough in it with very little ice cream. "Try this part. It's not so bad."

I shake my head and wrinkle my nose. "No thanks. You can eat it."

He tries to look annoyed, giving me a cold, hard stare, but it's more humorous than anything. "Nova, you have to have some of it; otherwise, I'm going to go home feeling guilty for eating all of your ice cream."

I wonder if he's this entertaining when he's not buzzed—I wonder if I'll ever get to find out. I overdramatically sigh, pretending it's a burden, gather my hair behind my head and lean over the table. He meets me halfway and puts the spoon into my mouth, licking his lips to suppress a grin as I suck the chunk of dough into my mouth. Sitting back, I chew on it.

"So," he says as he takes another bite himself, his eyes lingering on my mouth. "It's not so bad without the melted ice cream on it, right?"

I swallow the dough and let go of my hair. "No, it's worse," I lie, biting my bottom lip to keep from laughing.

He licks some ice cream off the bottom of his lip and I notice him eyeing my mouth again. For a second I wonder what his lips would taste like after he's eaten all that ice cream, but then guilt creeps over me as I picture Landon and his lips and how he was the only guy I'd ever really wanted to kiss. The calm bubble that discreetly formed around us pops, and I start counting the tiles on the floor around our table, searching for an excuse to get up. Then a shadow casts itself over the table.

I glance up and I'm relieved to find Delilah standing next to the table. She has a cone in her hand, along with a napkin. "Hey," I say to her.

"Hey," she replies, giving me a questioning look, then her eyes wander to Quinton as she sticks out her hand. "Hi, we haven't really met yet. I'm Delilah."

Quinton sets the bowl of ice cream down on the table, wipes his hands off on the front of his shirt, and shakes her hand. "Quinton."

"Yeah, I know," she says, letting go of his hand. There's something in her tone—insinuation, maybe—that makes me wonder if she knows something about him. "You're from Seattle, right?"

His hands twitch as he balls them up and folds his arms on the table. "Yeah." His fists are so tight his knuckles are turning white and I wonder what he left back in Seattle. Or maybe who. He clears his throat and then scoots to the edge of the booth. "I have to go." He gets up, swings around Delilah, and then hurries for the door.

Delilah and I watch him as he shoves the door open, walks outside, and then dashes down the sidewalk with his head tucked down. Seeing him like that, so upset and disheartened, brings up a memory I'd almost forgotten.

"I don't want to talk right now," Landon had said to me once, and then he'd walked away, leaving me standing in the middle of the yard, totally confused because I'd only asked him where he wanted to go to college and if he'd still want to be with me. After I thought about it for a few minutes, though, I realized how huge the question was and how silly I was for putting it on him, so I didn't chase after him. I wished I had, though. I wished I had more than anything. Maybe if I would have chased him down and forced him to talk, things would have ended differently—maybe things would have never ended at all.

I start to slide to the edge of the booth, seriously contemplating chasing Quinton down, even though I don't know him.

"What are you doing?" Delilah asks as she sits down in the booth, stopping me from sliding out, and licks the top of her vanilla ice cream cone. "Don't chase after him."

I inch back inside the booth, slip my flip-flop off, and tuck my foot under my leg. "Why?"

"Nova, you barely know him," she says. "I mean, it's great to see you smiling like that, but you should probably learn more about him before you go chasing him down."

My shoulders slump as I reach across the table for the bowl of ice cream. "He looks so sad." I frown at the empty bowl. "Like really sad. I wonder why."

"So do you," she remarks, licking the top of her cone. She keeps licking and slurping on it and it starts to drive me nuts. "Okay, I'm going to tell you something about him, and then

I'm going to let you decide whether you want to go there or not, because you've been through a lot, and you deserve to know what you're getting into before you dive in."

Deserve? Who's to decide what I deserve? I shove the bowl to the side and lean forward, crossing my arms. "You're making me worry. Is there... is there something wrong with him? Quinton, I mean?"

She drums her fingers on the table. "Sort of."

I swallow the lump in my throat, fleetingly glancing at Tristan and Dylan over at the counter, chatting it up with the cashier guy. They look so happy and they make it look so easy. I fix my gaze back on Delilah. "Please just tell me."

She dabs some ice cream off her lips with a napkin and starts to open her mouth, when Dylan strolls up to our table.

"Hey, babe," Dylan says over-cheerfully as he puts his arms around Delilah. He has dirt on his cheek, and he smells like beer and cigarettes. He kisses the top of her head and glances up at me. "Hey, Nova." His eyes travel to the empty seat across from me. "Where'd Quinton go?"

I point over my shoulder at the window. "He left." I eye Delilah over, wanting to hear what she has to say about Quinton, but she shrugs, obviously not wanting to talk about it in front of Dylan.

"Where'd he go?" Dylan asks as he shovels up a spoonful from the ridiculously large bowl of ice cream he's holding.

"He probably just needed to get some air." Tristan struts

up to the table carrying a bowl of ice cream that's piled with marshmallows. "He does that sometimes."

I note the slight annoyance in Tristan's tone. "Is he okay?" I ask. "Maybe someone should go check on him."

Tristan stares at his ice cream, then his eyebrows elevate. "He's fine."

Something's up and the longer no one says anything, the more awkward things get. Finally Dylan and Tristan sit down in the opposite seat and start chatting about the concert. Delilah keeps saying we're going to go, even though I said no earlier. I'm too distracted to argue, though. I can't stop thinking about how similar Landon and Quinton are, and the longer I compare them, the more I realize I should have chased Quinton down, just like I should have done with Landon, and I make a silent vow to do better this time, no matter what it takes.

Chapter Six

Quinton

I'm not sure if I'm running away from my feelings, the past, or Nova. Probably the combination of all three.

I was sitting there in a place that looks like it's straight out of Willy Wonka's Chocolate Factory, actually talking to Nova about fucking ice cream, and I have this tone in my voice, the one I used to use on Lexi, when I was trying to charm her. And Nova is smiling at me and I can tell she doesn't smile that often by how hard it is for her. It's like she wants to be sad, which makes me want to make her happy, maybe then I could make up for some of the sadness I put in the world.

Then her friend Delilah comes up to the booth and starts asking me about Seattle. Unlike Nova, she seems determined to get my past out of me. In fact, I think she already knows about it, but she wants to actually hear me say it. Even though I'm pretty much ripped out of my mind, the panic and the guilt gets to me as I think of Lexi and the promise I made to her. The need to escape gets to me, and I'm up and out the door, running away from my problems.

I walk all the way back to the trailer park, which is about three miles, and I'm freaking thirsty as hell and tired. After I drink a beer and smoke a bowl, I pass out on the bed and pretty much stay that way for the next few weeks, drifting in and out of reality. Somehow, in the midst of my dazedness, Nikki and I end up in my room, screwing multiple times, even though I barely remember her coming into the room. Then she lays in my bed and starts yammering about what color she should dye her hair. I keep blinking at her, wishing she'd disappear, and finally, Tristan comes in, kicks her out, and then steals his pipe back. Somewhere along the line, I start to lose my buzz, finally diving to rock bottom. I'm exhausted, and even thinking feels like a huge fucking project, but I need to find a job because I'm running out of money and weed and I need to start paying rent.

I wasn't always this way. I used to be responsible. In fact, it was something my mom always took pride in when she was bragging to her friends. I was supposed to go to a good college, probably with Lexi, where we'd date until we graduated, then we'd get married and start our lives together. At least that was the plan. But that plan's no longer possible, and even a plan for a day seems pretty much out of my reach.

❧

June 28, Day 40 of Summer Break

I sit up in bed and swing my legs over the edge. I'm stretching my arms above my head when someone knocks on the door. "Come in," I call out, thinking it's probably Tristan coming to lecture me again about getting out of bed.

But when the door opens up, Nova is on the other side. Her hair is pulled up, and wisps frame her face. She's wearing a short black dress with red stripes and slender straps that show off her bare shoulders and collarbone. There's black liner framing her blue eyes, and her full lips look glossy. But other than that I don't think she's wearing any makeup, because I can still see the freckles on her nose.

She stares at my bare chest as she clutches her phone in her hand, and I'm suddenly very hyperaware that I'm only in my boxers. She can see the nasty scar on my chest, leftover from the accident that nearly ripped me in half, both mentally and physically, and the tattoos on my bicep of everyone I killed that day. Her cheeks flush, but surprisingly she doesn't leave the room. She points over her shoulder at the hallway. "I came here with Delilah, and Dylan said that you'd been back here sleeping for quite a while and that I needed to come wake you up."

"He did?" I shake my head. I don't know much about Dylan, but the longer I stay here, the more I realize that he seems to like starting trouble. I stand up and head to my dresser, working to put a smile on my face. "All right, you did your job. I'm up."

She nods and I expect her to leave, but she dithers in the doorway. Then, looking nervous as shit, she takes a deep breath, steps over the threshold into my room, and starts wandering around. There are clothes and sketches all over the floor, the dresser, and the bed. She assesses each one closely, and I squirm uncomfortably as I take a shirt out of my dresser.

She stops at my bed and eyes the drawing I made back in high school of Lexi wearing nothing but her underwear and bra. I wonder what she's thinking. If she's offended? Do I care if she is?

Her head tips to the side as she reaches out to pick it up, and I open my mouth to tell her not to touch it because it feels wrong somehow, seeing Lexi's picture in another girl's hand. But then she decides against it, pulling her hand away.

She glances over her shoulder at me. "She's pretty."

I nod, swallowing the lump in my throat, and then slip my shirt over my head. "Yeah, she was."

Her lips part a little when I say *was*, which I didn't mean to say. In fact, I wish I could take it back. Luckily, Nova seems to be understanding and she steps up to my wall and starts studying a drawing I made of vines weaving around a bag of Skittles. I made it when I decided to take a hit of acid, because weed wasn't doing anything for the internal agony. It turned out to be a very bad idea and did nothing for numbing my emotions, instead bringing out a very dark, almost insane side of me.

"This one's interesting," she muses, glancing at me. "What were you thinking when you drew it?"

I reach for a pair of jeans in the top drawer of the banged-up dresser that only has two of the four drawers. "Honestly, I don't remember." I unfold the jeans and transfer my weight to one leg so I can slip them on. "I think it had something to do with the fact that I'd smoked a lot of weed and did...other stuff, and then fell in a rosebush that day and went home and ate some Skittles."

She laughs, looking bewildered, and I find myself smiling, too. "Do you do that a lot?"

"What? Fall into rosebushes? Or eat Skittles?" I ask, zipping up my jeans.

She sucks her bottom lip in between her teeth, and I catch her gaze flicking to my hands as I button up my jeans, which makes me wonder what she's thinking about. "No, do you smoke weed a lot? I'm just curious."

The light mood she created plummets, and I feel deflated. "Yeah," I say truthfully, knowing it's probably going to scare her off.

She glances around at some of the drawings, then holding her dress in place, she crouches down to get a closer look at one. "Yeah, so do Dylan and Tristan, but you probably know that since you live with them."

I grab my wallet off the dresser. "Yeah, I guess."

I'm not sure what Dylan's and Tristan's reasons are for smoking an abundance of weed; whether Tristan does it just because or if it's how he deals with the death of his sister, Ryder. All I know is that I do it to deaden the pain inside me.

It was something I discovered after countless therapy sessions, prescriptions, and trying to draw my way through my inner turmoil. Nothing was working, and one day, while I was hanging out with the only friend I had left, he took out a joint. I'd never tried pot before—never cared to. But then I realized that I really didn't have anything to care about anymore, so I tried it, and when it alleviated the heaviness in my body and clouded the dark thoughts inside my head, I knew it was the only way I was going to survive. I've been doing it pretty much every day for nine months now, and it's part of life for me. Without it, acceptance of what my life really is—what I've become—would be unbearable.

Nova stands back up, smoothing the wrinkles out of her dress. When she looks at me, her eyes are enormous and crammed with worry. The abruptness of her shift in demeanor throws me off balance.

"So everyone is pretty determined to go to that concert in Fairfield," she says, slipping her fingers below the bands on her wrist. She scratches at the skin, seeming anxious and out of her element. "And it's like a weeklong event or something."

"It could be fun." I stuff my wallet into the back pocket of my jeans. "You should go."

"Yeah…Delilah keeps pushing, but like I said, I'm not really a fan of concerts anymore."

"Because they're too noisy?"

She nods as she coils a strand of her hair around her finger. "Plus, I'd be there with Dylan and Delilah and sharing a tent with them and they'd probably want to do stuff... They wouldn't even care that I could hear them."

"Isn't Tristan going?" I ask, grabbing my watch off the bed. "You could share a tent with him."

"Yeah, but... I don't know. It'd be weird with just the two of us." By the way she says it, I suspect she knows Tristan has a thing for her and that she doesn't like it. She unravels her hair from her finger and then stands up straight. "You could go, too, and then I wouldn't have to share a tent alone with Tristan."

I fasten the buckle on my leather band watch. "But why would you want to share a tent with me, too? You barely know me."

She skims my body and then steadily maintains my gaze, even though her hands are trembling at her side. I feel very vulnerable, as if she's reading me like an open book. It's like she's been hiding this fiery personality from me, and it's starting to show. I'm not sure if I like it or hate it or if I should even be analyzing it. "That's okay. Then I can get to know you," she says.

"You don't want to do that," I assure her, doing her a huge favor. I start to step around her, but she matches my movement, cutting me off.

"Please." Her tone carries a silent plea. I have no idea where it stems from, but I get the feeling it has nothing to do with me. But I know I should say no, because I promised Lexi that no matter what, I would never forget her, and Nova seems like the kind of girl a lot of guys could get caught up in: sad, vulnerable, determined. And those goddamn big blue eyes of hers... they're seriously getting to me. I rub my hand across my face, preparing to turn her down, but when I open my mouth my answer completely contradicts my thoughts.

"Okay," I tell her and my hand falls to my side. I'm stunned and thoroughly pissed off at myself. I'm about to tell her I didn't mean it, but her eyes light up.

"Good," she says and then she takes a step forward, lifting her hands up. I have no idea what the hell she's doing and she looks as baffled as I feel. And terrified. Then all of a sudden she's wrapping her arms around me and giving me a hug. Her heart is knocking in her chest, going about as fast as mine.

I tense, unsure what to do. Then I start to pull back, but like a moron, gravity pulls me forward and I fold my arms around her waist, giving her a hug back, feeling guilty from the gratifying contact, but completely consumed by it at the same time. I blame it on the weed still lingering in my system, because I'm normally more careful than this. I've become a pro at pushing people away, and now suddenly I'm fucking careless—it has to be the weed.

"Look... Nova..." My eyes shut as I inhale the sweet scent of her. "I don't think—"

She rapidly pulls away. "So I think Dylan or Delilah will drive. Or maybe Tristan. I think everyone's still deciding who's driving."

Does she know what she's doing? Does she know that I

don't want to go, so she keeps talking so I can't get out of it? "I'm not a fan of road trips," I lie in a lame attempt to get out of it without making a big deal.

A smile accentuates her lips, and it enhances the green specks in her eyes. "Neither am I, but it's only like a four-hour drive." She playfully pinches my arm, stunning me, and I flinch. "And you can sit by me." Before I can even begin to respond to her extreme flip of attitude, she turns toward the door and opens it. "Everyone's hanging out in the living room. You should come out there." Then she walks out and closes the door.

I stand in the middle of my small, shitty-ass room, stunned and speechless. This isn't how I work. I don't just go on road trips and go to concerts with a girl who obviously wants to hang out and get to know me. I get high, I draw meaningless shit, and I fuck. That's it. Because if I do anything else, my life will have purpose, and I deserve to be miserable until my life comes to an end, which is hopefully soon.

Nova

I run straight to the bathroom to throw up, moving so swiftly I don't have time to count my steps. I'm not even sure why I get nauseous; whether it's due to the fact that I pretty much made a commitment to go to the concert or because I'm nervous to be flirting with someone or that I feel guilty over flirting. I was never good at flirting, and it always made me come off as an awkward weirdo. That's why I lucked out with Landon. He did all the pursuing, otherwise we'd never have gotten anywhere past just being friends.

I burst into the bathroom and I barely make it to the toilet as vomit burns at the back of my throat. After I barf up the chicken sandwich I had for lunch, I spread a towel down on the grimy linoleum floor and sit down on it. There's very little space between the toilet and the bathtub, and I have to keep my elbows tucked in from touching either one, because they both look equally disgusting. I tap my finger on the video icon on the screen of my phone and then hit record.

I look pallid on the screen and my eyes are red and watery. "It's been a few weeks since I saw Quinton at the ice cream parlor and I've been spending a lot of time feeling adrift. A couple of nights ago, I woke up from this dream, where Landon was still alive and we were married and happy. In the grogginess of exhaustion, I ended up getting out of bed and wandering across the street in the middle of the night to the hill where I last saw Landon alive. For a moment, I swear I could envision us both lying there in the grass together, but then Landon slowly faded and eventually so did I.

"I'm not even sure what compelled me to go there, but I couldn't seem to find a reason to leave until morning when the new owners of the house came out and yelled at me for trespassing. I think they thought I was high or drunk or something, and that's kind of how I felt—so detached. I've been overanalyzing why I did it…why I just walked over there in the middle of the night, like I was sleepwalking or something, and honestly I have no idea . . ."

I fight to keep my voice even as I tuck my hair behind my ears. "Anyway, I woke up this morning and forced myself to feel different—less weighted. I randomly decided I needed a change from the lack of purpose and that I needed to do something magical." I pull a disgusted face at my cheerful choice of word. "Well, maybe *magical* isn't the right word—more like *out of the ordinary*, at least for me, which is a really big deal because I don't do out-of-the-ordinary very well." I tip the camera to the side as I pull my knees up and wrap one arm around them. "So I did something completely and utterly difficult for me—I did the first thing that popped into my head and came over here to ask Quinton to go to the concert with us, even though the idea of going to one makes me want to vomit. I think it might be my inner conscience telling me that I need to get to know him. Delilah says he's been through a lot, but Dylan and Tristan wouldn't give her the details. They'll only say that he's had a lot of death in his life lately and that he's messed up in the head."

I pause, picturing the heavy sorrow in his honey-brown eyes, and then I picture Landon's. They match, at least in my head they do. "I want to help him, though." I bite at my lip. "I blame it on the dream I had about Quinton last night, which is a complete change from the ones I've been having about Landon. Quinton was drowning in the ocean, which is weird because I've never been to the ocean, but anyway, he was drowning and I was watching him drown and he was begging me to help him, but all I would do was stand on the shore and watch him drown." Guilt clouds my eyes and they look strange on the dim, low-resolution screen. "God, that makes me seem really twisted, doesn't—"

I hear knocking on the door. "Nova, are you in there?" I flinch as Delilah's voice carries through from the other side.

"And are you talking to yourself?" she asks. "Or are you making a movie in the bathroom, because that would be weird."

I quickly shut the camera off, stand up, and hang the towel back on the rack before opening the door. "I was actually going to the bathroom." I point over my shoulder at the toilet. "That *is* what those things are known for."

She sticks out her tongue, then stands on her tiptoes to peek over my shoulder. "Are you sure you weren't doing anything weird in here? I'm picking up a vibe."

I shake my head and gesture her out of the door as I shuffle forward. "You're crossing the lines of our friendship boundaries, Delilah. Seriously."

"I guess so," she says, sounding suspicious, but she shrugs and ambles up the hall, tracking her finger along the wall. "So what'd you say to him?"

"Who?" I count the cracks in the paneling on the walls as I follow her.

She tips her head to the side and peers over her shoulder at me. "Quinton. Dylan says he's been in his room for like three days and he just came out. Plus he suddenly decided he was going to go to the concert."

"I just asked him," I say with a casual shrug, but my heart squeezes in my chest a little. He's been in his room for *three days*. "And he said okay."

She eyes me skeptically as she stops at the end of the hall and bends her knee, bringing her foot up to refasten the strap on her sandal. "Just be careful." She returns her foot to the floor, tugs down the bottom of her leather skirt, and then leans in toward me. "Guys like Dylan and Quinton are not easy to date, if that's even what they'll call it."

"You should take your own advice," I tell her in a low voice, flicking a piece of ash out of her hair and it lands on her arm.

"I'm a lot different than you, Nova," she says, dusting the ash off her skin. "Besides, my mom raised me to be a skank, so that's what I am."

"Delilah…," I start, but she scowls at me, so I wrap my arm around her shoulders and pull her in for a hug as we round the corner.

Quinton and Tristan aren't in the living room, but Dylan is sitting in the torn-up recliner near the television. Music flows from the speakers—"Blue" by A Perfect Circle—and two lit joints are balanced on an ashtray on the coffee table. There are blankets hanging over the windows, blocking out the sunlight and reducing the circulation, and it makes the air misty and fortified with smoke.

"Shit, what'd I miss?" Dylan asks. He takes in the closeness of Delilah and me, and his eyes shadow over. He has his boots kicked up on the table and a newspaper piled with green flakes on his lap. "And why was I not back there watching it?"

Delilah picks up a cup on a nearby table and chucks it at Dylan's head. "Don't be such a pervert. If you want a show, watch some porn."

He doesn't move quickly enough. The cup hits him in the forehead, and some of the liquid in it spills on the weed. "Fucking watch it, Delilah, or I'll kick your goddamn ass out." There's a sharpness in his voice; he's no longer playing around as he shifts his weight forward and carefully lifts the newspaper away from his lap.

Delilah narrows her eyes as she marches up to the coffee table in front of Dylan with her hands on her hips. "Don't you talk to me like that. I'm not one of your little sluts. You can't just do and say whatever you want to me."

His eyes darken as he sets the newspaper down on the table and rises to his feet. A bright red welt is forming on his forehead from where the cup hit him. "That's not what you said last night," he says darkly as he slowly stalks around the table toward her. A vein in his neck bulges. "In fact, if I'm remembering right, you were pretty much begging me to do whatever I wanted with you."

"I was..." She peeks back at me and her expression tenses before she looks back at Dylan. "I was high, okay? I would have said anything."

I press my back against the wall, fiddling with a strap on my dress. I wonder if she lied to me when she said she hadn't smoked weed since college—and if she did, why? Why is everyone always trying to shelter me from it? I'm not about to ask her in front of Dylan, though, who's pretty much scaring the hell out of me at the moment.

Dylan's eyes stay fastened on Delilah as he gets in her face with his hands balled at his sides. "Is that the real reason you're with me? For my fucking pot?"

She shakes her head and lets out an uneasy breath as she cautiously places her hand on his chest. "You know that's not true."

"Then prove it," he says and then his hands dart forward, fingers curled, mouth set in a line.

I think he's going to hit her, but instead he roughly snags her by the waist and picks her up from the ground. She goes a little rigid as he grabs her butt and forces her legs around him. Then he strides by, nearly running into me, and heads for the hallway, carrying her with him.

I give her a what-the-hell look as her eyes lock on me from over his shoulder. "Delilah..."

She shakes her head and mouths, *I'm fine. Just wait out here.*

I don't want to wait out here. I want her to do what she wants to do, and from the look on her face, she doesn't want to go back with Dylan, but she leans away and kisses him deeply as they duck through the curtain and disappear down the hall.

She makes me so nervous sometimes. Dylan's always been a jerk, but that was a little intense even for him. I wonder if he was really contemplating hitting her and then backed out at the last second. If he'd tried, would I have really tried to stop it? I'm not sure, because from past experiences, I've never been one to intervene in people's personal business. Maybe it's time, though. Time to start living life differently. But which direction is the right one to follow? And what are my choices even? Go to school, pick a major, and hope it'll make me happy?

I drop down on the couch and stare at the pile of weed and the joints burning in the ashtray, wondering if I should put them out because there's a lot of potent smoke flooding the room. But my hands remain on my lap as I ponder what the world looks like after someone smokes it. What did it make the world look like to Landon? Why does Delilah do it? Or Quinton? Or even Dylan and Tristan? What is so enticing about the stuff? Or is *enticing* the right word? Addictive?

My thoughts drift to the first time I ever found out Landon smoked weed. We were sixteen, and I was so naïve, I thought his bong was some crazy art piece—he was always creating weird sculptures all the time.

"Don't touch that," he'd warned when I'd gone to pick it up off his dresser.

"Oh, sorry," I said, backing away, letting my hands fall to my sides. "Is it breakable or something?"

He let out this low laugh, the one he used on me whenever

he was amused by my aloofness. "Yeah, but that's not why you can't touch it."

My gaze swept around his room and I noticed that there was smokiness to the air. "Wait a minute…is that…" My eyes widened as my gaze landed back on the dresser. "Is that a bong?"

He used the laugh on me again and it made me flustered. He shook his head, and then wound around the foot of his unmade bed, coming to a stop in front of me. I tipped my chin up to meet his sad eyes, and he cupped my cheeks in his hands.

"I love that you have no idea what it is, Nova," he said, grazing the pad of his thumb down my cheek, almost looking like he was going to cry. "You're too good to know what it is."

"I know what it is," I protested. "But why are you doing that stuff and how did I not know about it? I thought we knew everything about each other."

He smiled sadly as he traced a path with his finger across my bottom lip. "Trust me, Nova. You're better off not knowing half of the shit that goes on inside my head. You're too beautiful and good for that." He nodded his head at the bong on his dresser. "For any of this."

But I'm not. Just talk to me was what I thought. But what I said was nothing. *Nothing.*

I blink the thought from my head, rub my watery eyes, and pluck a flake of weed from the pile and hold it between my thumb and my finger. "Who were you to decide what I wanted to know?" I mutter, my chest aching, along with my heart.

"Why wouldn't you ever just tell me things, instead of deciding for me that I was too good to know? Why couldn't you just tell me and let *me* decide? Why wouldn't you just talk to me, instead of deciding to leave me? Here. Alone. With a head full of fucking numbers. I feel so lost all the time..."

Suddenly the potential for a new, magical day is gone. The longer I sit there, the more pissed off I get, which only makes me feel guilty, but then the guilt makes me feel angry, and suddenly my head's spinning and I can't even remember sitting down.

Somewhere through the spinning and racing thoughts, I hear the door creak open, and Quinton comes walking inside. I quickly toss the flake down onto the pile, but it's too late; he's already seen me holding it. As he pushes the door open wider, he arches his eyebrow at me with curiosity written all over his face.

"What are you doing, sitting here by yourself?" he asks as Tristan walks in carrying a large cardboard box, his face red and beads of sweat coating his skin.

"Nothing." I slump back in the chair, trying to ignore the stinging in my eyes. "I'm just sitting here."

He looks at me suspiciously as he closes the door, then he saunters to the back of the couch and launches himself over it, landing on the cushion with a hard bounce. "Where did you run off to when you left my room?" he asks, kicking up his unlaced boots onto the table. He has three holes in the hem of his shirt and one in the collar, along with a few smudges and spots of ink and charcoal.

I shrug, fold my arms around myself, and grip my phone tightly in my hand. "I've been here the whole time. I promise."

"Holy shit." Tristan's arm muscles are flexed as he drops the box down on the countertop. He wipes the sweat from his forehead with the back of his hand. "This thing is fucking heavy."

"Well you didn't have to take all the pipes," Quinton calls out. His glazed eyes are still fixed on me. "You could have just taken one or two."

Tristan starts searching around in the box, taking out pipe after pipe and lining them up on the countertop. "And what? Turn down free pipes? That'd be fucking stupid of me."

Quinton seems like he wants to argue with him, but he clenches his jaw shut and directs his attention to me. "But you disappeared for a while, right? Because when I walked through here just a bit ago, you weren't here."

That's because I was in the bathroom, barfing my guts out because I think you're hot, but I feel guilty about it. And then I decided to make a video about my twisted thoughts about you. I'm starting to grow flustered, so I try for a subject change. "Do you guys have anything to drink?" I blink my eyes against the smoke and then press my fingertips against my eyeballs. My head's feeling a little heavy and lopsided.

Tristan peeks up from the box, and strands of his blond hair fall into his eyes as the corners of his lips tug upward. "Like a Corona or two or three?"

Staring blankly at him, I hold up my finger—not the

middle one, even though I want to, which is a little blunt for me, but at the moment being blunt seems awesome. "One time."

"One freakin' memorable time," Tristan teases, clutching a pipe in his hand. When I narrow my eyes at him, he starts laughing, and accidentally drops the pipe onto the ground. He bends to pick it up, stumbles a little, and bumps his head on the side of the counter. "Shit." He stands up, rubbing his head.

I stare at the joints in the ashtray, a thin stream of grayish smoke slithering from them, and blurred, disjointed thoughts run in an uneven flow inside my head. "Why do you guys do it?" I ask, because I really want to know—understand— what Landon's fascination was with it all the time. Why did he smoke it? How did it make him feel inside? Why was he so dead set on thinking that I was too good to smoke it and feel what it's like to be high, yet he didn't think he was good enough? Why? God damn it. There are always so many questions about him, about how he saw me, and I'll never get an answer, because he's not here anymore. The only way I'll ever even possibly begin to know is to try and find out for myself.

Quinton tracks my gaze and then his face drops, like he just realized the joints were there. "Fuck, who left these burning out here?"

"They were like that when I came out," I say, picking at my fingernails.

"Why didn't you put them out?" Quinton asks me, allowing his feet to fall to the floor.

"I don't know." I rack my brain for my real answer and the one that comes to me is kind of frightening. *Because I was thinking about smoking it. Because I wanted to see what it was like—what it was like for Landon. Why he thought I was too good to see what it was like.*

He leans forward, picks them up, and scrapes the tips gently along the edge of the table, putting them out. "You don't want this shit, Nova. Trust me. You're too good for it."

His words tear at my heart, because they're so similar to what Landon used to say to me all the time. But they also annoy me. I want people to stop telling me I'm good when I don't even know if I am. I'm not sure if my irritation is directed at him, though, or if I'm just lashing out on him because I'm frustrated with Landon for leaving me. Or maybe all the secondhand smoke in the room is bringing out an ugly side of me. "How do you know what I want? You don't even know me."

"And you don't even know me," he says calmly as he places the unlit joints on the table. He glances over his shoulder at Tristan, who's distracted by the pipes in the kitchen, and then he leans in toward me and lowers his voice. "So let me give you a little insight. You don't want to be here, sitting with me, talking to me, or asking me to go to concerts. You don't want to know me, or this fucking fucked-up world I live in, Nova. Trust me."

With a neutral expression, I slant forward and snatch a lighter and one of the unlit joints from off the table. "You don't know me, either, and you don't know what I want, so don't try and tell me you do." I know that what I'm doing is probably wrong, or at least that's what I used to believe. Right now, I feel different. I don't care about right or wrong. I don't care about anything.

With an unsteady hand, I place the joint in my mouth, and ignoring both their protesting looks, I cup my hand around the end, and flick the lighter, figuring I can handle it. Nothing can prepare me for the fiery burn, though. As soon as the smoke hits the back of my throat, I cough and gasp for air. I lean forward, sticking my hand out, with the joint pinched between my fingers, wanting to get the joint as far away from my face as possible.

"Shit, Nova, are you okay?" Tristan hurries around the couch, removes the joint from my hand, and extends his hand out to the side of him, with the joint between his fingers, to get the smoke as far away from my face as possible. "What are you doing? You don't do this shit."

"You don't know me either." I sit up straight, still coughing while my eyes water.

Quinton frowns as he retrieves the joint from Tristan's hand, and Tristan gives me a pat on the back, although I can tell he's trying hard not to laugh at me.

Quinton positions the joint between his fingers, then he places the end between his lips, and his chest rises as he takes a deep inhale and holds it in. He balances the joint in the ashtray and relaxes back in the chair, letting his head fall back as he breathes out the cloud of smoke toward the ceiling. "Nova, you should go home," he says in a sluggish voice, rubbing his hand over his face, as Tristan drops down in the sofa beside him, his eyelids growing heavy.

It feels like I should still be irritated at him, but I can't really feel anything. My mind and body are numb and the counting and need for control are silent. *Silence.* Without even knowing what I'm doing, or whether I'm doing it because I want to understand, because the secondhand smoke has clouded my judgment, or because I actually want to do it, I slide my arm across the coffee table and grab the joint. Quinton turns his head and watches me as I place it into my mouth. Copying his exact movements, I let my chest expand as I suck in a breath, then I trap the smoke in my lungs, standing on the edge of the unknown, waiting and waiting, then finally I let it out, falling off the edge completely, wondering how hard it's going to be to climb back up. Or if I'll even want to.

Maybe this is what I've been searching for during the last year. Maybe I've been waiting around to fall. Maybe I don't know what I want or who I am without Landon, and maybe this is all in desperation to figure stuff out.

Or maybe I'm just lost and I have no idea what the hell I'm doing.

Chapter Seven

Quinton

This is an honest-to-God first for me. I'm ripped out of my mind, nearly floating to the ceiling—or falling to the floor, depending on how you look at it—and I can't bask in the detached feeling. Nova's got me preoccupied. Her blue eyes are red as hell, her pupils glossy, and I can tell she's struggling to keep her eyelids open. I don't like how caught up I am—how worried I am about her. I get high so I don't have to worry or think, but somehow she's more powerful than the drugs, but what I'd like to figure out is why. What makes her so different? What makes her so consuming?

I tried to talk her out of smoking the joint. The old Quinton—the good, sober one—would have snatched it right out of her hand, because it's obvious she's never smoked weed before and she's doing it to cover up something. But I'm too far gone, and before I know it Tristan, Nova, and I are squished on the couch, sharing a king-sized bag of Doritos, staring at the movements on the cracked computer screen as the screen saver dances to the beat of the music.

"Do you think it's trying to tell us something?" Nova asks with a dazed look on her face as she analyzes the pink-and-green streams on the screen.

Tristan snorts a laugh as he grabs a handful of Doritos and drops them into his mouth; half of them fall onto his lap. "Yeah, that we should stop assessing lights on the screen."

I have my arm draped on the back of the couch and Nova's hair is scattered on it. "I think it's trying to coexist with the lyrics."

She brings her lip in between her teeth as she glances up at me. "That's insightful."

Normally, when a girl looks at me the way she's looking at me, I'd take her back to my room and lose track of time for a little while. But the good inside me is conflicting with the bad, and I can't seem to bring myself to say anything to her.

"Not insightful," I say. "Just thoughts."

She nods, like she gets what I'm saying, but how could she, because I'm not even making sense to myself. "Do your thoughts ever get jumbled in your head?" she wonders, rubbing at her eyes with her fingertips.

I can tell we're about to head down that path, paved of weed, smoke, and senseless nonsense that can only be found when the mind hits an idyllic state of stupidity, and I don't want to do that. I don't want to get to know her, because it'll mean too much and I don't want meaning in anything in my life. It's the point of existing in the state I'm in; the one where nothing matters except getting high and feeling numb, because once things start to mean something, it becomes harder to follow the wrong path.

"I think we should find a way to get you home," I say, lowering my feet to the floor. I mean it. I really want her to leave, not just so she'll quit messing with my emotions, but because she doesn't belong here in this house—in this lifestyle.

She frowns, seeming hurt. "Why?"

I glance at Tristan, hoping he'll chime in and help, but he has his head tipped back against the sofa and his eyes locked on the ceiling. "Because...I don't think you should be in a place like this."

She looks as if she's struggling to get mad, her cheeks tinting pink, like she wants to be angry with me. "Delilah's still back there with Dylan, and I can't leave her here. Plus, she's my ride home."

"We can find you another ride," I say. Tristan lifts his head up and looks at me inquisitively. "Maybe we can ask Frankie."

"Who's Frankie?" she asks, her head falling back as she tries to look me in the eyes. My arm is still on the back of the couch, and her head is resting in the crook of it. Her neck is curved back and her chest is sticking out a little from her top, giving me the slightest view of the curves of her breasts. Under normal circumstances, with a different girl, I'd just take her back to my room and fuck her, then tell her to leave. But she keeps blinking up at me, looking helpless, and all it does is make me want to hold her. It's driving my goddamn body and mind crazy. *It's definitely time for her to go.*

"He's the neighbor." Tristan stands up, collecting the bag of chips off the table. "And Nova can stay here if she wants."

"I want to," Nova says, slowly picking her head back up. She blinks and gathers fallen strands of her hair behind her ears.

"I don't think that's a good idea," I object, despite my body's opposing reaction. I'm about to add a list of reasons why someone like her should not be sitting here with us, when the front door opens and two guys come strolling in like they own the place. One of them has a backpack on and the other has what looks like a closed pocket knife in his hand. He's probably carrying in case Dylan or Tristan tries to screw them over with whatever they're dealing. It's only a threat, warning everyone not to mess with them, but when you've got a room full of illegal substances and a bunch of paranoid people high out of their minds, things can get ugly fast.

"What's up?" Tristan says to the shorter of the two as he winds around the sofa, yawning. They slap hands and bump fists, and then the taller one's eyes land on Nova as she sits up in the sofa. He's got sores all over his face, his teeth are yellow, and his gaze drinks Nova in like she's a dose of heroin as one of her straps falls off her shoulder. She shifts uncomfortably, leaning into me as her shoulders slump in.

I position the strap back up over her shoulder, then slip her fingers through mine as I stand up, pulling her with me, despite my initial reaction to go over there and see what they're dealing—see if I want it. "Have fun, man," I say to Tristan, leading Nova toward the curtain.

Tristan waves at me, totally distracted by the idea of getting drugs, and I'm not surprised. Yeah, he may have a little bit of a thing for Nova, but when you've tasted the addiction of drugs, it's pretty much all that matters when it's in front of you.

Nova more than willingly follows me toward the hall, grasping my hand, and one of the drug-dealing crackheads says something about having a ride with her when I'm finished. He thinks I'm going to screw her, but there's no way I'd try to, especially when she's this far out of her mind. She's too sad and lost, and the last thing I want to do is ruin her more. But the good-guy thought process is the old Quinton seeping through, and by the time we reach my room, I'm panicking, trying to decide whether to run out of the room and leave her here alone, or scoop her up, lay her down on the bed, and rip her clothes off.

Nova instantly makes herself at home, strolling up to the iPod dock and picking up my iPod. She bites on her bottom lip as she scrolls through the songs, her head swaying from side to side as she contemplates the song list.

"You have good taste in music," she observes, peeking up at me through her eyelashes.

I run my fingers through my hair as I linger near the doorway, with my hand on the doorknob, ready to bolt. "Yeah, I guess."

She taps the screen, puts the iPod in the dock, and seconds

later lyrics fill up the room. She sinks down on the edge of my bed, tucking one of her feet underneath her ass, and then her eyes lock on me. "Quinton, why did you move here?"

Every single one of my muscles winds into overly tight knots. "I really don't want to talk about it."

"Okay," she says simply, and then looks around at the drawings that are tacked on the wall. When she spots the one of Lexi, she stares at it for a very long time, and her eyes start to fill with water. "I used to have a boyfriend that sketched like you." She angles her head to the side and a tear slips out and falls down her cheek. "But he's dead, so he doesn't anymore." Blinking frantically, she forces her eyes from the drawing, and looks desperately at me, like she wants me to say something to make her stop talking.

Tristan told me her boyfriend died, although he never explained how. Death is a sensitive subject for the both of us and we always try to dodge around it, even though it's always there, existing, an invisible wall between us.

"Nova, we don't have to talk," I say, finally daring a step away from the door. "We can just go to bed or something."

She glances at the bed behind her and then her cheeks turn a little red. "Like have sex?"

The depressing atmosphere lightens a little, and I rub my hand across my face, trying not to laugh at her. "No, like lie down, shut our eyes, and go to sleep."

"But I'm not tired."

"Really?"

"Yes, really." Contradicting herself, she yawns and stretches her arms above her head. "Well, maybe we could lie down for a bit, I guess."

I nod and she instantly collapses onto the bed. Her brown hair is sprawled across the pillow and her eyes look lost, like she's floating away from reality. My fingers long to grab a pencil and paper from the dresser and capture the perfection in her face, her eyes, and her body, but I promised never again and I need to stick with it. Drawing someone, in these circumstances, is way too personal.

Breaking the moment, she turns onto her side and faces the wall with her back to me. Her dress barely covers her ass, and one of the shoulder straps is falling down again. Some guys would have completely and utterly taken advantage of her at this point, but as much as I've slept around, taking advantage is something I can't do. Even with as far as I am in the fucking dark, the good Quinton still has a vague amount of control over certain things.

I lay down on the bed beside her, careful not to touch her, keeping one arm under my head and one on my side, as I scoot back so I'm barely on the bed.

She rolls over, facing me, and then stares at me for so long, it almost drives me crazy. "Did you love her?" she finally asks.

"Who?"

"The girl on the wall."

My heart pounds inside my chest, nearly cracking my lungs. "Yeah…but I don't want to talk about her."

126

She looks perplexed, drifting off into her thoughts. "Okay...I understand." She releases an uneven breath before shaking her head. "What's your favorite color?"

I arch my eyebrows, wondering where the abrupt subject change came from. "Huh?"

"What's your favorite color?" she repeats without an explanation.

I search her eyes for a reason why she's asking, but I don't know her at all, so I can't figure her out. "I don't know...black onyx."

Her lips curve upward. "That's such an artist answer. Most people would say like purple or blue, but you...black onyx." She laughs under her breath, and it seems a little more natural than the other couple of times I've heard her laugh. But she's high, which means it's not real. None of this is, which makes it easier.

"What about you?" I ask. "What's yours?"

She mulls it over, pressing a smile back. "Indigo."

"Is that really your favorite color?" I inch forward slightly on the bed to keep from falling off the edge. "Or are you just trying to impress me?"

She shrugs, rolling her tongue in her mouth, amused. "What's your favorite food?"

"Chicken teriyaki," I reply, wondering if we're entering a game of twenty questions or something. "Nova, where are you going with this?"

She shrugs again. "I'm just trying to get to know you."

"You don't want to do that." I roll to my side and straighten my arm out so I can reach my cigarettes on the dresser. I pull one out, grab my lighter, and then turn back over. "In fact, I should have never brought you back here."

"Then why did you?" she asks, watching me intently, as I light up the cigarette and toss the lighter onto the foot of the bed.

I slant my head to the side to avoid blowing smoke in her face. "To get you away from those guys."

She assesses me closely, like she's trying to unravel what I'm thinking. "What's your—"

I cover her mouth with my hand and shake my head. "No way. I get to ask one now."

Her lips curve upward against my hand. "Okay."

I lower my hand to my side. "First car."

"Never had one," she answers, her voice shaking and off pitch. "Well, besides the one my dad gave me."

I want to ask her how he died, but that'd be bringing up the subject of death. "Favorite band?"

She rolls her eyes. "You can't have a favorite band. It's not possible."

"Bullshit," I argue, reaching behind me to ash the cigarette on the floor. "There's always one that outweighs the others just a little bit."

She points a finger at me. "Then you are not a true music lover, my friend."

"I am, too," I say, slightly offended but entertained at the same time. "I promise. But I do have a favorite band."

"Who?"

"Pink Floyd."

"Total guy copout answer." She smiles and I love the sight of it. It makes me want to continue on in this little flirty state we've arrived at and keep going, move forward, at least until I sober up and life and reality return to me.

"I can prove it," I insist and take a drag from the cigarette. She looks me over with inquisitiveness. "How?"

"Name a random band—one you think I'll never know— and see if I do."

Her eyes briefly wander to the ceiling as she considers my challenge. "Okay, but if you lose then you owe me something."

I smile amusedly. "Owe you what?"

"Something," she says, and her blue eyes sparkle.

"Fine." I sit up and put the cigarette out in an old soda can up on the dresser. "But if I win, then you owe me something."

She sticks out her hand. "You have a deal, Quinton..." She trails off, "What is your last name anyway?"

I've never been a fan of telling people my last name. That way if I decide to bail out of their lives, it makes things easier because it makes it harder for them to track me down. I've been going through the last year introducing myself to people as Quinton, giving them as little detail about me as I can. And no one ever asked me to offer more. "Carter," I say. "My name is Quinton Carter."

"All right, Quinton Carter." She pushes her hand at me. "You have a deal."

129

I place my hand in hers, noting how warm her skin is, and how long and thin her fingers are. "Okay, you have a deal, Nova Reed. Now give me a band."

We're still holding hands, but I don't try to let go. I'll give us this little moment until it's over and then I'll walk away from it forever, because that's what I need to do, at least that's what the good side of me—the old side of me—is telling me to do. Or maybe it's the new side…I'm having a hard time distinguishing between the two at the moment. *Good. Bad. Right. Wrong.*

"Brand New," she finally says.

I stare at her stoically, so she can't read my expression. I know the band, but I want to make her think I don't. "Brand who?"

"New," she enunciates, and I can tell by the pleased look on her face that she thinks she's won.

I fake uncertainty for a few moments longer, and then let a grin spread at my lips. "Oh, Brand New."

"I know you don't know them." She props up on her elbow and rests her head against her hand. "I checked your iPod and they weren't on there."

"That's because you didn't check the playlists." I slip my fingers out of her hand, and her lips part as I climb off the bed and walk over to the dresser. I pick up the iPod, scroll to the Hidden playlist, compiled of songs I used to listen to when I was with Lexi. I hesitate, knowing that there's a good chance that turning it on is going to fling me down memory lane. But

I want to win, to prove that I know music, to prove to her that I listen to the same music as her, and honestly because I love the idea that she'll owe me something, even if I probably won't ever act on it. With an unsteady finger, I tap my finger on the Brand New section and hit Play on "Me vs. Maradona vs. Elvis." The song clicks on, and I shut my eyes with my back to Nova as the soft lyrics and nearly soundless tune takes me to the last time I listened to it: a year and a half ago, when my life had direction and purpose.

"What would happen if I ran away?" Lexi had asked as we sat in my car, staring out at the town below the cliffs. We'd driven up to the turnout, a place where teenagers went to make out, which we had done plenty of, but then Lexi went into thinking mode, and suddenly we were talking about life.

"Well, I hope you won't run away from me." I laced my fingers through hers as I pulled the visor down to block out the piercing pink glow from the setting sun. The song was playing in the background, turned down quiet enough that we could talk without yelling, but loud enough that it was known it would be forever linked to that moment.

She'd stared at me for a moment, and then glanced down at our hands entwined together. "But what if I wanted to run away from my life? You're a huge part of that, Quinton, so if you came, I really wouldn't be running away."

There'd been something about her, maybe the look in her eyes or the tone of her voice, but it seemed like she'd actually thought about this before.

I brought her hand up to my lips and grazed them across her knuckles. "Lexi Davis, if you run away, then I'd run away, because even though you don't want to admit it, you and I belong together."

Most girls would have melted, but Lexi had always been tough to win over and to read. It'd taken forever to get her to go on a date with me and even longer to make the commitment of being my girlfriend.

After a minute or two of pretending to be unaffected, she'd finally given in and leaned over the console to kiss me. That night we'd had sex for the first time. It was one of our greatest moments, full of meaning and connection, something I know I'll never have again.

Forcing myself away from the realness of the memory, I return to the fakeness of my room. I turn back to Nova, surprised to find that she looks like she's been crying. "I told you I knew them," I say, kicking a shirt out of the way as I make my way back over to the bed.

She smiles, but it looks forced. "Yeah, you win."

Instead of getting on the bed, I squat down beside it, so I'm at eye level with her. "Are you okay?" I ask, searching her eyes, which are still red, but a little more alert.

She nods slowly. "Yeah, I'm feeling a little less foggy headed ... but I'm getting tired."

"Do you want me to go find Delilah?" I ask, but she instantly shakes her head, and then straightens her arm above her so her head falls to the pillow.

"I'm just going to shut my eyes for a few seconds." Her eyes start to pool with tears and I have no fucking clue what to do or say to calm her down. She smashes her quivering lips together, sucking back the tears. "Can you stick the song on Repeat and then just lie down with me?"

There's something in her expression that makes it impossible to say no, like she'll crack if I do. So even though I don't really want to, I backtrack to the dresser, hit the Repeat button, and then situate on the bed beside her, making sure to leave some space between our bodies.

She straightens her arms above her head, still staring at me like I'm a ghost, like I'm not real. She starts scratching below the bands on her wrist, and I notice a thin white scar that runs horizontally along her skin. It could be just a coincidence, a crazy accident that left her with it, but it also could be something else. It's in the right area, just above the vein below the bottom of her hand. I could ask her about it, but then she might ask me stuff, like where the scar on my chest came from or what my tattoos mean. And I can't give her those answers. So I keep my lips fastened, letting things remain uncomplicated between us, simple, like my favorite color, food, and band. That way when it's all gone, it won't hurt as bad.

But she continues to keep her eyes on me, with her hands under her head, and the longer it goes on, the harder it becomes to keep my hands and thoughts to myself. She looks like she's going to start crying again, and I feel like I'm on the verge of joining her.

"Quinton," she whispers as a few stray tears escape her eyes. "Can you do something for me?"

The heart-wrenching sadness in her voice makes me want to do anything for her at the moment, if it'll get her to smile again. "Sure. What?"

"Will you..." She sucks her lip up into her teeth as more tears stream down her cheeks. "Will you kiss me?"

That wasn't what I was expecting her to say at all. My mind starts racing, flooded with disturbing thoughts. "I don't think that's a good idea... not like this." *Not ever.*

Tears cascade out of her eyes as she nods and releases her lip from her teeth. "Okay."

My heart is thumping and each of her sobs triggers it to thud faster. I bring my hand forward and wipe some of her tears off her cheek with my thumb. "It's not that I don't want to." It's a partial lie because I do and I don't at the same time. "I just don't think it's a good idea, considering we're both a little out of it."

She nods again and doesn't say a word, her eyelashes fluttering against the tears as she struggles to get them to stop. The look on her face is rupturing my heart, and as she rolls over to turn away from me, my willpower fractures. I grab her arm, and without saying a word, I draw her back to me. I can feel my own tears forcing their way up into my eyes as I realize that I'm going to kiss her and it's going to actually mean something, not just to Nova but to me.

Grappling to breathe, I secure a finger underneath her chin, tip her face up, and press my lips to hers. She sucks in a sharp, stammering breath, then kisses me back like she's been trapping her breath for ages and suddenly I'm supplying her with oxygen. I know I should pull back, but it's been a long time since the emptiness inside me hasn't been so hollow, and I find myself slipping my tongue into her mouth and kissing her back with way too much passion behind the kiss.

Things only get more intense when she traces her hand up the nape of my neck, then runs her fingers through my hair, drawing me closer, and the voice that's haunted my head—the one telling me to stop—abruptly shuts up. I roll to my side, positioning my body over hers, lining us together, as I explore her mouth with my tongue. A few tears drip from my eyes and fall onto her cheeks, which are soaked with her own tears. She keeps gasping, pulling me closer, pressing her body against mine, like she needs me near her or she'll die. Her legs circle my waist, and the dress she's wearing slips up and her bare legs graze the outside of my jeans. My hands start to wander downward toward the bottom of her dress, wanting to feel the softness of her skin. But when I reach the bottom of the fabric, I can't seem to go through with it, and at the same time her hands leave my hair. Just as quickly as it started, we stop it. Together. Both of us pulling away, panting, our eyes glossy with tears and regret as we roll onto our backs.

She cries soundlessly, with her arm draped over her head,

and her chest wrenching as she cries. But I stop crying, staring at the cracks in the ceiling, letting myself die all over again.

Letting the hollowness take back over.

Nova

I'm bawling my eyes out and I can't seem to stop. I kissed Quinton and touched him while he touched me. He's so much like Landon, and kissing and being with Quinton momentarily gave me a twisted sense of peace. It almost felt like I was with Landon again, and for a moment I think about just letting myself go, allowing things to heat up as much as they want to without holding back. I'd never done that with Landon. Every time we'd reach the point of having sex, I'd always backed out. I let my fear own me and take away my chance of ever being with Landon completely. I'll never get that chance again. And I don't want to feel that kind of regret again. Ever.

But eventually I had to accept the excruciatingly painful reality that Quinton isn't Landon. They smell and taste so much different because they *are* different. I *kissed* Quinton. I kissed someone else besides Landon. Oh my God...And for a moment I actually liked it. I actually wanted to be on the bed with him, letting his tongue slide into my mouth while I ran my fingers through his hair.

Guilt and confusion take me over. I feel sick to my stomach, like I'm going to throw up, and tears continue to pour out of my eyes. I cry for what seems like an eternity while Quinton stares silently at the ceiling beside me. Somehow I fall asleep and then next thing I know I'm being shaken awake. Moving past the grogginess, the headache, and the hunger rumbling in my stomach, I open my eyes to Delilah kneeling on the bed beside me. Quinton is gone and his bedroom door is agape.

I sit up and she scoots back to give me room. I rub my eyes and yawn. The music is still playing and I'm very unsettled on the inside, like each of my nerves is supersensitive. "What happened?" My voice is hoarse and my throat feels dry, like I just drank sand.

She inspects me closely, leaning in to examine my eyes, her hair falling into her face, and I notice the giant purplish hickey on her neck. "You tell me." There's speculation in her tone. "Nova, did you... did you smoke weed? Or have you been crying?"

I tug the elastic out of my hair and secure it around my ponytail. "Both."

"Why were you crying?"

"Because."

She waits for more details that I'll never give to her. "Why did you smoke weed then?"

"I don't know," I answer truthfully. "I'm still trying to figure that out."

I wait for her to lecture me, chew me out for being so stupid, so I can call her a hypocrite, but she simply sighs and then backs off the bed.

"Let's go," she says, motioning for me to get to my feet.

137

"Dylan wants us out of here, for some reason, and honestly, I don't want to stick around and find out."

My knees wobble a little as I stand up and tug down the bottom of my dress. "Why do you sound mad at him? What did he do to you?"

"He didn't do anything to me, so drop it." Her eyes turn to ice as she yanks open the bedroom door.

I raise my hands in front of me as I head for the door. "Sorry, it just seems like you're really upset about something."

"So do you," she says, glancing over her shoulder at me, assessing my tearstained eyes. "What were you doing back here anyway?"

I shrug. "I came back here with Quinton."

"To do what?"

"Nothing," I say, but the lie sticks in my throat. "We just laid around and talked...listened to music." *Kissed*.

"*Slept* together."

"Yeah, but in the sense of actually sleeping," I reply in a snippy tone, bracing my hand against the wall as the room starts to spin. "I didn't have sex with him." Just kissed. And it wasn't him with me. Not really. At least that's what I'm trying to tell myself.

She halts at the end of the hallway and I crash into the back of her. It only seems to aggravate me more, and I seriously consider pushing her to the floor because of it.

She turns around and sighs, placing a hand on each of my shoulders. "I know you didn't have sex with him. And relax.

You're coming down, and it's only going to get worse before it gets better."

I'm too tired to say anything else, so I nod, and we duck through the curtain and exit the hallway together. There's a bunch of guys in the living room and a few girls in skimpy dresses that barely cover their thighs and boobs. It's really loud and really bright and it's making me edgy.

Nikki is one of the girls there. She's sitting by Quinton on the larger sofa, laughing at something as he sips on a beer. He's smiling and it irritates me, but everything's irritating me at the moment, even the way my legs feel like two rubber bands weighted down by bricks.

Delilah leans over Dylan's shoulder and whispers something in his ear. He shoots her a harsh look, then reaches up and cups the back of her neck, roughly yanks her in for a violent kiss. At first Delilah tries to pull back, but then she gives into him and kisses him back. I pretend to be engulfed in my thoughts, pressing my fingers to the brim of my nose, but my head is hollow, and I'm very aware of all the sounds and noises going on around me. I want to count to regain some control over the situation, but it seems too much like a project, so I stand near the wall, while Dylan and Delilah make out, wanting to shout at everyone to shut the hell up.

While I'm scratching at my wrist, trying to keep myself together, Quinton looks over at me. I can tell by the way his expression drops that he's not happy I'm looking at him. I'm not happy, either. I fight for my expression to remain neutral and tell my legs to move slowly as I head toward the front door. His eyes follow me, though, and it's hard not to run as the past nips at my heels and raw emotions fire up in my heart.

Once I'm outside, in the summer air, I can breathe again, and my head starts to clear. As I lean over the railing, wanting to rest my head and go to sleep, I take in everything I've done. I tell myself never again. *Never.* But deep down, I'm already desperately longing for the brief silence the weed gave and the split second of comfort kissing Quinton brought me.

Chapter Eight

July 12, Day 54 of Summer Break

Quinton

I've felt like shit for the last couple weeks, even though I'm smoking more weed than usual. Dylan bought a bunch of weed from various dealers and he's got the three of us testing them, to see which kind is the best. Why, I'm not sure. Either he just really wants some good weed, or he's planning on selling some on his own and wants to check out the competition. I'm guessing the latter, since Tristan's mentioned him dealing before.

After sampling the fifth bowl, I drag my ass to my room, grab my sketchbook, and flop down on the bed, planning on letting my hand go crazy and letting it draw some tripped-out picture. But as I sit there, with my legs crossed and the blanket bunched up at my feet, all I can picture is the way Nova looked the last time I laid eyes on her and how soft her lips were, the way she felt underneath me, the scent of her hair, and the sound of regret as she sobbed.

141

I'd woken up in the bed with her, feeling guilty, not just for kissing her, but because I'd let her get high. I realized I should have ripped the joint out of her hand, but instead I'd stood by and watched her basically jump off a fucking cliff. Some people can handle the fall pretty well, and they climb right back up, but there are others, like me, who don't care enough to figure out how, and I wonder which one Nova is.

Then I ended up fucking up even more by kissing her, because it wasn't the same as when I kiss someone like Nikki. With Nova we'd talked before making out, she'd made me smile, and I'd made her smile. And for a second, even through the fog of drugs, the moment I spent searching her mouth with mine had altered into realness.

I'd left her sleeping in my bed, hoping to run away from the feelings intensifying inside me; the ones telling me that I need to fix the mess. I ended up making it worse, though, when Nova saw me talking to Nikki. I could see the hatred in her eyes, and I knew she'd stay away after that, and I haven't seen her since. It's a good thing, at least that's what I tell myself.

"Hey man," Dylan says, interrupting my thoughts. I blink at my drawing, realizing that through my daze, I've managed to draw Nova's eyes. "You up for that concert in a few weeks, because we're trying to make plans and decide whose car to take?"

I set the pencil and sketchbook down on the bed, shaking my head. "Nah, I think I'm going to bail out…maybe…" I trail off remembering how Nova begged me to go and how I told her I would, unintentionally. Part of me wants to do what

I said I'd do, while the other part is begging me to stay away from Nova, like I have been. "I don't know what I'm doing yet, honestly. I'm still deciding."

He backs out of the doorway with his hands in the pockets of his jeans. "Tristan will probably be fucking relieved if you decide not to go."

"Why?" I sit up and stretch my arms above my head.

He pauses just outside the door, bracing his hands against the door frame. "Because he thinks you have a thing for Nova."

"How does me not going prove that I don't have a thing for her?"

He shrugs. "It doesn't, but it'll give him time alone with her." He rolls up the sleeves of his plaid shirt, reaches for his cigarettes in his pockets, and pops one into his mouth. "I don't really get why, though. The girl's seriously crazy sometimes."

"Crazy?" I push up from the bed and head over to the dresser. "She seems normal to me."

He lights the end of his cigarette and puts the lighter into his back pocket. "Yeah, but she's not. Delilah said she went off the deep end when her boyfriend killed himself and she even tried to slit her wrists." He makes a clicking noise with his tongue as he traces his finger over his wrists. "But who can blame her? I mean, she was the one who found him dead. That seriously has to screw with someone's head..." His eyes widen as he pulls an oh-shit face. "Fuck, I completely forgot... Shit, man..." He rubs his bald head with his hand that's holding the cigarette. "Look, I didn't mean it."

"Yeah, you did," I say in a tight voice, not just pissed off at him for bringing up my painful past, but because he insulted Nova and is talking about her like she's some kind of freak show. Me, I deserve it, because I caused the agony in my past, but Nova, she didn't do anything. Something happened to her and it fucking makes me ache, like physically hurt on the inside and out. "Now can you get the fuck out so I can change?"

His eyes turn cold. "You better watch how you talk to me. You're a guest in my house, and I'm not going to let you stay here for much longer if you don't start paying for rent."

I head for the door, my hands balled into fists, wanting so badly to punch him in the face. "I'm working on getting a job."

He slams his hand against the door as I start to close it. "If you need a job, I can get you one."

I look him over skeptically. "Doing what?"

He takes a drag from the end of the cigarette, and smoke eases out of his mouth and envelops his face. "I think you know."

I do, but what I'm not sure is if I'm that desperate yet. Yeah, I do drugs, but dealing is a whole other level of crap. "I'll think about it."

He lowers his hand from the door and steps back. "Well, don't think for too long, otherwise you're going to miss your chance."

I nod, and he backs out into the hall so I can shut the door. I turn in a circle, looking at the pathetic little room that's become my home, trying to remember how I got here, but the path leading from Lexi's death to this exact moment is nothing but a blur. I wonder if that's how Nova feels. I wonder if that's why she looks so sad all the time. To see something like that— to see death. It's the kind of thing that scars people on the inside. And not just small scars, but long, thick, jagged ones that never go away. The kind of scars that alter the appearance of things, change people. Ruin them. The only difference is that I put the scars on myself by crashing the goddamn car, while Nova's were forced on her by someone else's decision.

I glance down at the drawing of Nova's eyes and then at the drawing of Lexi on my wall. Images devour my thoughts, yanking me back to the dark moment that changed me forever.

"Quinton," Lexi whispers, and even though her eyes are open, they're glazed over and I can tell she can't see me. "Just promise me that..."

Tears stream from my eyes as I lift her head up from the ground and move it onto my lap. Blood immediately soaks my jeans, and in the glow of the moon, I can see blood all over her, me, the ground below us. "It's okay, baby..." I fight back the tears, knowing I have to be strong because I'm not the one hurting. In fact, I feel numb. "I won't let anything happen to you. I promise."

She shakes her head from side to side as her breaths become ragged, and she clutches my arms. "Just promise me that you'll never forget me, no matter what. That you'll always love me more than anyone else."

"Of course," I say, with my fingertips pressed to her wrist. I can feel her lethargic pulse, and the longer time goes on, the more time goes on between each beat. "Lexi, that's a stupid thing to say, though, because you're going to be fine." I'm lying. She knows it. I know it. Blood is gushing from her body and her limbs are contorted in odd, unnatural angles.

But I found her phone, and the naïve part of me thinks that if the ambulance can just get here in time, everything will be okay; they can fix her, mend her, put her back together, and erase this entire night.

I focus on the uneven rhythm of her breathing, knowing it's fading but praying to God she can hold on. If I can just keep concentrating on it, she'll keep breathing. She has to.

"Quinton," she says in a feeble voice, and I can no longer choke back the tears. Hot tears spill down my cheeks, and I reach up and wipe them away before she can see them. "I'm sorry for sticking my head out of the window."

I start to cry, my body trembling as I feel her heart slowing down. "It's not your fault." I manage to get out. "I should have just pulled the damn car over. Lexi, I'm so fucking sorry. I promise I'll make this better somehow. I'll never let go of you. I promise."

"Always trying to make things better." She tries to smile, and it looks crooked and wrong. "One day you're going to make someone really happy…"

"Yeah, you..." I trail off as she shuts her eyes. It's the last thing I say to her, and I wish it was the last thing I ever say. Maybe if I lie down with her and try hard enough, I can get my own heart to stop beating.

I wince, wrenching myself out of the memory. Tears drip from my eyes. I gradually walk up to the drawing of Lexi on the wall beside the window, study the dark lines I put on the paper when I wanted to capture the perfection of her body. "Is it breaking the promise if I'm friends with her? Because I want to be friends with her, despite how much I don't deserve it. I used to think it was breaking my promise to you, but I don't know anymore... I blame it on the fact that the old me is trying to push his way through and make me be a good guy again, because she looks so sad and lonely." I pause, waiting for some sort of sign or answer.

The room stays silent and I sigh, rubbing my hand across my face, knowing that I should just get it over with. End my life. Say good-bye. Leave the thoughts and memories and self-hatred behind like I've wanted to do for a year now instead of wasting space and breaths. But I don't seem to have it in me. It's like I'm waiting around for something to happen, even though nothing ever does.

I back away from the drawing, toward the door, taking more steps into the future, even though I want to remain stuck in the past.

Chapter Nine

July 10, Day 56 of Summer Break

Nova

I've been taking a little break from trailer parks and guys for the last couple of days. It's been neither a good break nor a bad one, which is becoming the story of my life. Nothing is good. Nothing is bad. Everything just exists, like me floating through life with no direction or meaning.

Despite my break from trailer park guys, I can't seem to get Quinton or his sadness out of my head. I want to learn more about him, perhaps find out about the girl in the picture, but he seemed so upset that I even brought her up. I tried to search him on the Internet, even though it felt kind of wrong and nosy on my part. But I was trying to find something else about him, other than he likes art, he lived in Seattle, and he smokes weed. But there are too many Quinton Carters, and I couldn't find the one I was looking for, not even on Facebook or any other social media network. The more I search and come up empty-handed, the more frustrated I get, but I think there's an underlying reason to my frustration, stemming from how I connect Landon to Quinton. It feels like I've stepped back into the past again, meeting the sad, haunting guy that carries the weight of the world on his shoulders, and I can't figure out the reason why.

I wake up a couple of mornings after it happened, feeling more jumbled than I usually do. I count the seconds it takes the sun to move over the hill line, just like I always do, but there's no sense of order and comfort this morning. I get out of bed and take a shower, then head to my computer desk and open up Landon's video file. The longer I stare at it, the more I start wondering what exactly he said on it. Are there answers to my questions? About him? About his life? His thoughts? Stuff about us? Shit, what if there is? What if this whole time the answers have been right here, but my fear and anxiety have been getting in the way.

I put my finger on the mouse pad and let the cursor hover over the file, something I've never done before. My finger shakes as I consider tapping the mouse, clicking the file, letting it open up. I'd get to see his eyes again, watch his lips move as he spoke and took breaths. His heart would be beating and he wouldn't be silent in a wooden box, at least for the moment of the clip.

My heart picks up in my chest. What does he say on it? How does he look? What does he feel? How will I see it— see him?

I instantly pull my hand back, shaking from head to toe, my nerves so contorted and confounded I can barely breathe. I'd almost turned it on, which means what exactly? That I'm starting to move on from him? That I'm starting to move on in my life?

"No...no...no..." I shake my head and shove away from the computer, turning it off, and counting as I race to the bathroom. Running away from the problem, like I always do.

❧

It's late afternoon, and this morning's episode is a shadow of a memory in my mind. After a lot of counting, I was able to calm myself down. I'm sitting on my bed with every picture of Landon I own scattered around me, along with a few psychology books. Beneath the bed is a locked box of Landon's drawings. They've been there since his parents gave them to me. The window is open, the fan on, and I pulled my hair up in a ponytail, trying to reduce the sweat forming on the back of my neck. But even in my denim shorts and gray tank top, my skin is getting a little salty.

I have the computer opened up and the web camera aimed at me as I search through photo after photo, looking for something in his eyes or expression that'll give me a clue to why he did it. I can spot sadness in almost all of them, but there has to be more to it than that. He couldn't have just decided to give up because he was sad.

"I know there are more pictures than this," I mutter to

myself. I uncross my legs and scoot off the bed, heading for the garage. My mom boxed up a lot of stuff when I went away to college and stacked the boxes on the garage shelves.

As soon as I step into the garage, I instantly regret it. Too many memories swarm around the drums set in the corner, covered up by a sheet. I haven't touched them since Landon died; my passion to play died right along with him. He was the one who encouraged me to play, bought me the drums, and shared my love for music. But now it all seems pointless, and I can't even bring myself to pick up a set of drumsticks.

I skitter around the drum set and head toward the 1967 sleek, cherry-red Nova parked in the middle of the floor and the bike leaning against it, the last thing my dad touched before his death. Painful memories of everyone I lost hit me from every direction, and I start to count each step as I maintain a steady stride around the car, dragging my hand along the shiny hood. I was never into cars, but my dad always was, and he always tried to get me into them, so I wasn't surprised when he left the Nova to me in his will. What did surprise me was that he had a will, like he knew he was going to die young and wanted everything planned out before he went.

Sighing, I remove my hand from the car and grab the box labeled "Nova's Photos" on the bottom shelf near the back. Then I go back to my room and dump the photos out, trying not to cringe at the mess I've made or the fact that there are too many photos to keep track of. Landon and I never really went anywhere important, but I loved taking pictures of him.

He was so beautiful, and his beauty was only amplified in pictures—like a piece of art that looks plain and ordinary from a distance, but up close the angles and shapes and colors fit perfectly together and create something so amazing it couldn't possibly exist.

"Knock, knock," Delilah says as she enters my room. I haven't seen her since I got high at Dylan's house, but that's because I've been avoiding Dylan's house and she's been spending most of her free time there. She has an iced coffee in her hand, and her hair is divided into two braids. She's wearing a pink shirt and cutoffs, she has no makeup on, and she's wearing a backpack for some reason.

"Planning on making a trip back to high school?" I tease as she shuts the door.

"Huh?" Her face contorts in puzzlement.

I point at the backpack. "What's with that?"

She glances at the bag on her back. "Oh, that." She jumps on the bed, landing on her knees, and the mattress bounces underneath her weight. The ice swishes in her cup, pictures start to slide to the side, and I work to keep them together on the bed. "I brought goodies."

"Goodies?" I ask, grabbing a stack of photos and putting them on my lap.

Her eyes light up as she removes the backpack off her back and drops it onto the bed. She unzips it, and I'm starting to get really curious about what the hell she's doing when she takes out a glass pipe and a small plastic bag full of weed.

"Where did you get that?" *And why did you bring it here?*

She opens the bag and picks up a pinch of weed. "From Dylan, duh?"

I align the stack of photos that are on my lap. "Okay, then why did you bring it here?"

"Because I thought we could have a nice relaxing day together now that I know you're cool." She fills the pipe with weed and grabs a lighter out of the backpack. "You know, I used to try and keep this as far from you as possible, but after the other day..." She trails off as she glances up at my shocked expression. "Okay, well, maybe I totally just misread you. Was it like a onetime thing or something?"

"I don't know what it was." I try not to look at the pipe and remember how I felt when the smoke first hit my lungs, but it's hard not to stare at something so wonderful yet potent. "Delilah, why did you lie to me when I asked you if you were smoking weed again?"

"I just didn't think you'd be cool with it. You always seemed like you weren't, or at least you acted like you didn't want to try it," she says, shrugging. "Besides, I didn't technically lie. I hadn't been doing it since I left for school...I just started up again."

"Why, though?"

"Why did you do it the other day?" There's accusation in her eyes, like I have no right to be talking about this with her. And she's right. I really don't. The truth of the matter is I did smoke weed the other day, and for a few moments I'd actually felt content and soundless on the inside, something I haven't felt in a long time.

"So do you want to smoke a bowl or not?" she asks with a slight impatience in her tone.

I wonder what she'd do if I said no. "What about my mom? She's home... what if she comes in here?"

"Actually, she just left," she says, setting the pipe down on her lap. "But if you don't want me to, then I won't."

"Won't she smell it, though? When she comes back?" I ask, staring at the pipe. I can almost feel the burn of the weed just from looking at it, along with the brief contentment that followed afterward, and I'm surprised how much my mind craves it.

"Well, turn the fan on and spray some air freshener around or something," she replies. "Besides, you're nineteen. What the hell is she going to do if she catches you? Ground you to your room?"

I honestly could picture my mom trying to rationalize it as me mourning and let me off the hook, because she does that a lot, like when I got really drunk and threw up on the kitchen floor, and she found me the next morning passed out beside my vomit.

"It's okay, Nova," she'd said, helping me to my feet. "We... we all make mistakes when we hurt, but we need to find a way for you to deal." She kept saying we like it was her and me going through it together, like we did with my dad. But not this time. This time it was just me.

"If you want to smoke it, you can," I tell Delilah, selecting a picture of Landon and me lying on our backs in the grass from the seemingly endless stack. I was holding the camera and held it above us to snap the shot. I'm laughing in it and Landon looks like he wants to be anywhere else but getting his picture taken. If I remember right, though, he was particularly irritated that day with everything.

I keep sorting through the pictures while Delilah turns on the ceiling fan, relaxes against the headboard of my twin bed, and starts smoking the weed. Smoke fills the room quickly, moving lazily around my face, and the air stinks like some sort of pungent weed burning in a field.

"You two look really beautiful together," she says, leaning forward and examining the photos closely.

"Yeah, I guess," I mumble, because honestly I always believed Landon was out of my league in the looks department.

"You look happy," she remarks. "I've never seen you that happy."

"Do you need anything to eat or something?" I try for a subject change.

She shakes her head and takes another hit, and her lips pucker as she blows out a cloud of smoke. "Do you ever think you'll love someone again?" she asks, and I frown at her. "What? I'm just curious."

"You've never been curious before." *Which is why I love hanging out with you.*

"I know, but it doesn't mean I don't wonder." She sighs and inhales from the pipe.

I try to stay focused on the photos, but the room's getting cloudier, along with my head. Eventually she places the pipe and lighter on my nightstand and lies down, staring at the ceiling.

"So my mom had this guy over the other day," she divulges. "And he grabbed my ass."

My head whips up from the photo. "What?"

She nods, without looking at me. "Yeah, but it's how it's always been, ever since, you know—" she points at her chest "—these bad boys came into the picture."

Delilah rarely talks about her mom, but from what I've picked up, she works for a "service" that helps men with their problems. I'm not sure if it's an escort service or a phone chat service or what, and I've never met her mom, because Delilah's never taken me over to her house before.

"Are you okay?" I ask.

"As okay as I've always been," she replies emotionlessly.

She reaches for the pipe and puts it to her mouth, holding the lighter above it as her eyes remain on the ceiling. I look at the large quantity of photos on my bed, then press my fingers to the bottom of my eyes, my head pounding from the smoke and the emotions flowing through my body. From the outside, these pictures create a life spent together, and I wonder what I would be doing if Landon was still around. If I would be somewhere else, with a future ahead of me, with him. Or would I have ended up in this exact place, getting high and trying to find out who the hell I am without Landon? Maybe we wouldn't have lasted and I'd have ended up crushed by a breakup instead of his death. Maybe I was destined to get to the exact moment. Maybe this is where I really belong. Perhaps he really knew this was how I would turn out, and that was why it was so easy for him to leave me behind.

Delilah starts coughing as smoke rings around her face. "Are you sure you don't want any?" She offers me the pipe.

I try to think of a reason why I shouldn't do it, but again I can't find one. So I take a hit, both terrified and relieved that I do it because it's still so unknown yet vaguely familiar and brings me so much quiet. I couldn't even count to ten if I wanted to, and my thoughts are just a haze in my head. We lie on my bed, talking about music and classes and the time I barfed my guts out in the campus garbage cans after I downed nearly a half a bottle of tequila.

My mom eventually comes home, and we hurry and spray perfume everywhere and throw open all the windows. She sticks her head inside to check on me and asks if we want anything to eat. She either doesn't notice the smell or doesn't want to admit she does. Or she's just letting me off the hook again.

"I have cookie *dough*," she tells Delilah when Delilah asks for cookie dough ice cream. Her tone is clipped and she seems very uncomfortable. My mom's never been a fan of Delilah or her reputation around town, but she'll never say anything rude directly to Delilah. It's not the kind of person she is.

"That works," Delilah says, swiveling in the computer

chair as she pretends like she's been looking through my CD collection.

"And what about you, Nova," my mom asks me, looking a little bit upset. I wonder if she can smell the weed or see it in my eyes. Does she know what I was just doing? "Do you want anything to snack on? You can come help me cook dinner if you want. I'm making your favorite."

"What is my favorite?" I ask. Delilah laughs, but I wasn't trying to be funny. I really don't know anymore what my favorite food or color or even song is.

"Fettucine alfredo," my mom says, and her blue eyes look like they're watering up.

Feeling a ping of guilt, I gesture at the photos on my bed. "I'm going through these right now. Sorry."

She sighs, heartbroken, and I feel my heart crack, but the numbness from smoking instantly seals it up, and then I can't feel anything at all. She backs out of the room and leaves us alone in our dazed stupidity and all I can think is: *Where do I go from here?*

The only answer I get is silence.

Chapter Ten

July 27, Day 69 of Summer Break

Nova

I've been getting lost a lot lately. Not only from my counting and thoughts of Landon, but also because I've been spending a lot of time with Delilah and doing and smoking things I shouldn't, and I keep doing it because honestly it makes me feel better, at least for a moment, until it's passed through my system, and then it feels like I'm impatiently waiting around for the next better moment to come around again.

I still stick to my morning routine, though, counting the seconds it takes for the sun to rise over the hill, then I get out of bed and take a shower. I always spend my five minutes in front of the computer staring at Landon's video file. I haven't come close to clicking on it again, and I'm thankful for it. I don't think my mind could handle another panic attack over it or handle actually clicking on it and watching it. I only stare at it, letting my mind know it's there—letting me know he's there.

Delilah was over here about an hour ago, yammering about the concert, while we shared a joint, something we've been doing a lot. She's been pushing me to go for the last two weeks and I keep declining, because: (a) I'm afraid of what memories will surface, because Landon and I used to go to concerts all the time; and (b) I'm terrified of being around Quinton. I avoided him since our awkward kiss, and I'm nervous about what he'll say when I see him again and what I'll say too because deep down I know I'm not one hundred percent seeing him as *him*.

It's stifling today, but I'm outside anyway, in my cutoffs and a really thin purple tank top with my hair pulled up. I smell a little like smoke mixed with the scent of the perfume I used to try and cover up the stench of the weed stuck in the fabric of my clothes and in my hair. I'm sitting on the swing that's on the front porch of my little one-story home, counting every single time it moves back and forth, trying to air my hair and clothes out. Just diagonal is a large oak tree that holds one of my most genuine, life-changing memories. It's centered in the middle of the green grass that lines the front of the two-story house that Dylan used to live in. I have my foot under me and the swing rocks back and forth.

"All right, Nova, we're heading out," my mom says as she walks out the front door. She has a purse on her shoulder, the car keys in her hand. She's wearing slacks and a satin top, and her hair is in a bun.

I remember when she was with my dad, and her hair was

long with tangled waves and tiny braids throughout it. She would wear long, flowing dresses, and she reminded me so much of a hippie, all love, peace, and happiness. I miss those days; the ones where she'd laugh freely and her smile would brighten up her face. She's a different person now, and although I don't doubt that she's truly happy, I wonder about the difference between her happiness when she was with my dad versus her happiness with Daniel. She's more of a controlled happy now. She finds different things funny, and in a sense she's a different person, one who's harder to talk to.

I wave at her as Daniel walks out the door wearing a polo shirt and black slacks. He's pulling a suitcase behind him and has a granola bar in his hand. "If you need anything, call us," he says, stepping down the stairs, dragging the suitcase along with him. They're going to a resort for the weekend to celebrate their four-year anniversary, but I can tell my mom is hesitant to go and leave me behind. She's been talking about canceling it for the last week, pretending like she's too busy.

"Okay." I stand up to give my mom a hug good-bye.

She wraps her arms around me, squeezing me way too tightly, and I wonder if she can smell the weed on me or if I've aired out enough. "If you need anything—anything at all, call us." She shakes her head. "God, I feel guilty for even leaving at all."

"I'm nineteen years old," I tell her. "And I've been living on my own for almost a year now. I'm fine." I draw back. "Now go have fun on your trip."

She presses her lips together and stares at me directly through my sunglasses, and I wonder what she sees. Does she know what I've been doing? Can she tell how lost I am? That I don't know what I'm doing? That I'm not sure who I am anymore? Can she still see her daughter thriving inside, or is the Nova she gave birth to, raised, tried to shape into a good person with values, gone?

She sighs, hitching her thumb under the strap of her purse and heads for the stairs. "I love you, Nova."

"Love you too." I sit back down on the swing again, feeling guilty about all my bad decisions, but it quickly vanishes through the lingering high inside my head. They load up the car and back out of the driveway, and she watches me the entire time, looking away only as they reach the corner. Then everything gets quiet; even the neighborhood has decided to bask in the silence. I rock in the swing for a while, and even though my eyes aren't focused on his house, my mind still is.

I take my phone out of my pocket, flick the screen to turn on the video, and aim it at Landon's old house. "He doesn't live there anymore or anything, but I kind of feel tied to it. Maybe it's because I spent so much time there, engulfed in everything he did." I wiggle my foot out from beneath me and place it down on the concrete patio. "Not too long after he died, his parents moved out, and now the porch is littered with bicycles and toys, and in the backyard on the hill where I once lay beside him, there's now a swing set." I slant to the side, so I can get a shot of the backyard and the hill that dips down to the fence line. "It's like he doesn't even exist anymore...like he never did...but he still does to me, inside my heart. In fact, he still owns it."

The door creaks open, and my heart pounds deafeningly inside my chest...It matches the beat of the music as he hangs lifelessly from a rope...His skin is so pale, like snow, and his eyes are still open, like he's still there, holding them open...

I slap my hand across my face, *hard*, wanting to get the hell out of my own head. My sunglasses fly off my head, and the pain erupts up my cheek as my ears start to ring and my eyes start to water. My skin is tender; I clutch my cheek, tears stinging my eyes, sorry for not thinking before I act. It hurts. Badly. But so does the memory.

I wait until my heart settles and my adrenaline balances out. I take a deep breath and another, then sit up straight and rotate the camera around, so I show up on the screen. There's a bright red handprint on my cheek, and I wonder if it's going to leave a bruise. "Sometimes I wonder how unhealthy my attachment is to him. I mean, is it normal to feel like this after over a year has passed? But who's to say what's normal and what's not. Who's to say anything, really, because it always seems like everyone is saying a bunch of different things and we don't make sense to each other. At least that's how it is for me. Nothing makes sense anymore..." I trail off, glancing up as Delilah's truck pulls into the driveway.

I'm surprised, because I thought she was heading out to the concert. She parks the truck and hops out, waving at me, and I notice that there are two other people in the truck. The passenger door swings open and Quinton jumps out, followed by Dylan.

"Hey, Nova Dova," she singsongs, energetically skipping around the front of the truck. She's changed her outfit from this morning into a pair of maroon corduroy shorts and a white tank top. Her auburn hair touches her shoulders, and she has an array of colorful bracelets on her wrists. "Are you making one of your videos?" Her jaw drops as she nears me, her eyes fixing on my swollen cheek. "Did you get in a fight while I was gone?"

I drop the phone to my lap and click off the recorder. "No," I lie. "I fell out of the swing and hit my face on the floor."

"Are you okay?" She trots up the steps.

I nod. "Yeah, I'm fine."

Quinton and Dylan are talking to each other in hushed voices at the bottom of the steps, and Quinton looks like he's getting annoyed. Dylan's got a hood pulled over his head, which doesn't make any sense since it's blistering hot. Quinton has on a black shirt and a pair of faded jeans. His jawline is scruffy and there's a tiny bit of black smeared on the upper section of his cheekbone.

"What are you doing here?" I ask as she stops in front of the swing. "I thought you were taking off for the concert."

"We are but we came here to pick you up," she says, folding her arms.

Dylan steps up to the porch and drapes an arm around her shoulders, his gaze focused on me. "Whoa, what happened to your face?" He slides the hood off his head and rubs his hand over his bald head.

"I fell," I respond robotically, covering my cheek with my hand.

His face contorts as he takes in the gnarly welt. "You look like shit."

"Thanks," I answer dryly.

Delilah elbows him in the gut. "Don't be a dick."

His gaze bores into her, and Delilah cowers back as his jaw tightens. "So are you down, Nova?" he asks, still scowling at Delilah.

"Down for what?" I ask nervously, rocking the swing.

"For the concert." He diverts his attention to his watch, and Delilah releases an uneven breath. "We have to go buy some camping shit from the store, go back to my house and get Tristan's fucking car packed and then hit the road soon if we're going to make it in time to hear the opening band."

Quinton steps up beside them and leans back against one of the porch columns. I pretend he's not there, looking at me with those honey-brown eyes I've been hiding from.

I slip off my sandals and let my feet drag against the floor as I swing back and forth. "I already told Delilah that I changed my mind about going." *I can't do it. I'm not that strong. It's too much.*

Delilah shakes her head and waves a finger at me. "No way. You said you'd go and you're going. I will not let you sit around here and mope all week."

I sift through my thoughts, trying to think past the numbers floating in my head. *One, two, three, four, take a deep breath.* "My mom needs me home this weekend," I lie, scowling at her, because I know what she's up to. She thinks that because she showed up here with Quinton, she can get me to go.

"Your mom left for her vacation." She elevates her eyebrows accusingly. "I was here this morning while she was packing, *remember*?"

"You know, you're the only reason I'm going." Quinton straightens out his leg across the porch and nudges my foot with his. His eyes are bloodshot, like they almost always are, and I can smell the scent of pot flowing off him. "It's pretty fucked up to bail out now and leave me hanging." He gives me a smile and I get caught up in it for a minute, until I remember everything that happened between us and how he just walked out and started talking to Nikki, forgetting about everything in the time it took for me to catch my breath.

"I'm sure you'll live," I say. "And I'm sure you'll find someone else to take."

His tongue slips out of his mouth and he licks his lips, and then presses them together, looking remorseful. "No, I can't. And I don't...and I don't want to."

Delilah teasingly swats my arm. "Come on, Nova, just come and have fun." She skips over to the front door and fumbles with the handle, before opening up the screen. "I'm going to go pack your stuff up, and then we have to make a stop at the sporting goods store." She walks into my house and Dylan tags along behind her, the door banging shut behind them.

I get up from the swing and trudge toward the front door, preparing to fight with her over going when Quinton's fingers enfold around my arm and he lures me back to him. "Hey... about what happened? I didn't mean any of it."

I glance over my shoulder at him, the sunlight blinding and reflecting in his eyes. "You don't need to apologize. I know I'm not as much fun as Nikki is to hang out with. And I'm really sorry I cried when you kissed me..." I swallow hard. "That wasn't really about you."

"Then what was it about?" he asks, sounding genuinely interested.

"The past..." My gaze aimlessly wanders to a house on the other side of the street. "And the fact that it all caught up with me."

His brows groove and then he shakes his head. "I didn't mean to leave you in the bed like that. I just kind of woke up and panicked, you know, because you were there in my bed."

I don't get what he's saying and with the way he keeps blinking, I doubt he even does. "Quinton...what do you want from me?" It's a strange question and a glimpse into the awkwardness that once used to radiate from me. "I'm sorry," I apologize and turn for the door. "That came out weirder than I planned."

He hauls me back before I make it too far, maneuvers me around him, and steers me back against the railing, until the wood is scraping at my skin through the fabric of my shirt. He scans my face over and his lips dip downward at the sight of my cheek, then he quickly wrenches his gaze away from it, like it hurts to look at it—or me.

He bends over a little to look me in the eye and the nearness of him is overpowering to the point that I actually want to touch him. "I know I don't know you that well and I'm not that good with people, but I'd like us to be friends."

Friends. Is that what I want from him? I cross my arms behind my back so I'll keep my hands to myself. "You want to be friends with me? Really?"

He nods, delicately cupping his hand on my injured cheek, careful not to press down too hard. "Yeah, I like you, Nova. You're very..." He racks his brain for the right word. "Amusing," he finishes, and the corners of his lips quirk, but he battles the smile swelling through. "What do you say? Will you be my friend, Nova Reed?"

I feel like I'm a kid again and the boy across the street is asking me if I want to hang out. I want to say that I'm getting in over my head. That I'm too unbalanced and confused to be around him, but as he continues to stare at me with his honey-brown eyes, streaked red and brimming with despair, I feel my doubts melting and I find myself nodding.

"All right," I tell him. "We can be friends, if that's what you want."

He pauses with a flicker of misery appearing in his eyes, but it promptly disappears. "That's what I want." A smile expands at his lips, but I wonder how real it is. How can I tell? "Now, can you do me a huge favor?"

"Um...sure. What?"

"Can you please, pretty please, come to the concert with me? I don't want to be alone with those two." He nods his head at the front door.

"You won't be alone, though," I say. "Isn't Tristan going?"

"He is," he says with a teasing grin. "But it'd be weird with the two of us."

I roll my eyes, pretending to be annoyed, but the lightness in his voice is working its way into my heart. "I think you stole that line from me, but it really makes no sense when you say it."

His grin broadens and again, I wonder just how much of it—of him—is real. "I know, but it worked for you, so I figured it could work for me."

"Quinton, I really don't—" I start, but he places his other hand over my lips, silencing me.

"Please, Nova...I don't want to be alone." His skin is meltingly warm, and there's pleading in his tone that stifles the conflict inside me. I'm terrified to death of going and disrupting my order so much, but the way he says he doesn't want to be alone, with such anguish, temporarily kills the anxiety inside me.

"Okay, I'll go," I say, mentally counting the times Landon and I went to concerts—eight—tracking the past, while I move toward the future. *I'm actually doing this? Oh my God.*

What's going to happen? Am I going to lose control? Going to fall apart?

He smiles, drawing both his hands away, and taking a step back, putting a little space between us. "Now do you want to tell me why you have a handprint on your cheek?"

Sealing my lips together, I shake my head, knowing I can't say I fell because he noticed it was a handprint. "No," I say, rubbing my finger along the smudge of charcoal on his cheek, something I used to do with Landon all the time.

"Okay." He flexes his fingers at his sides as I pull my hand away. "Would you at least let me put some ice on it?"

I nod, and he offers me his hand. I take it, knowing I'm choosing to put myself out on a tightrope, and all I can do is cross my fingers that I'll make it across and that there's something to make it across to.

Chapter Eleven

Quinton

I'm a terrible fucking person. I've known it for a year and three months now. The once-good guy who wanted to be an artist and start a family died in the accident and was never revived. Now there's just loser, stoner, drifter Quinton.

I used to be the kind of guy who loved to help everyone, even when it meant helping Lexi mourn over her dead dog. I was the kind of guy in high school who was friends with pretty much everyone. I volunteered to tutor the kids who had a harder time in school, and every year I'd help out at the homeless shelter during Christmas and Thanksgiving, just like my mom did, although I never did get to see her in action. I just heard stories, on the rare occasions my dad would talk about her, and saw a few pictures. I guess I stupidly believed that being good like her would bring me closer to her, but the only time I really got closer to her was when I was lying on the ground after the accident with my chest bleeding out as my heart willingly stopped beating. I'd made peace with dying, and now I made peace with the dark road I'm stumbling down.

But there are always a few rare instances when the good and the bad coexist, and sometimes I can't figure out if I'm making a good decision or a bad one. Like when I asked Nova to be my friend. I haven't had any real friends for a very long time and for a lot of good reasons. But even though I'm fucked up, for some goddamn reason I still think I can help her not look so sad. And after the moment passes, and I realize that I can barely keep myself together let alone help someone else deal with their own problems, it's too late and I'm already in a sporting goods store shopping with her. Dylan and Delilah went out back with one of the cashiers to make a deal and left me and Nova to get everything on the list. We're wandering around, looking for tents and coolers and "hot dog pokey stick thingys," as Nova put it.

"Hot dog pokey stick thingys?" I question with a cock of my eyebrow as I steer the cart around the corner while reading what's on the list.

"Yeah, you know." She makes this weird stabbing movement with her hand like she's trying to reenact the shower scene in *Psycho*. "Those metal pole things that you use to roast hot dogs over fires."

I restrain a smile. She's being too fucking cute for her own good. "I think they're just called hot dog forks."

"Really." Her expression twists with disappointment as she clutches her phone in her hand. She's been holding on to the thing since we left the house, like she's worried if she puts it away she'll lose it or something. "That totally lacks creativity."

I toss a sleeping bag into the cart. "Yeah, I like your name for them better."

"Me too," she says, detouring down one of the aisles. She pauses to lean over my shoulder and read the list. Her hair tickles my cheek, and the contact nearly drives my body mad. "Jeez, outdoor concerts must be a big deal or something... there's so much stuff we have to get."

"You've never been to one?" I stop the cart when she halts in front of the flashlight section, examining it with her hands on her hips.

She shakes her head, leaning away from me. "Nope, you guys get to pop that cherry." Her face instantly turns red as soon as she says it.

Millions of comments run around my head, but I decide to let her off the hook. "Well, the list says we'll need sleeping bags, tents, lanterns, foam padding, and a lunch box."

Still looking embarrassed, she picks up a yellow flashlight from the shelf. "What about flashlights instead of lanterns? They're cheaper."

I shrug and stuff the list into my back pocket. "All this shit is for Dylan. I already have most of it."

She makes a disgusted face and drops the flashlight back on the shelf. "Then we better get everything on the list," she says with a frown.

"Not a fan of him, huh?" I ask, pushing the cart forward again.

She pulls an apologetic face. "Sorry, I didn't mean for that to come out so rude. He just makes me uneasy."

"Me, too."

"Really?"

I nod. "Yeah, really."

This seems to make her happy, and her steps lighten as she walks into the next aisle. She has a funny way to her walk, like she's trying to make all her steps even, and I'm not sure if she's doing it on purpose, but she keeps stepping over the cracks in the tile. I thought I smelled a hint of weed beneath her perfume when we were back at her house, and I wonder if she'd been smoking it or something. Maybe she's high, and that's why she's acting a little off. I'm not sure, though. Since she doesn't look very stoned. And I don't get why she'd be smoking it. It didn't seem like she was an expert when she smoked it at my house.

"Nova, are you okay?" I ask, as she continues to walk up the aisle, staring up at the signs above our heads. There's a really old-school song playing from the store speakers, and her lips are moving to the lyrics.

She peers over her shoulder at me, her skin looking soft under the light, her eyes a dark blue, and her lips shiny with gloss. "Yeah, why?"

I glance down at her feet. "Because it looks like you're walking funny."

She stops walking and stares at her flip-flops. There's this gnarly scar on the top of her foot. "Yeah, my feet hurt a little bit."

I inch the cart up to her. "Hop in then, and I'll give you a ride."

"Seriously?" she says looking alarmed.

"A...yeah." I'm really confused.

She eyes the cart and then me before she climbs in, situating herself around the boxes and sleeping bag. She looks uncomfortable with her knees pulled up and her chin resting on them as she grips her phone in her hand. "Don't crash it, please," she says.

Her words stab me like a piece of jagged metal, and my heart pulses beneath my scar, reminding me how I got here and who I am and how in no way do I deserve to be here, in this world, this life. With her.

Nova

When he tells me to get in the cart, I seriously about have a heart attack. Because I'm walking around, counting each step, making sure to step over the cracks in the floor while I clutch my phone for dear life.

When I went into my room to pack, I'd realized just how bad my routine was going to be disrupted. Not only would I be surrounded my madness and disorder, but my morning routine would be ruined. Sure I could count the seconds it takes for the sun to rise over the hill line, but I couldn't stare at Landon's file for the usual five minutes, and the idea of not being able to nearly made me flip out. I tried to take my computer, but Delilah gave me this huge lecture about computers not belonging at concerts. In a panic, I'd sent the file to my phone, and now I can't seem to let my phone go, afraid that I'll lose the file or something.

And I've never been to this store before, and I don't know where anything is. Plus, there's these giant animal heads mounted on the wall in chaotic, uneven rows, and it's making me anxious.

Then he gives me an out to the controlled footsteps and I want it, yet I don't at the same time. I end up climbing in the cart, clutching my phone and asking him not to crash it please. For some reason, that makes him tense. Then he pushes the cart forward, without saying anything, and I can tell he's upset and I don't want him to be.

My dad used to say then when someone's upset and you don't know why, say something random because it'll make them smile. I never did this with Landon, because I was too afraid he'd think I was crazy, and I'm not particularly fond of randomness. I don't know if Quinton will smile, but it's worth it if it means getting him to smile again.

"Do you know that bears are bowlegged," I say and try not to laugh when he gapes at me. I point up to one of the bears on the wall. "You can't tell because only half of the body is up there, but it's totally true."

He stares at me blankly and then with his forehead creased, he starts laughing. "Please tell me why you chose to share that little fact with me."

I shrug. "I have no idea, but it got you to smile."

Shaking his head, he tries to gain control over his smile, but finally he gives up and grinning, he pushes the cart forward. We start talking about music as we load up the cart around me with all the stuff on Dylan's list. When we reach the tent area, Quinton insists that we need to try out the ones on display in order to know which one is the best to buy.

So I stand up, finally put my phone into my pocket so that I can swing my leg over the cart. He takes my hand and helps me to the floor safely. Then, still holding hands, we crawl into one of the smaller domed tents and lie down on our backs.

"What do you think?" he asks, our hands intertwined between us. "Is it first-time-cherry-popping worthy?"

I bite down on my lip. I couldn't believe when that slipped out of my mouth, and I'm blaming it on my current inability to make good, coherent sentences before I speak. "Maybe, but I thought this was Dylan's tent."

"It is," he says. "I was just curious."

"About what kinds of tents I like?"

"About the things you like."

He waits for me to say what I like, but I can't, because I really don't know anymore what I like and what I want.

We climb out of the tent and start wandering around the store again, trying to decide which tent to get, still holding hands for no other reason than neither one of us can seem to find a reason to let go.

"I like the purple tent," I say as we stand in the section where the boxes of tents are stacked. I have my free hand on my pocket, reminding me that my phone is there—the video is there.

He rakes his fingers through his brown hair, using the hand that's holding on to my hand, so I get to feel how soft his hair is. "Yeah, I'm not sure if Dylan will be too stoked to have a purple tent."

"Yeah, you're right," I say.

He cocks his head to the side as he studies the selection and then fixes his eyes on me. "You know what, he can have whatever tent we get him, since he's the one who made us do his shopping for him."

I giggle as he picks up the purple tent and drops it into the cart. He smiles at the sound of my laughter, and I smile, too, as we head up to the register. With our fingers still laced, we use our free hands to load up the conveyor belt. It's extremely awkward, maneuvering around the cart together, but I'm finding it amusing and kind of fun, which makes it hard to let go of his hand.

"You know, we should make a game of this," he says, setting a sleeping bag down.

I take a lantern out of the cart. "Out of what?"

He glances down at our hands clasped together. "Out of how long we can do this."

I feel a little guilty that we're still gripping onto each other, but it's comfortable—familiar and comforting—and I don't want to stop. "What does the winner get?"

"Well, technically we'd both be winners since we both would let go at the same time."

"Good point."

Smiling to himself, he resumes piling stuff on the belt, and I do, too. But the longer our hands stay joined, the sweatier my hand gets, and finally the comforting sensation leaves my body and I pull away, noting that it was my hand that left his first.

Chapter Twelve

July 28, Day 70 of Summer Break

Quinton

Nova and I finish up at the store, keeping our hands to ourselves, making light conversation that in no way gives me any insight as to who she really is inside. Sometimes she seems happy to be with me and sometimes sad, and by the time we make it to the trailer park she looks like she's going to cry. She wanders into Dylan's room with Delilah, and I have a suspicion that they're getting high. Part of me wants to go back there and stop her, but the part of me, the druggie inside, knows I'd be a fucking hypocrite if I lecture her for doing something I do every day, so instead I stay outside and load up the car. Eventually Nova and Delilah come back outside and start cooking hot dogs over a rusty barbecue grill on the porch. We all eat them and then get ready to hit the road.

We leave later than planned. It's a little after midnight when we pile into Tristan's Cadillac, with our suitcases, tents, sleeping bags, and all the other shit Nova and I picked up at the store piled in the trunk. The stars are out, but it's a little cloudy, so they look like distant dots hidden by a wispy veil. I'd sketch it because it's one of those rare sights that should be recorded, but I'm squished between the door and Nova, who's searching through videos on her phone.

Tristan is driving, and Dylan made Delilah sit in the backseat, even though she said it makes her carsick. He told her he didn't give a shit, and I really don't think he does. He wants to sit up front where it's roomier and he can rest back and get some sleep. Nova chooses to sit by me, and I both love and hate that she did. And it really makes me want to get high, but I won't smoke in the car. I'd never put any of their lives at risk by smoking in the car and getting everyone, including the driver, stoned.

"It smells like dirty socks," Nova remarks, scrunching her nose as she scrolls through video clips on her phone.

Delilah giggles next to her. "It's probably Dylan's feet. They stink."

"Shut the fuck up," Dylan complains from the front seat, kicking his boots up onto the dashboard. "I still have my shoes on."

Nova's eyes elevate from her phone and settle on me. "Is it you?"

I shake my head, confining a smile. "I still have my shoes on, too."

"But you always have your laces undone." She says it more

as a question than a statement. Her fingers wrap securely around her phone and she hugs it against her chest.

"Because it makes it easier to slip them off," I say, trying not to dig too deep into the fact that she noticed this minor detail about me. "And easier to put on."

"Oh." She glances back at her phone, but doesn't do anything but stare at the black screen.

"It's my feet," Tristan shamelessly admits as he veers the car onto the desolate highway. "But if I'm stuck driving, you all are just going to have to deal with it, because I'm going to be comfortable."

"No one made you drive," Dylan says, cracking the window so he can smoke. "You just did."

"Because no one else offered," he retorts, flipping on the high beams. The road in front of us lights up, every twist and turn, and every single tree. There's no one on the road, and it makes me apprehensive. It's not like I haven't been in a car since the accident, but I'm also usually high whenever I get into a vehicle. I didn't have time to light up before we drove off, and there's no way I'm smoking it in the car when I have other people in it. Being sober in a car painfully forces me to think about the accident and how in a blink of an eye we all could be gone.

Nova lets out an exhausted sigh as she drops her phone on the seat between Delilah and herself. "We should play a game," she says.

"Like spin the bottle," Tristan suggests, smiling at her in the rearview mirror.

She frowns as she tips her head down, pieces of her hair curtaining her face. "No, like I spy or something."

"That's the stupidest game ever," Dylan snaps from the front seat. His head flops back against the headrest, and his hand rests on the windowsill so the cigarette ashes can blow freely outside. He's been pretty moody lately—well, moodier than normal—which means he's probably coming down from something a lot rougher than pot.

Delilah unfastens her seat belt, and it makes my stomach somersault as she slides forward in the seat to massage the back of Dylan's neck. "Relax, babe," she says, moving her fingers in circles along his neck. "Try to get some sleep."

Dylan mutters something as he puffs on his cigarette. "This is such bullshit."

I move my attention from them to Nova, because looking at her makes my heart calm down a little, especially since she has her seat belt on. It gives me a sense of peace, even though I don't have my own on.

"How's your face feeling?" I ask her, observing her enflamed cheek.

She pouts out her bottom lip as she covers her cheek with her hand. "I think it's going to bruise, even after you put the ice on it."

"The ice was for the swelling." I resist the urge to put a hand on her cheek, because I need to stop touching her so much. "And it'll probably bruise, but it'll go away eventually."

"I know," she replies, disheartened. "But it hurts and I

need a distraction. That's why I wanted to play the game. Well, that and my dad and I used to play it all the time when we'd take road trips." She sucks her lip between her teeth, looking sadder than someone whose dog just died. "Sorry, that probably makes me sound like a little kid, doesn't it?"

"No, it makes you sound like someone who misses her dad." I stare out the window at the lofty trees and fence lining the road, thinking about my dad back at home, all alone, living in a house packed with memories of my mom. "I spy something green," I say. I wait for Nova to say something, but when she doesn't, I turn my head toward her. "What? Now you don't want to play?"

Her expression is unreadable. "No, I just didn't think anyone would actually play a game with me."

I shrug. "What can I say? I guess I'm a sucker for those sad, puppy-dog eyes of yours…" As soon as it slips out, I want to retract it. It's not a friend thing to say. It's a flirty, I'm-going-to-try-and-fuck-you-later thing to say. And I shouldn't be flirting with her or thinking about fucking her. Plus, Tristan's in the car and the last thing I want to do is piss him off, especially after how nice he's been to me, all things considering.

By the look on Nova's face, I think she knows I'm flirting with her, and I bite my tongue, wondering what the hell is going to come out of her mouth.

"The grass," she guesses breezily, letting me off the hook.

I frown, disappointed by her answer. "That's seriously your guess?"

"What." She bats her eyelashes innocently at me. "It's green."

"Nova." I shake my head, pretending to be severely displeased in her answer. "Your lack of creativity is alarmingly disappointing."

"Well, not all of us are artists," she retorts. "But if you think you're so creative, then let's see how good you are." She thrums her finger on her chin as she glances around at the forest on each side of the road. "I spy something...green." She smiles at me, amused by herself, which makes her at the moment completely and utterly the most wonderful person that's ever existed, at least in my book.

"Did you just copy me?" I question with an arch of my brow.

She exaggeratedly presses her hand to her heart. "No way. How could I when I don't even know what the answer was?"

"Yeah...I guess..." I focus on her, pretending like I'm trying to read her thoughts, and it makes her squirm. Maintaining an impartial expression, I give her an answer she'll never expect. "Your eyes."

She points a finger at me, grinning. "My eyes are blue."

Even though my mind is resistant, I raise my hand and touch my fingertips to her temple. "Actually, they're blue with little specks of green in them. It's one of the first things I noticed about you."

She presses her lips together so forcefully the skin around them turns purple. "You did?"

I nod, my guilt consuming me, and I want to retract everything I've ever said to her. But like I know way too well, you can't just take stuff back. The decisions we make from the moment we definitively make them stick with us forever. Like deciding to take the responsibility of being the driver for the night, which may not seem like a big thing, but in my case, it drastically altered my life forever.

"Oh my hell," Delilah declares, still massaging Dylan's neck. "You two are fucking adorable."

The color drains from Nova's face and she rotates in the seat, looking away from me, and slumping back in the seat. If I didn't learn about her past, I'd question why she did it, but now that I know, I understand, at least to an extent. I turn around in my seat, crossing my arms over my chest, and the car grows quiet.

Nova starts fiddling with the bands on her wrist that she wears to cover the scar. I lower my hands to my lap and drum my fingers on my knee, remembering how I felt after Lexi's funeral, even though I'd never made it there. But the idea that she was gone, buried in the ground, made me feel helpless, and I had the intense need to turn everything off. Was that how Nova felt after her boyfriend died?

Without even knowing what I'm doing, I slide my hand across the seat and to Nova's lap. She flinches from the initial contact and I almost expect her to jerk away. But she remains motionless and I wrap my fingers around her wrist, pressing them against the small, bumpy line on her skin, just below the bands. She rests her head back against the seat, her heart rate quickening, before returning to a steady, consistent beat. The feeling of it calms me down, because it reminds me that there's life in the world, and that hearts do keep beating even after they break.

Nova

"I can't believe you bought me these," I say, staring in disbelief at the pink drums set up in front of me. Landon and I are in my garage, and the door is shut to lock out the icy air, the snow, and the outside world. It's my birthday and I came out here with him, thinking he was going to drive me somewhere, but instead, there are wonderful, girly drums.

"Do you like them?" he asks, his arms crossed over his chest. He looks really worried, like I'm actually going to hate getting pink drums.

I spread my arms out to the side. "Of course. They're pink drums."

A fleeting smile sneaks through, and for a second the brown in his eyes almost looks golden. "Good, because I was worried you wouldn't."

I press my hands together, circling around the drums, bouncing with excitement. "Why? You know I've always wanted my own set. It gets so annoying using the school's, especially because all the guys think it's a guy's instrument and that I shouldn't be playing with them."

"They're just jealous." He drops down in a camping chair by the steps. His hair is damp from walking over to my house during the snowstorm, and his cheeks are a little flushed from the cold. He has a black hooded jacket on with the sleeves rolled up, and there's a ring of murky water around the bottom of his jeans. "Go ahead, Nova Reed, show me what you got."

I sit down in the stool and pick up the sticks. "But you already know what I've got. You've heard me play like a thousand times."

"Yeah, for a crowded room." He relaxes back in the chair. "But I want you to play just for me."

I air-jam for a moment. "What do you want me to play?"

He shrugs. "Whatever you want. Make it mean something, though."

I hate it when he says that, because he's the kind of person who's always looking deeper into things than a normal person, like me. I search my brain for the perfect song, but each one has a flaw, is either too fast or too slow, or I can't play it as good as I want to just yet. Finally I decide just to play my own song, one that I haven't been able to get out of my head since the day he first kissed me.

"Okay, I have one, but you have to promise not to laugh at me."

"Why would I laugh?"

"Because I made it up," I say. "And it's probably not very good."

"I'm sure it is," he assures me. "Besides, I would never laugh at you." He's no longer joking, and I love him so much for it. I want to tell him right there that I love him, even though I've known for a while, but like always, I chicken out.

Sighing to myself, I elevate the sticks above my head, pretending like I'm going to slam them down and make a lot of noise, but when I touch them to the drums, I hit soft, but with meaning and purpose. I start playing the song, getting more into it the longer I play. At one point I shut my eyes and let my hands lead the way, getting lost in the beat, getting swept away to another world while I think up lyrics in my head and whisper them under my breath. If I didn't know any better, I'd swear I'd died for a moment and left my body peacefully.

But then the song ends, and the moment of peace floats away and is replaced by nervousness. I open my eyes and realize that the camping chair is empty. I glance to my left and then my right, panicking when I don't see him anywhere.

"Was I that bad?" I wonder aloud, frowning at the sticks in my hand.

"No, it was perfect." The sound of his voice right over my shoulder causes me to jump.

I spin around in the chair, dropping the drumsticks, and pressing my hand over my racing heart. "Shit, you scared me."

He doesn't laugh at me, nor does he smile. He simply studies me with a perplexed, somewhat astonished look. "That was beautiful," he conclusively says and traces his fingers across my cheekbone. "Happy birthday, Nova," he whispers.

My eyelids flutter shut as his hand travels down my jawline, to my neck, to the collar of my shirt. He tugs it down a little and slips his fingers inside my bra as he lays me back against the drums. My head bumps against the cymbal, but I'm too consumed by his thumb grazing my nipple to care about the ringing in my ears.

He moves his mouth toward mine. "Nova...I..." He struggles to say something and I force my eyelids open, despite my body's protest. Our gazes lock, and for a second I think he's going to break up with me because he looks terrified and conflicted and completely torn apart on the inside.

"I love you," he whispers.

I swear to God time stops.

"I love you, too," I say with zero hesitation.

He starts to smile but it quickly fades, and then his lips connect with mine. He kisses me, caresses my body, drinks me in until my head becomes so cloudy I can barely remember my name. It's the perfect birthday. One

*I know I'll remember forever, because the guy I want to
be with forever finally said he loves me.*

When I open my eyes, the car has stopped moving, and
I'm lying in the backseat with a piece of paper on my forehead.
Blinking away the disorientation, I sit up and take the note off
my head.

Dear Sleepyhead,

Once you wake your lazy ass up, meet us out in the
tent area.

Delilah

Shaking my head, I ball the note up and stuff it away in
my pocket. The car is parked at the outskirts of a dirt field
that's packed with people flocking toward a massive stage set
up near the forest line. There are drums and amps and every
other musical instrument that my heart secretly desires to play
set up on it, along with lights strung along the front. The sun
is intoxicatingly warm, and it makes the leather seats below me
hot and the backs of my legs sticky. There's no one else inside
the car with me and the doors are locked. There are already
so many things wrong with being here, like the sight of the
drums up onstage, the fact that I missed counting as the sun
came up, and the fact that I'm waking up in the backseat of a

car I've only rode in once. So much unfamiliarity and my heart is already speeding up, slamming against my chest in unnerving thumps, and I start to take deeper breaths as I veer toward hyperventilation. I don't know what's about to happen next, whether I'll lose control, think of Landon too much, panic and do something irrational.

There's only one thing that can maybe get me back on track. I take out my cell phone and open the file, the sight of it slightly settling my heart rate, and gradually my breathing returns to normal. The longer I look at it, the more at peace I become, and again I have the urge to open it, my mind whispering at me that if I do I can see him again. *Get an understanding.* I don't, though, and once the five minutes pass I turn off my phone since the battery is half dead.

Scooting to the edge of the seat, I tuck the phone into my pocket, work the lock up, and climb out of the car. I stretch my legs and then tug the elastic from my hair, combing my fingers through the tangles as I start the hike across the field. The atmosphere is lively and buzzing with excitement, and I start counting my steps as I turn to the side and weave my way around groups of people smoking cigarettes and drinking beers. I have no idea where the tent area is or if there's even such a thing as a tent area.

Forty-eight...forty-nine...fifty...

My head is hurting. The air is spicy and sticky and smells like sweat, cigarettes, and weed. I pause in a small gap in the crowd, turning in a circle, trying to get my bearings.

Fifty-seven... fifty-eight... fifty-nine...

My heart throbs, and I place my hand on my forehead, trying to spot something familiar. The atmosphere is already getting to be too much, and I've been out of the car for a whole three minutes. This is exactly what I was afraid of. I knew I'd get like this, be overwhelmed by people and the fact that I have no idea what's about to happen in the next second. My mind starts to race and dash toward thoughts of Landon and me at concerts, listening, singing along, kissing...

"Hey." The sound of Quinton's voice blankets around me and puts a stop to my mental counting insanity. It's the most amazing thing I've ever experienced, and I want to grab on to it with everything I have in me.

When his hands graze my hips, my body settles even more and a strange quietness surfaces in me, one that I've only been able to get through weed. My hand falls from my head as I turn around and angle my neck to look at him. There are red rings around his eyes, not from being stoned but from exhaustion, and a few strands of his brown hair are sticking out on the side of his head. He has a half-finished beer in his hand, and a pack of cigarettes is poking out of the front pocket of his T-shirt.

"You look tired," I call out over the voices of the people around us.

"I'm fucking exhausted," he admits, leaning in toward my ear. His breath smells like beer. He tucks a strand of my hair behind my ear. "I don't like car rides... And I can't sleep when I'm in a car."

I put my lips beside his ear, trying not to breathe in his scent, but it's impossible. "You should go take a nap or something, then."

Shaking his head, he steps back and motions around us. "And miss all this fun?"

I frown at the crowd as I refasten my hair into a secure ponytail, leaving a few strands loose to frame my face. I reach for the cherry ChapStick I carry in my back pocket. "It's really noisy," I comment and move the stick over my lips. He watches me through hooded eyes, but I'm going to blame it on the sun.

"It's a concert, Nova." His tongue slips out of his mouth to wet his lips, and then he tips his head back and takes a sip of the beer, his neck muscles moving as he swallows. "It's supposed to be full of noise and chaos."

I put the ChapStick back in my pocket and wrap my arms around myself, tucking my elbows in as a group of guys walk. "So when does the music start? Because I think once it does I'll be able to handle it better."

"That doesn't make any sense. Music is noisier." He reaches up to scratch his forehead. Watching his fingers move reminds me of how he touched my scar—or my pulse—in the car. I haven't figured out which one yet, and I'm not sure which is better. Either he was touching the scar that clearly gives away what I did that day on the bathroom floor or he was feeling my pulse, which seems intimate and, even though I hate to admit it, beautiful—because, seriously, who does that? Who feels the heartbeat of another person like it's important?

"Music is settling to me, especially songs that I know," I tell him, standing on my tiptoes and inclining toward him so I don't have to yell over the bustle of the crowd. "And it'll settle me down." Maybe. As long as I can't connect the song to Landon.

His forehead creases like he's deeply contemplating something, but all he says is, "Come on." Then he swings his arm around my shoulder and draws me close as he winds through the crowd, steering me with him. I wrap my arms around his midsection as smoke snakes around us.

"Oh and by the way," he says, turning us to the side to get around two trucks parked closely together. "Dylan was super-pissed about the purple tent." He smiles, pleased.

I smile too, matching my footsteps to his, and somewhere along the way I lose track of how many I've taken. I don't realize it until we reach the tent area, which is basically a bunch of tents set up in random places that have chairs and coolers near them, totally disorganized and a complete nightmare for me. I hold on to him tighter, breathing in his scent as we step out into the sea of tents, suddenly aware of how clear my head is and how much I don't want to let go of him. I'm not sure what to do with the revelation. Run? Embrace it? Cry?

I'm still clinging onto Quinton when Delilah and Dylan duck out from their purple two-person dome tent. Another, slightly larger tent stands to the side, and Tristan is working to get the poles in it correctly so it'll stand up straight.

The three of them notice us simultaneously. They all look

like they want to say a remark about us cuddling together; Delilah's will probably be sassy, Dylan's crude—and Tristan, by the look on his face, might snap something ruthless. But somehow, they manage to control themselves. I think about backing away from Quinton, but I can't seem to get my feet to cooperate.

"So who's up for a little business?" Dylan asks, slipping his plaid jacket off. He balls it up and chucks it into the tent, while Delilah heads over to a red cooler that's between the two tents.

"I thought we were going to keep this strictly fun," Tristan says, squinting as he threads a pole through the fabric of the tent. "Wasn't that the deal?"

Delilah returns to Dylan and hands a beer to him. "Yeah, you said this was just fun."

"I said it could be fun for you." He pinches her ass and unscrews the lid of the bottle. "I have to work."

I'm not naïve enough not to know what kind of work they're doing—it's the same thing I knew they were doing out in the back of the sporting goods store, even though no one said anything to me. It makes me very aware of the environment I'm in, but I don't seem to care. I used to care about stuff all the time, then I lost the thing I cared about the most, and it seemed like everything left meant nothing or was insignificant.

My cheek is pressed against Quinton's chest, and his heart is striking rapidly from inside his chest, like he's uneasy, too. "I think I'm just going to relax," he says, moving around the chair and heading toward the cooler with his arm still around me. I shuffle my feet with his. "It's been a long fucking drive."

"It was four hours," Tristan grimaces, bowing the pole toward the ground. He's got his shirt off. His chest glistens with sweat, and his jeans hang low on his hips. "Besides, all your dumb ass had to do was sit in the backseat." His voice drops to a mutter as he stabs the pole in the ground. "But then again, we know how great it is to put you behind the wheel."

I feel the volt of panic surge through Quinton's body, and every single one of his muscles tightens and he quickly jerks his arm away from me. No words are uttered, no looks are exchanged. He just hurries off, his expression blank, and seconds later he vanishes into the crowd.

I'm left standing there with my jaw hanging to my knees and the impulse to chase after him, wondering where he's running off to. I should go after him. Not let him go. But once again, I just stand there, not doing anything.

I turn to Tristan and without a second thought say, "Why did you say that?"

Tristan avoids eye contact with me, keeping his head down. "If you want to know, then go after Quinton. You two seem to be hitting it off so well."

I stare at him in disbelief, trying to figure out what the hell is going on. Why would Tristan make a comment like that? Was Quinton in an accident or something?

Delilah steps up beside me and loops her arm through mine, jerking on my arm and tugging me away from my staredown with Tristan. She has a white tank top on and the bottom is folded up so her stomach is showing. Her shorts are ripped in the front, and her auburn hair is in a messy bun on top of her head. "How about Nova and I go try and snag some water bottles off someone, since you two jackasses thought it wasn't necessary to bring any," she says.

Dylan sits down on the cooler and crosses his legs out in front of him as he drinks his beer. "That's what the beer is for."

"And that's what causes dehydration," Delilah snaps with a shake of her head. "Fucking idiots," she mutters, pulling me with her as she stomps toward the crowd.

But I don't want to go with her. I want to go find Quinton and find out what's wrong. That's what I want—*need*—to do, like I didn't do multiple times with Landon. My thoughts are racing a million miles a minute as we approach the edge of where the crowd thickens, and I veer toward having a panic attack. Because I can't see Quinton anywhere. I can't see *anything* at the moment, and it's scaring the shit out of me.

I slip my arm out of Delilah's and take off after Quinton. "I'll catch up with you later," I call out, waving.

"Hey, where the hell are you going!" The sound of Delilah's voice hits my back and I sprint off before my mind decides to turn back.

I push people out of my way as I hurry through the mob, knowing that the probability of finding Quinton is very low. But I have to try, otherwise I might end up regretting it.

Forever.

Quinton

I take off through the crowd, my mind racing a million miles a minute as I'm painfully reminded of who I am and what I did. I need to get away from here— from Nova. From everyone. I don't deserve any of this. I don't deserve anything.

It's like one moment everything is fine, and then a few honest words are muttered and suddenly I remember who I am. Tristan had every right to say what he said. I killed his sister—it's my fault that he can't see her anymore. It's all my fault. But it pisses me off a little that he said it only because I had my arm around Nova. He has a thing for her, and I know I should take a step back and let him have her—she'd be better off with him. Kind of, anyway. Honestly she'd be better off with the old version of me, the one who was going to go to college, open his own art studio, and paint and take pictures, and start a family eventually. It was a boring plan, but it was what I wanted, but everything got erased that day and now I'm here, roaming around in the world without any direction, waiting for it to come to an end again.

I wander around the crowd for what seems like an eternity, engrossed in my thoughts, on the verge of crying as the past stabs at my insides and makes me feel like I'm bleeding out, just like I did on the side of the road after the accident. If it'd gone on just a little bit longer, if the ambulance would have driven just a little bit slower, then maybe they wouldn't have been able to revive me. Then I wouldn't have to be here in this world, living a fucking life I don't want. I'd made peace that night as I lay beside Lexi, but then my peace was taken away from me when they brought me back to life. And now I'm left with the guilt of their deaths rotting away at the side of me, like I'm buried in the ground with them, but I'm not. Maybe that's what I deserve, though.

As tears start to spill out, I take a deep drag of the cigarette that has a flake of weed shoved into the tip, trying to stop crying. It's a discreet way to smoke in front of people, although I'm pretty sure that no one around here gives a shit who's smoking what. Then I run into Delilah and Dylan, and Delilah proceeds to chew me out, saying that I need to be careful around Nova, because she's breakable.

"Don't hurt her," she says, jabbing a finger into my chest so hard it hurts. "I mean it. She's been through a lot, you know. I mean her boyfriend killed himself, for Christ's sake."

Her eyes are bulging, and I'm fairly certain she might be spun out of her mind. I haven't seen it actually go on with her, but there have been a few times where I've noticed Dylan up about as high as someone can go and then suddenly he's at the bottom, furious at the world. I actually knew a guy once that did meth a lot, and that was pretty much how he was all the time. But he also lived in a shed out in the backyard of his parents' home and he had no job and no teeth, and he liked to talk about conspiracies a lot. I don't get why a girl like Delilah would do it. She's beautiful and seems mildly intelligent. What's she hiding from? Or is it just Dylan's influence?

But I don't ask and tell her what she needs to hear. "I'll take care of her. I promise." *Promise. Promise. Promise me.* Tears form in my eyes again. I'm making promises about Nova and breaking my promise to Lexi, and half of me wants to break that promise.

Dylan gives me a hug, because he's spun out of his mind and probably has no idea what he's doing or where he even is, and I refrain from the urge to punch him in the face. Then they leave me, holding hands, and talking about a million miles a minute. And I stand there in the middle of the crowd, with my thoughts and my guilt, surrounded by people, but somehow feeling utterly alone.

Nova

I can't find him anywhere and it's pushing me toward a panic attack. I keep thinking about how upset he looked when he took off— how upset he always looked. I keep running and running deeper into the crowd, even when a voice flows through the speakers and is echoed by a strum of guitars. Then the opening band begins playing, and music and sweat and enthusiasm deluge the field, along with the enthralling scent of smoke. I stop in the middle with my hand on my head, trying to hold on to reality and figure a way out, searching the ground and the sky for something to count, but I can't find anything.

"Hold on to my hand," Landon shouts over the music as he holds his hand out to me. But I hesitate, looking around at the people tripping out of their minds, high on music. *"Nova."* His voice brings me back to him. *"I'm not going to let anything happen to you."*

I place my fingers in his and he pulls on my arm, steering me in front of him, so he can walk behind me with his hands protectively on my hips. The band that's playing is usually a rough, edgy band, but their playing one of their softer, sultrier songs.

We're in a dome building, but as I stand in the crowd, listening to their lyrics and watching them pour their hearts out onstage, I can't help but wish that we were outside, underneath the sparkling stars, because it would add to the magical feeling building in me.

"Are you enjoying yourself?" Landon whispers in my ear, his breath damp against my skin.

I nod, then realizing I've shut my eyes, I open them. *"I am,"* I say, tilting my head back so I can look in his eyes. *"Are you?"*

He nods with a hint of a smile on his lips. *"I am. You're like the only person I do have fun around while I'm sober."* He says it as a joke, but the haunting hollowness in his eyes makes me wonder if he's lying.

I turn around and loop my arms around his neck. *"Why? What's so special about me?"*

"I'm still trying to figure that out," he says with his hand against the small of my back and his forehead wrinkled.

It makes me feel small and ugly and unimportant to him. I let out a breath, moving my arms away, because I'm about to cry. But he presses me closer, shaking his head.

"No, I didn't mean it like that, Nova," he insists. "In fact, that came out very wrong."

I force down the strangling lump in my throat. "Then what did you mean?"

Looking down at me, he strokes my cheekbone with his fingers. "I'm not sure." He stares into my eyes, like he's trying to read his own thoughts through his reflection in my pupils. Then he grabs my arm, twirls me around, and tugs me back against him, wrapping his arms around my waist. "Let's just enjoy ourselves."

"Okay..." My voice gets lost in the music as he kisses my neck, sucking on the skin, even biting at it. "I love you, Nova...I always will...no matter what."

I blink from the thought as a stray elbow rams me in the side. I'm being smashed into as people demand more room, flailing their arms and bobbing their heads. And everywhere I look I see Landon's honey-brown eyes and inky-black hair, only sometimes the hair shifts to short and brown and suddenly Quinton is everywhere, a sea of replicates that need to be helped. And then I see the one image I loathe more than anything.

The rope is slightly frayed, like it was about to break, and all I could think as I fell to the floor was: Why couldn't it just break?

"God damn it." I clutch at my head and my knees buckle as I collapse to the ground, knowing that there's a good chance that I'm going to get trampled, especially if I'm near the mosh pit.

But I don't care. I'm too lost in Landon. He would always say that, that he'd love me no matter what. At the time, I thought it was just something he said, but now I wonder if he was always saying it because he wanted me to know he loved me, even if he took his own life. The thought of this brings me no sense of relief, because that would mean that pretty much the entire time we dated, he was thinking about leaving me. Then he did, and now he's gone, and I'm left sitting in the dirt at a concert that I really don't want to be at. My hands are getting stomped on and I'm getting kicked, but I can't get up. I'm starting to have a panic attack, which has happened a few times. My therapist always told me to breathe through it and that it would pass, but how the hell can I when my lungs are shriveling up and oxygen is getting restricted?

"Nova, what the fuck?" A voice rises over the shouting and music. A hand grabs my shoulder and someone lifts me from the ground.

It's not the voice I want to hear, neither Landon's nor

Quinton's. Instead, Tristan stands in front of me, holding my arm, and he looks pissed off for some reason.

"What are you doing?" He grips my elbow and hauls me to the right, thrusting his hand out in front of him to create a narrow walking path for us. "You can't just sit down in the middle of this shit."

I trip over my own feet as I aimlessly let him lead me through the people. Ultimately we break free from the chaos and step out into the mellower tent area. My head empties a little, but not a lot. In fact, the noise and loudness that's diminished around me is replaced by noise and loudness screaming inside my head. *You didn't find him… didn't help him.* "Why did you say that to him?" I wiggle my arm out of Tristan's grasp as we reach our tents. "That thing about being the driver?"

"Because…" He drags his hands through his hair, smoothing it out of his eyes, and he leaves his hand on the top of his head, his elbow bent out to the side. "Look, I fucked up, okay? I shouldn't have said it. It doesn't bring anyone back." He turns around, clutching the back of his neck as he hikes over to the tent.

I know very little about Tristan, other than he's my age, he does drugs, but he's actually really smart. Even though he failed most of his classes, he always did well on tests, but he just never turned in his homework. I don't know what his likes and dislikes are, or what he does besides smoke a lot of weed and drink. I've never met his parents. I don't know if he has any sisters or brothers. But he's always seemed like a nice guy, and so it doesn't make sense to me that he would intentionally say something to Quinton that would hurt him.

He ducks in the tent and zips up the door. Seconds later, smoke seeps out of the screens on the side. I trudge over to the cooler, open the lid, and take out a beer. I pluck the fragments of ice off the glass, wipe the condensation on the side of my shorts, then sit down on the cooler and drink the beer while I survey the crowd from a safe distance. Delilah and Dylan's tent occasionally shakes, and I'm pretty sure they're having sex inside it.

How did I get here? To this place? This moment? This life?

I sit on the cooler for a while, drinking the beer, watching the stage, listening to the rhythm and the musical poetry flowing from the stage. The more alcohol that enters my system, the more calm I feel. The sky dims, and Delilah and Dylan come out and wander off somewhere while Tristan stays in the tent. I'm guzzling beer when Quinton emerges from the crowd. He's got a cigarette in his hand, his brown hair is wet, along with the top of his shirt, and it looks like he's been crying.

I lower the bottle from my lips and wipe my mouth with the back of my hand. "Why is your shirt wet?"

He points over his shoulder without making eye contact with me. "Some asshole dumped a bucket of water on me when I walked by."

"Are you okay?" I ask, not really referring to the water.

He shrugs, reaching behind his head, and tugging off his shirt. "It's just a little water." He tosses the shirt toward the tent and then motions for me to stand up.

I obey, getting to my feet as I take in the lines of muscles carving his chest and stomach, along with the coarse-looking scar running vertically down the middle, right over his heart. He opens the lid to the cooler and grabs a beer, the muscles of his arms flexing with his movements, and the names tattooed on his arm ripple. *Ryder* and *Lexi*. There's also the phrase *no one* below the names. Who are Ryder and Lexi? Why do they mean so much to him that he'd permanently tattoo a reminder of them on his body? And who's no one?

When he stands up straight with a beer in his hand, he notices my gaze. I start to ask him what they mean, but he covers the tattoos with his hand, and the harsh look in his eyes makes me snap my mouth shut. He unscrews the cap off the beer, and then he lets his head fall back as he nearly guzzles half of it in one large gulp. Lowering the bottle from his mouth, he licks the remaining alcohol off his lips.

"Where's Tristan?" he asks, staring at the stage.

"In the tent."

"Doing what?"

"I don't know. Smoking weed, I think."

He twists his head in my direction with his eyebrow crooked. "How would you know that?"

I shrug. "I smelled and saw the smoke coming from the tent."

He pops the end of his cigarette into his mouth and gradually inhales. "Yeah, you're probably right." He holds the breath in for longer than seems necessary, and his lips part as a stream of smoke rises out of his mouth and surrounds his face.

I'm confused because it smells like weed, but he's smoking a cigarette. His eyes look glassy, though, and his pupils are immense. He continues to drag on the cigarette, looking more and more out of it with each breath. Finally he grabs one of the fold-up chairs in front of the tent and sits on it. I'm trying to figure out what the hell to do or say to him when Tristan exits the tent, his shirt still off and his blond hair disheveled.

I stand there awkwardly as the two of them pretend that the other one isn't there. Tristan goes over to the cooler and takes out a beer, and then he stares at the ground in front of his feet while he rotates the bottle around in his hand.

"Sorry, man," he mutters, freeing a breath from his chest. "I really didn't mean it."

"It doesn't matter," Quinton replies without looking at him. "I deserved it—deserve more."

"No, you don't."

"Yeah, I do."

"I don't think it was your fault."

"But it was."

"No, it wasn't. Shit just happens and I was just being a douche bag because . . . of stuff."

"Because I deserved it."

Tristan drags a chair next to Quinton's and sits down. "How about we agree to disagree?" He tilts the top of his beer bottle in Quinton's direction.

Quinton sighs and taps his bottle against Tristan's. "You

should really start acting more like your parents toward me. And my father."

"My parents are fucking idiots," he says. "And your dad's always been a dick, even before."

Quinton doesn't respond, and silence sets in as he hands Tristan his cigarette. I stand just behind them, gripping my beer bottle, wondering if I should leave because they seem to be having a little bonding moment. I feel awkward, because I have no idea what's going on and the moment seems so personal.

"Nova, are you alive back there?" Tristan asks without looking at me.

"Yeah," I reply and then finish off the rest of my beer before tossing it in the trash bag just outside the tent.

"Do you want to sit down?" Tristan glances over his shoulder at me. It's getting dark and his blue eyes look like sapphires. "Or do you prefer sitting in the dirt in the middle of the crowd?" The corners of his mouth tug upward, and it's like nothing even happened, as if there had been no fight between the two of them.

My eyes drift around our little area. "I'm fine. There are no chairs anyway."

"Why were you sitting in the dirt?" Quinton glances at me for the first time since he returned, and I have this crazy impulse to hug him and say I'm sorry for not being able to find him, but I don't.

"I went looking for you," I say with a shrug. "And then everyone went crazy when the band started to play."

"So you just sat down?" he asks, gaping at me unfathomably. "In the middle of a fucking concert?"

I shrug again. "Just another thing to make me amusing, I guess."

The two of them gape at me and then they bust up laughing. I feel kind of stupid and all the problems and worries I'd been having shift to the fact that they think I'm insane. I debate whether to pretend I have to go to the bathroom or just dive into the tent.

Their laughter dies down and Quinton wipes a tear from his eye as he beckons to me. "Come here," he says.

I briefly dither and shuffle over to him. "I told you concerts are too noisy. It's messing with my head."

He sets his empty beer bottle into the cup holder on the arm of the chair and stretches his arm out to the side, keeping the smoke as far away from me as possible. "Did you really go looking for me?"

I nod. "Yeah, you looked sad."

I can feel Tristan's eyes on me, even though it looks like he's staring at the crowd.

Quinton scans my face and then reaches up and spreads his fingers around my hips. Pulling me down, he sits me on his lap, then he sweeps my hair to the side, and places his lips next to my ear. His breath is hot against my skin and smells pungently of weed. "I'm really okay. You don't need to worry about me." He moves away and releases my hips from his grip.

I'm uncertain if he wants me to stay on his lap or get up, or if I want to stay put or run like hell. "Yeah, I do," I say, and we trade a look that neither of us really understand. All I know is that something is changing inside me. I don't know what it is or if it's good or bad, because it's unknown and unplanned and surprising and new. I'm terrified, because it feels like I'm tumbling off a cliff and I have no idea when I'm going to hit the bottom. Or if I ever will.

Chapter Thirteen

Quinton

She's sitting on my lap and she shouldn't be. For many different reasons, one being that Tristan is sitting right next to us. But he's pretty stoned and doesn't seem to care. He even says something to a few girls that wander by with their tops off, smiling when one of them blows a kiss at him. Still, I don't deserve any of this. Nova. Tristan's forgiveness and understanding. What I deserve is to be fucking dead instead of Ryder and Lexi.

But Nova said she went looking for me. No one ever goes looking for me or cared enough to worry about me. When she says it, I'm pretty certain my worthless heart shatters inside my chest, and she steals one of the pieces. If it didn't already belong to someone else I probably would have handed her all the pieces right then and there.

She sits on my lap for an eternity, chatting about music, while Tristan and I take turns passing the cigarette back and forth. She seems happier than she did a little while ago, and it makes me happy watching her eyes light up as she talks about lyrics and her favorite bands, always putting an emphasis on the *s*.

"No way," she disagrees with something Tristan has said, and he grins because he has her attention. "They're not better, and their drummer totally sucks."

Leaning over, Tristan grabs the handle of the cooler and hauls it over. He puts it in front of his chair and uses it for a footrest. "What makes you the expert?" he asks Nova.

"Because I'm a drummer and therefore I know these things." Nova shoves his feet off the cooler and, bending forward, she lifts the cooler lid. Her shorts slip down a little as she digs a beer out of the ice, and I have to fight back a smile because her panties are black and lacy. Honestly, I would have pinpointed her as a white-cotton kind of girl, considering how embarrassed she got when she made a joke about popping her outdoor-concert cherry.

"Just because you can play the drums"—Tristan grazes his thumb across the bottom of the cigarette, scattering ashes onto the ground "—doesn't mean you can decide who plays the drums better and who sucks."

"Yeah, it does." Nova's getting sassier with the more beers she drinks. She extends her arm out toward the cigarette, like she's going to grab it and take a hit.

This time I choose to do things differently and put a moment of good in the world, despite the fact that I have to be a hypocrite to do it. I swat her hand out of the way and shake my head. "No way."

"Hey," she protests with a frown. "What the hell was that for?"

I shift my arm so my hand falls down into my lap, just beside her hip. "So do I ever get to see you play?" I dodge around the subject to keep her mind diverted from getting high.

"The drums?" she asks, still frowning. When I nod, she seems reluctant to answer. She tips her head back and places the mouth of the bottle to her lips, sipping out the beer. Her hair falls down her back and softly brushes my arm, and it sends a silent quiver through my body. She lowers the bottle and licks her lips. "I don't know…" She inquiringly looks me in the eye. "Do you want to watch me play?"

"Of course," I say, reminding myself that we're just friends. *Just friends.* "That's why I asked."

She wets her lips with her tongue, deliberately this time, and I wonder if she's doing it on purpose so I'll focus on her lips. "When we get back to town…if you want…you can come over and watch me play." Her voice shakes as she says it, like the words are thick in her throat and she's struggling to enunciate each letter.

"Hey, what about me?" Tristan asks, offended, as he flicks the cigarette onto the ground and stomps on it with his bare feet. Then he starts cursing as his skin begins to burn. "Shit, that's hot."

She ignores him, her eyes fastened on me as she takes a faltering breath, balling her hands into fists. "But I get to pick which song."

I nod, nervous about how personal this is getting. "Okay, sounds like a plan, Nova Reed."

Tristan huffs a frustrated breath, then takes his cell phone out of his pocket and starts texting.

Nova rotates around so her back's to me and she's facing the stage. She relaxes against my chest with her legs hanging over my knees. I tense, but she doesn't seem to notice. In fact, I think she's extremely comfortable, and the more she stays there, the more comfortable I get.

"My dad taught me to play," she says and downs another mouthful of beer. "When I was six."

"He taught you to play the drums?" I keep my tone light, remembering how when I first met her she told me her dad died.

She nods, spinning the bottle around in between the palms of her hands. "He also played the guitar, but for some reason I could never figure out that instrument."

She sounds like she's choking up, and I want to console her. I open and close my hands, then place my palms on the tops of her thighs, so she's trapped between my arms. Her leg muscles spasm underneath my touch, but she doesn't move away.

"How old were you when he died?" I ask, kneading her soft skin with my fingertips. *What the fuck am I doing?*

"Twelve." Her breath hitches in her throat. From the stage, the singer shouts out something about every girl taking their top off. She clears her throat multiple times. "Can I ask you a question?"

Even though I'm certain I'm not going to like her question, considering the topic we're on, I nod. "Sure."

She wavers, staring up at the stars across the ash-black sky. "Have you ever lost someone close to you?"

I hear Tristan cough several times beside me and then he turns to the side in his chair, like he wants to escape this conversation. The band starts playing again, hammering on the drums and shouting in the microphone, and Nova starts thrumming her fingers on top of her legs to the rhythm.

It takes me a while to respond. "Yeah, I have."

She nods and doesn't say anything more. Most people would have asked me who and how. I remember right after the accident everyone wanted to know what happened, not just to Lexi and Ryder but to me, too. I was in the hospital for quite a while. Miraculously the guy I hardly knew that was kissing Ryder in the backseat barely had any bruises and scrapes, and the driver of the other car broke her leg. That was it. Two with minor injuries and three deaths, if I include myself, which I do. Even though I was revived that day, I still think of myself as dead.

"Are you okay?" Nova turns her head to look at me. "You seem tense."

"I'm fine," I assure her.

"Are you sure?" She looks doubtful as she searches my eyes.

It's been a while since someone has been so concerned

about me. Not even Lexi worried about me this much, even when I'd get low about my dad's distant parenting tactics.

"I'm sure," I tell Nova. "Now stop worrying about me."

"Okay," she says, working to smile, like she doesn't believe me. She coils a strand of her brown hair around her finger. "Do you think that somewhere in the world, at this very moment, someone is doing this exact same thing?"

"What? Sitting around and getting high?" Tristan jokes, glancing up from his cell phone screen.

"No, sitting under the stars, listening to music." She unwinds her hair around her finger.

Tristan shrugs, sliding his finger across the screen of the phone as he gets to his feet. "You're a very strange girl," he says and heads for the tent, then at the last second veers off in the direction the topless girls went.

"I'm just curious," she mutters to herself. "About what other people do with their time... with their lives."

I sit there for a while, drinking in her words. Somewhere between the weed, watching her lips move, and her strange yet insightful words, I get caught up in it all—in her—and suddenly I'm pressing my lips against hers. I've done this a lot before, as a way to distract myself from my life. But this isn't the same. This *means* something, but I'm still trying to figure out what and if I want it or even deserve to get it.

At first she stiffens, but then she hooks her arms around the back of my neck and inches closer, opening her mouth to me as she spreads her legs open, and my hands travel higher toward the bottom of her shorts. She tastes like beer and smells like pot. Tristan's gone, but he could come back at any moment. I should stop this. I should care enough to stop Tristan from seeing this, but my will to care about doing the right thing at this moment has died. My thoughts are blurred by the lingering high and the scent and feel of Nova. All I seem to care about is caressing her tongue with mine and feeling her skin because it's soft and soothing, and in another life I'd touch it all the time.

I'm about to pull away, because emotions are prickling inside me, when she swings her leg over me so she's straddling my lap, then she grips the sides of my neck and pulls me closer. She kisses me fiercely, to the point where it feels like my lips are going to bruise, then she's crushing her chest against mine as she gently rocks her hips. I dig my fingers into her waist, bringing her even closer, before I push her back, breaking the connection.

She's panting, wild-eyed, her hair falling out of the braid. She glances at Tristan's empty chair and then looks back at me.

"We should stop," I say, but it sounds like a lame attempt, my voice drifting off at the end.

"W-why?" She stutters a protest and I have to admit that it's nice there are no tears in her eyes. "I don't want to."

I brush her hair back from her eyes, and let my fingers linger on the bruise on her cheek. "You don't even know me, Nova. I'm no good for you...you deserve so much better." *Please run away. Because I can't seem to do it myself.*

Her jaw tenses, like I struck a nerve. "I think I should get to decide that."

"Whether I'm good enough for you?" I ask.

"Yeah, which I can only decide if I get to know you," she says.

I motion my hand in front of myself, pressing the point. "This is pretty much it. What you see is what you get."

"That's never the case," she disagrees, flattening her palms onto my bare chest right over the scar and my body goes rigid. "In fact, most of the time people hide who they really are." Her throat bobs up and down as she swallows hard. "Most of the time you think you know someone, but you really have no clue."

I think about her boyfriend and how he took his own life, and I can't even begin to imagine what that did to her. I wrap my fingers around her scarred wrist, still concealed by bands, and graze my palm along it as the truth pours out of me. "But sometimes people are exactly who they are. And what you see is what you get." I press my fingertips down, feeling the beat of her erratic pulse. "I'm exactly who I am. I have no job, I get high and drunk all the time, I have no purpose. Even my fucking art doesn't have any meaning anymore."

"But it did once." She glides her free hand over my shoulder and grips my shoulder blade, her skin searing hot against mine. "And all those things are what you do, not who you are." Her hand is trembling, and her pulse throbs with the beat of the bass coming from the stage. "Please, let me get to know you, Quinton." Begging laces her voice and her big blue-green eyes, and I wonder if this is about me anymore, or someone else, and I should get up and walk away because she's too good for me to be kissing, but she's also so sad and the little tiny piece of my old self—the one who loved to help everyone— wants to make her happy, make her smile, make her laugh— help her. Even if it's completely unrealistic.

Then she's kissing me again and lightly tugging on my shoulder and I still have my fingers on her pulse and my hand is gripping at her waist. Passion and heat consume our bodies as she traces her finger up the back of my neck. I gently pull on her wrist, drawing her even closer, until there's no more room left between our bodies, then I slip my hand around to her back and underneath her shirt so I can feel the heat exuding from her skin.

She lets out a gasp as I move my mouth back, gently biting at her bottom lip. Then I descend lower, down to her jawline, sucking soft kisses on her neck, and she arches it back. When I approach the top of her chest, I can tell she gets nervous by the acceleration in her pulse. She moans as I start to slip the straps of her shirt down, and the sound nearly drives me crazy, my body responding in ways it hasn't in a long time, as my mouth reaches the curve of her breast. I picture myself standing up, taking her to the tent, and peeling her clothes off, knowing that if I slipped inside her it would feel different than it did with the other women I've been with over the last year. I'm trying to decide if I want it—the connection—when someone in the crowd shouts something profane at us and it's followed by whistling, and the moment scorches into ash and separates into pieces.

We break away from each other, and I'm relieved to find that she's not crying this time around and neither am I. But this time is different, and maybe it's because it's not the first kiss. Or maybe it's because I understand her a little bit better, and that she's not just some girl that giggles and laughs and doesn't get what it means to hurt inside. She's been through stuff, and for some reason, I'm drawn to her. Why she's not crying, though, is a mystery.

Her lips are a little bit swollen and her chest is heaving. "Maybe we shouldn't be doing this out in the open," she breathes, tracing circles on the back of my neck, as she eyes the tents behind us.

"Do you want to try and get close to the front?" I ask, trying to avoid going into the tent with her, because I know what will happen if I do. "I think that band you said you love is about ready to start playing."

She cranes her neck and looks over her shoulder at the stage with uncertainty in her eyes. "I'm not sure if it's worth it."

The people surrounding the stage are rowdy, and a lot of girls have given in to the singer's demands and are walking around topless. It's a really bad scene, and a year and a half ago I'd never have dreamed of coming to a place like this. But sometimes stuff happens and we find ourselves lost, and suddenly we're standing in a place we don't recognize and can't remember walking—or falling—there, and we're unsure how to get back or if we even want to.

I place a hand on her cheek and she quickly looks back at me, holding my gaze. "I won't let anything happen to you. I promise." *I promise. I promise. I'm so sorry, Lexi.*

She nods, like she completely trusts me. I stand up, clutching the backs of her thighs. She starts to climb off me, but I delve my fingers into her bare skin and lift her back up. She gasps in shock as I press her up against me and firmly hold on to her legs.

"So you don't panic and sit down in the dirt," I say and hike into the crowd, carrying her with me.

At first she seems reluctant, but then she locks her ankles behind my back and clings to my shoulders. She angles her face forward and brushes her nose against mine, closing her eyes. "You remind me of someone I used to know," she whispers, as I maneuver my way through the crowd toward the stage.

"Oh yeah." I turn us to the side and squeeze through two guys with their topless girlfriends on their shoulders, which seems to be a growing theme at this concert. "Who?"

Her eyes flutter open and the light from the stage reflects in them. "Just someone."

"Care to share who that someone is?" I trip over my untied shoelaces but quickly recover my balance. The air smells rank, like stale beer, salt, smoke, and pretty much every other foul scent.

She shakes her head. "Not yet."

"But you will someday?" *Is there ever going to be a someday with us?*

"Maybe...one day...when I can."

We remain quiet during the rest of our journey toward the stage. It's dark, the stars are shimmering, and the vibrant stage lights illuminate the faces in the crowd. The air is still hot, but there's a gentle breeze, and goose bumps start to dot Nova's arms.

I get us as close as I can, then set her on the ground. She faces the stage, wrapping her arms around herself, and I keep my hands at my sides. Then the band comes out onstage and starts playing a song that's depressing and genuinely honest in a way that gets under my skin. It talks about life and death and how we're all connected to both. That even after someone's gone, life moves on, no matter what we do.

Halfway through it, Nova shuts her eyes and starts swaying her hips to the beat, her lips matching the singer's. "I love this song," she says with her eyes shut and her hands are on the back of her neck.

My eyes trace the curves of her body and the enthralling way she moves. "I love watching you," I whisper so softly I know she can't hear. I dig my fingertips into my palms, trying to resist the compulsion to place my hands on her hips and move with her.

As the song keeps playing, though, I become more and more hypnotized by her, and the way she lets herself go, when usually she's so contained. For the briefest second I'm glad

I'm there with her, which makes me feel confused and guilty, because I should want to be with Lexi. Thoughts are drifting through my head, in long sequences that don't match, yet they do when they're put together in a different order, and suddenly, for a fleeting, guilty, irreversible moment, I'm glad my heart decided to beat again.

I step forward, not sure what's driving me, but I give in to it regardless. I wrap my arms around her and pull her nearer, closing my eyes as the sound of her voice caresses my ears. She leans back against me, and we sway together as the music encases us. I wish I could keep my eyes shut forever, because then I'd never have to go back to reality. I don't try to kiss her or feel her up. I just hold her and let our bodies stay linked, wanting to know her and understand her more than I have with anyone since Lexi. For an instant, I have something to hold on to again, a reason to keep breathing, to live.

Chapter Fourteen

Nova

Somehow the night gets abruptly lighter as I lose track of time and direction and the need to count everything that exists around me. I'm not sure how it happens. Maybe it's because we're both a little buzzed and the substances are making us act like two completely different people at the moment and later it will catch up with us. Or maybe it's the simple fact that we're getting caught up in the music and each other, and the fact that the night feels unreal, like it belongs in the pages of a book where everyone gets their magical night without having to face consequences later.

After we dance and sing for hours, sweat drips from our bodies, and my arms and legs get tired, Quinton guides me back through the crowd, his fingers entangled with mine. I keep getting bumped into by people as one of the more energetic bands violently play their instruments onstage and everyone starts to go crazy, screaming, shouting, and thrashing their heads around. Finally, Quinton steers me in front of him and then spans his arms out to the side, creating a wider route, bumping anyone who gets in his way. It makes a lot of people angry, and by the time we reach the tent area we've been yelled at a lot. I find it funny for some reason and so does he, and by the time we stumble into the tent, we're laughing our asses off.

"I'm surprised you didn't get punched," I say, collapsing onto the sleeping bags as he zips up the tent. Tristan's not here, and I haven't seen him since Quinton kissed me on the camping chair. I don't really wonder where he ran off to, though, because I can barely focus on where I'm headed to. *Where am I going? What am I doing? Do I want this?*

Quinton turns around, stooped over to avoid hitting his head on the tent's low ceiling. He still has his shirt off, and a trickle of moonlight shines through the thin fabric of the tent, highlighting his scar and making his eyes look like charcoal.

I'm deciding how I feel about this moment, whether it scares me or what, when he gets down on his hands and knees and starts to crawl over to me. "You're beautiful." He says it so simply, like it's a fact that he needs to say. He stations his body over mine, and then propping up on his elbows he outlines the brim of my nose with his finger. "You have these freckles... I'm actually pretty mesmerized by them."

"By my freckles?" I ask, because it's the first time anyone's ever said anything about them.

He nods, pressing his lips together as he studies me through the dark. "I...I think about drawing them all the time."

My hands are at my sides and my hair fell out of the braid

a long time ago and it's a tangled mess around my head. I'm not sure if I can let him draw me, whether I can pass over that moment to him. Just thinking about it is frightening, especially since I told him I'd play the drums for him, and I think I actually meant it.

"Your lips are soft, too." He grazes the pad of his thumb along my bottom lip, sighing, and then he moves his hand up to my hair and tangles his fingers through it, tugging at the roots a little. It feels so good, and my eyelids start to grow heavy. "We should try to get some sleep," he whispers, and I nod, knowing if I don't go to sleep soon, pulling away from him is going to be harder.

He shifts his body off me and I pivot to my side, flopping my arm out and feeling around for my sleeping bag, ready to pass out.

"Shit," he mutters, lifting the sleeping bag off the ground, and peering beneath it. "I think Tristan left one of the sleeping bags in the trunk. I'll go get it."

I flip back over and grasp onto his arm, his muscles constricting underneath my fingers. The music is still booming outside, and there are a lot of people shouting near the tent. "Wait, don't leave me."

"Nova, I'll be right back," he promises. "Or you can come with me."

"I'm too tired." I yawn, covering my mouth with my free hand. "And I don't want to be left here... what if something bad happens?"

I must have pushed the right button because he gives in easily after that, settling back down on the floor on his side.

"You can use my sleeping bag," he says, reaching for a pillow. "And I'll use Tristan's until he comes back."

"Then what?"

"Then I'll move to the floor."

"Won't you get cold?"

He suppresses his laughter as he fluffs the pillow and tucks it underneath his head. "Nova, it's like seventy degrees in here. I'm pretty much sweating."

"But the floor's hard." I rotate to my side onto the sleeping bag and Styrofoam padding. "You can just . . . you can just share with me."

It takes him a second to respond. "Are you okay with that?"

I nod and then realize it's too dark for him to see it. "Yeah, I'm perfectly fine." My voice is unsteady though, replicating my nerves. I flip the sleeping bag open and climb in it, wiggling back until I'm at the edge, almost ready to fall out the other side.

He remains motionless, looking like a statue in the dark. A perfect statue, one carved of marble but that has small nicks and chips in it, and I want to figure out what put them there. I can't hear him breathing, and when he puffs out a loud breath, I realize that he wasn't breathing at all.

He scoots to the side and then, with a small amount of reluctance, lies down beside me, bringing the pillow with him. There's quite a bit of space between our bodies, at least as much as possible with us both being in the sleeping bag. I debate whether to leave the space there or reduce it and irrevocably come to the conclusion that I'll regret later if I don't get close to him. Or at least I think I will, anyway.

I inch my body forward, until I feel the heat emitting from his skin. He holds perfectly still as I rest my forehead to his chest, right against his heart, which is pounding, rock solid and zealous. I can't tell if he's scared or excited or what. Then he fixes a finger under my chin and tips my head back. I stare into his eyes, which I can barely see, but feel that they're on me.

"Nova," he says in a strained voice. "Can...would it be okay if I kiss you?"

I'm not sure if he's in the same place as I was the last time I asked him that. Either way, I elongate my body and arch my back, so I can reach his lips with mine.

Do I want this?

I brush them softly across his, closing my eyes as his breath eases out and he starts kissing me again with so much fervor I nearly melt. His body ends up on top of mine, and my hands are on his chest, feeling the outlines of his muscles as I drown in his body heat. It's getting hot and I'm panting for air and everything seems to be moving in fast motion and my thoughts are having a hard time keeping up with what's going on. Then suddenly he's sitting me up and ripping my shirt off over my head, and I stop breathing altogether. His dark eyes drink me in, and my body quivers as he reaches around my back for the clasp of my bra. There's a fleeting moment where I think about shouting for him to stop, that I can't go any further tonight, but it passes in the blink of an eye as he unhooks my bra. It falls off my chest, and I sit there exposed to him in the heat and the moonlight. My head is racing, searching for numbers or structure, but I can't find it.

"You're so beautiful," he repeats, and he breathes deeply as he lowers his weight onto me, laying me back down. He supports himself on his arms, placing one on each side of my head, and I open up my legs so he can situate himself between them, and my thoughts speed up as adrenaline courses through my body. It becomes too much, to the point where nothing makes sense and I can't really tell if I want this or not.

What do I want? Landon? Him? Something else entirely. I don't know anymore.

I'm trying to figure out if I want to stop him, but then I notice how unsteady his hand is as he touches my breast, stroking my nipple, and kissing my neck, as he grinds his body against mine. It calms me down that he's nervous, which is kind of twisted, but makes sense when I really rationalize it.

"Quinton," I groan, as my nipples harden under his touch. I start writhing my hips against him and his hardness, and it makes my body wake up from a very deep sleep. I feel myself climbing so high, I swear to God I'm going to drift off into the stars. I keep moving and he moves with me, completely in sync. This song is playing outside, one I've never heard before, but know I'll never forget because I'll never forget this moment.

It's one of those. The kind that gets branded into your mind and you can't get rid of it, even when you want to.

After we kiss for an eternity and our bodies are quivering with adrenaline and we're sweating with passion and overwhelming need and exhaustion, we break apart. I put my shirt back on and then we lay on our backs, neither one of us talking as we stare up at the tent ceiling gently flapping with the breeze. I should feel guilty, but for some reason I feel numb, and through the fogginess of my thoughts, I wonder how I'll feel in the morning. Landon was the only guy I'd ever done anything with. And now I'm here with Quinton, and he's alive and nothing makes sense anymore.

Gone. And just like that my head is filling with numbers, only they have no rhythm and I can't get them to connect. I clutch at my head, trying to breathe as noiselessly as possible.

"So what do you think about the band playing?" Quinton asks.

"They're okay," I reply, the numbers floating from my head as I listen to the vamped-up version of one of the band's more delicate songs, and my heart starts to beat rhythmically again. "But I like the softer version of it."

"I've never heard of them," he confesses, turning his head toward me.

"Wow, I can't believe you just admitted that to me," I say. "You know I can't be friends with you now."

"Is that what we still are?" he wonders. "Friends?"

"I'm not sure," I admit, sliding my hand down my face,

to my neck, then finally resting it on top of my chest. I count the beats of my heart each time it hits my palm. I think about Landon's and my friendship and how much we knew about each other, yet there was still so much stuff we didn't. "It feels like we barely know each other... but I want to get to know you." The overenthusiastic beat of my heart floods my mind as he stays silent.

"How about we play your little game of twenty questions again?"

"When did we play that?"

"In my room... back when... back when we were high."

I thrum my fingers against my ribs. "Isn't that a dangerous game? One where we both... where we both end up crying."

He reaches over and threads his fingers through mine so our hands are entwined on top of my heart. "We'll keep it light." He caresses the top of my hand. "Besides, it really wasn't the questions, was it?"

No, it was your eyes and that damn song.

"Okay," I say quietly. "You go first, though."

"What's your favorite vacation place?" he asks without missing a beat like he had it planned out the whole time.

Not a light subject at all, but I answer anyway, because my mind is too weary to conjure up a lie or dodge around it. "It was actually a road trip. Back when my dad was alive, we'd go on one each summer. My favorite was the one when I was eleven, though... right before he died. He took me to every carnival he could find. It was fun." Laughter escapes my throat. "I ate way too much cotton candy at one of them and ended up puking on the tilt-a-whirl."

He sketches a heart on the back of my hand. "Nova . . . how did he . . . how did he die?"

I yawn, zoning in and out of reality. "He had this heart condition. He didn't know he had it. We were actually out riding bikes up on these mountain trails and then suddenly he tipped over and he didn't get up. At first I thought he hurt himself . . . but then, the look in his eyes . . . he knew he was going to die and he was scared. I ran back for help and everything, but it was too late. By the time I came back, he was gone." I'm starting to choke up, because I've only talked about what happened with Landon, my mom, and therapists. I suck in a loud breath as the bitter burn of beer stings at the back of my throat. "I'm sorry. Here we're supposed to be playing a light game of twenty questions, and suddenly I'm babbling about death."

He slides his hand away from mine, up my chest and to my neck. Pressing his fingers to my jawline, he forces me to look at him through the dark. "I asked you the question after I told you we could make it light. I'm sorry. I should have kept my mouth shut."

"It's fine," I assure him, but it feels like the biggest lie.

"My mom died," he discloses in a subdued voice. "When I was born."

"I'm so sorry." I scan his face, but it's too dark to tell what he's thinking, but I wish I could tell what's going on inside of him. Does it match what I look like—what I feel?

"You don't have to be sorry," he replies with his fingertips still pressed to my jawline. "I just wanted to answer your question from earlier, when you asked if I'd ever lost anyone close to me."

My heart is throbbing in my chest as I wonder if maybe one of the names tattooed on him belongs to her. "What was her name?"

"Anna," he breathes so softly I can barely hear it. His fingers push harder against my skin.

But it's enough to know that it's not either of the names on his arm.

I let a breath ease from my lips. "Did your dad raise you, then?"

"Yes," he answers in a tight tone, pulling his hand away from my face. "But honestly, I pretty much raised myself."

I want to say something comforting, but I can't think of anything, so I say the first random thing that pops into my head. "If you could have one wish, what would it be?"

He pauses and when he speaks again, his voice sounds lighter. "Is that one of your twenty questions?"

"It is." I turn to my side and our fingers untangle from each other. "And you're already down to eighteen."

He captures my cheeks between his hands, bringing me back to him, and even though I'm drunk, I can feel the intimacy in the touch. "I can't tell you the one wish I would make right now, but I can tell you the one thing I want to do right at this moment." He sketches his finger down to my lips and brushes his thumb back and forth across the bottom one. "I'd...I'd like to hold you."

I don't know him well enough to know if he's feeding me a line, but the conflict in his voice, like he's afraid to say it, makes me believe that he's not. I inch my body forward so we're flawlessly aligned from head to toe, and then he brings his fingers away from my face, creating a path down my side. When he reaches my hip, he slips his finger underneath the bottom of my shirt, tenderly skimming my skin and eliciting heat between my thighs, and my body uncontrollably curls into him. But he only does it for a second, then he digs his fingers into my outer thigh and pulls on my leg, hitching it over his hip. Every single aspect of our bodies link perfectly together, and it feels amazing in the sense that it actually is him and me lying here together. There's no ghost memories, no need to figure out why Landon did it and who I am without him. There's nothing but silence.

"If you could have one superpower, what would it be?" I pick up right where we left off, because I want to continue with this seamless moment of simplicity.

He smooths his hand down the back of my head. "The power to forget. What about you?"

"The power to understand," I say, nuzzling my head against his chest as I yawn. "Or the power to save."

He keeps smoothing my hair down as he rests his chin on my head. I expect him to question me about my answer, but he doesn't, and I don't question him about his.

"What's one thing you're afraid of?" he asks.

"Unknown places," I say without a second thought.

"I'm unknown," he points out. "Does that mean I freak you out?"

I shake my head. "I already told you that you remind me of someone I used to know."

"So that makes me familiar?"

"Kind of... I guess... God, you probably think I'm crazy."

"I think you're the most interesting person I've met in a long, long time." His fingers envelop the back of my head, he slides his chin off the top of my head, and tips his chin down while I angle mine up. We meet in the middle, looking at each other at the precise moment my heart skips a beat.

"What if I kissed you right now?" he asks, his lips mere inches away from mine and his warm breath lightly tickling my skin. "Would that be familiar?"

"I don't know," I reply. "It wasn't at first, but now..."

He lightly grazes his lips across mine, gentle and barely existent. "Now what?"

My thoughts are muddled, and it's hard for me to picture anything but Quinton. I grip the front of his shirt and crash my lips against his. It's the fourth time we've kissed, and each time it gets easier. I'm still not sure who I'm thinking of when I kiss him. All I know is that at the moment my head is clear and at peace. And maybe that's my answer. Or maybe that's what I tell myself to make it easier to kiss him.

Chapter Fifteen

July 29, Day 71 of Summer Break

Quinton

I wake up the next morning feeling a lot more weighted than I did the night before. My first instinct is to slap Tristan awake and ask him where he put the stash. But then I look down at Nova in my arms, and I become conflicted, and I have no idea why. The bad in me wants to bump a hit and disappear, but the good wants to lie here, hold her, and make her happy. It's strange, because two months ago I had nothing and now suddenly I have something, but I don't know if I want it. I know I don't deserve it, but still, want and deserve are two different things.

I lay in the tent for a while, arguing with myself inside my head, and finally Tristan sits up. He starts rummaging around through his bag, humming to himself, then he notices I'm awake and he frowns.

"Have fun last night?" he asks, giving an accusing glance at Nova cuddled up against my side.

"It's not what you think," I say, my arm muscles tightening as I decide if I should pull away.

He opens the small plastic bag and starts packing the pipe. "What am I thinking?"

I glance at Nova. She seems content, motionless, her breathing soft, and I hope she's asleep. "You think I slept with her."

He laughs acerbically as he closes up the plastic bag and nods his head at Nova, who is sleeping soundly with her head resting on my chest. "Well, you did."

"Yeah, but we just slept. We didn't..." I lower my voice. "We didn't have sex."

"But you kissed her?" he asks, and when I don't answer he adds, "You knew I liked her."

"I know," I say, letting out a loud exhale and say the only thing I can think of. "I'm sorry. Fuck, I really screwed up...I always do..."

Shaking his head, he puts the mouth of the pipe up to his lips and positions the lighter over the bowl. "Sorry doesn't take back the fact that you kissed her." He flicks the lighter several times before he gets a constant flame to burn. "I mean, do you even like her, or is this just another one of your Nikki things?"

"It's not like Nikki," I tell him defensively, as smoke fills up the tent and my mouth begins to salivate.

He sucks in a deep breath, traps it in his lungs until his

eyes start to water, and then releases it. "Then what's it like?" he says, coughing, smoke puffing from his lips.

"I'm not sure yet," I say, my eyes fixed on the pipe, because every single part of me craves it so fucking bad. I know as soon as I take the first hit, most of my problems will be forgotten for the moment and my life will go back to how it was, where I'm contently high and my emotions are shut off. But do I want to go back to that? "I'm still figuring it out."

He assesses me as smoke fills the tent. "What if I said to back off? Would you?"

I feel light-headed from the smoke and the heat circulating in the tent. "Yes, but only because I owe you." It hurts to say it, but it's the truth. "Just say it—say you want me to back off—and I will." It feels like an invisible piece of sharp metal reslices the scar on my chest open because I know I'll do it, back off if he asks me, but it won't erase the feelings I'm developing for Nova, feelings I thought died over a year ago.

He keeps his eyes on me with the pipe and lighter in his hands. He glances at Nova, then back at me, and grabs a clean shirt out of his bag. When I first moved into the house, he talked about her a lot. I didn't get it, because he barely knew her, yet he seemed obsessed with her. But I'm realizing how easy it is to get caught up in her and her sadness and the way she gets nervous and embarrassed and how she seems to see the world in a different light. *God, how did I let myself get to this place?*

"I'll back off." He tugs the shirt on, scoots toward the door, and climbs out, taking his pipe with him and letting fresh air inside. Then he leans back in. "I just hope you know what you're doing, because from what I've seen you like to mess around, and she doesn't seem like that."

He's striking a nerve. I remember the first time I slept with someone after Lexi was gone. I was high and there was this girl, and even now I can't remember her name. She acted like she was into me, and my head was too obscured by alcohol and weed to do anything else but act upon it. After it was over, I felt numb, and feeling numb felt better than feeling the agony, loneliness, and guilt. So I kept screwing around and doing drugs, and after a while it became a part of life for me—a habit.

"Are you sure?" I say and it feels like my scar splits open even more.

"Yeah, I'm sure," he replies and I feel both relieved and terrified, because he's no longer an obstacle, which means I can actually be with Nova. *Shit.* Guilt, shame, and longing choke me. "I have sort of a thing going on with one of the girls from last night, anyway."

"You're going to take your pipe out there?" I ask, as he begins to zip the tent back up.

"Yeah...I got some stuff to take care of," he says, and then he gets the door zipped up entirely, leaving me in the tent with the lingering scent of my weakness. A few moments later, I climb out of the sleeping bag, leaving Nova alone, while I go chase down my addiction.

❧

After I find Tristan and get my much-needed hits, I don't go straight back to the tent. I'm not feeling better for some reason, and it's making me panic inside. Weed usually calms me—clears out the dark thoughts in my head—but now I feel guilty for smoking it, yet I feel guilty when I don't, and the amount of guilt colliding inside me brings me to the ground.

Luckily I've made it out to the car by the time my knees give out. I draw my knees up toward my chest and rest my arms on top of them, lowering my head. I keep taking deep breaths, telling myself to calm down and breathe, but the fucking problem is I really don't want to breathe at the moment. I want my lungs to stop working, along with my heart, and my thoughts, and my guilt, because I can't fucking take it anymore. I want to end my life and leave everything behind, but for some damn reason my body won't respond to what my head wants, like it's waiting around for me to change my mind.

Tears start to fall from my eyes and I keep my forehead pressed to my knees, begging for everything to go away. Begging for silence. And all I can do is go back and smoke some more weed and hope it gives silence to me.

Nova

I open my eyes to the sunlight blinding me and my cheek resting against someone's firm chest. At first I start to freak out as I search for the sun, bursting with the need to count the seconds it takes to move over the horizon. But I quickly realize that I'm in a tent, and I can't see the sun rising because it's already way too hot and bright for it to barely be waking up. It's already radiating into the tent and heating up the air in here, and there are a bunch of voices and noises outside that I don't recognize.

I'm not sure what to do with the abrupt shift in my routine. On the one hand, I'm glad from the break of lying in bed, waiting for the right moment when I can get up. But on the other hand, it brings an uneasy feeling to my chest because I'm waking up to the unexpected.

The air is a little steamy inside the tent, and the warm body huddled up against me makes it even hotter. Quinton and I are in a very intimate position; his arm is tucked under my neck and I have my hand on his chest, our bodies folded inward together, like two puzzle pieces.

I'd woken up in the middle of the night, after all the kissing and talking, panicking and feeling like I had a hangover. As I watched him breathing softly in his sleep, I became lost in everything that was him, and a part of me admitted that I was glad I was lying here, with *him*.

But now that I'm awake, and my blood is pumping freely again, along with my thoughts, I'm not so sure where I want to be or what I want to be doing. I'm confused. I'm always confused.

I sigh, wondering if there will ever be a time when things will be easy and crystal clear again.

"Good morning," Quinton says in a lazy tone, and I jump from the sound of his voice.

"Jesus, you scared me," I say, breathless, pressing my hand to my chest as I sit up.

His eyelids lift open, and it gets to me every time; the honey-brown shade pooled with even more sorrow. "I can tell."

I take note of his plaid shirt and black cargo shorts, which is a different outfit from what he was wearing last night. His eyes are red and puffy, but I can't tell if he's high or if he's been crying. "Have you been up already?"

"Yeah, I had to... I went to talk to Tristan." He pauses. "You know you wiggle a lot in your sleep."

"Well, you talk in your sleep," I say, rubbing the tiredness from my eyes.

"Oh, yeah." He arches his brow. "What'd I say?"

"That Nova is the most awesomest person in the world," I joke in a tired voice, resting my arm on my stomach.

He chuckles softly. "Yeah, that does seem like something I would say."

"You don't think I'm awesome?" I fake a frown.

He grazes his thumb across my lip. "I think you're beautiful."

I strangle down the urge to run out of the tent, because in the light of day—in my refreshed mind—the word is harder to hear. "You keep saying that."

He gives me a big, goofy grin that looks so out of place on his face it can probably only mean one thing. He's stoned.

"That's because you are." He explores my body with his penetrating eyes, making sure to cover every inch, and even though he's not touching me, it feels like he's touching me all over. When his eyes rest on mine again, he seems uncertain. "I think…" He shuts his eyes, his expression contorted in pain. "I really want to draw you, Nova."

"I'm not sure if I can let you," I utter softly.

His eyes open and the pain hidden in his pupils is magnified. "I'm not sure if I can." He massages his forehead with the heel of his hand, like he's trying to rub away the stress. His shirtsleeve slips down a little, revealing the names tattooed on his arm.

"Who are Ryder and Lexi?" I ask, extending my fingers to touch the names inked on his skin.

He stiffens and then slides his arm out from underneath me. "How about I go find us some breakfast or something?" His voice is tight, nearly a shout as he ruffles his hair into place with his hand. Without waiting for me to respond, he unzips the tent and leaves me alone with my question echoing in my head.

I start to get up to see if he's okay, but my stomach rolls with nausea from all the beer I drank last night, and I lay back down with my arm over my head. I stare at the ceiling, recollecting every time Landon had run away from me when I asked the wrong question. Then one night he'd taken off and never returned, just like that. Just like Quinton's doing.

Without taking my eyes off the ceiling, I stretch my arm out and feel around the side of the tent until I find my phone. I open the Landon file, staring at it, counting the seconds down. But when I hit two minutes, I feel too tired to keep going, weighted down by worry, anxiety, my bad decisions, and my exhausting routine. For the first time in over a year, I skip out on the last three minutes of my routine. My limbs and fingers feel heavy as I click the camera on, noting the paleness of my skin and the redness in my puffy eyes as I clear my throat before speaking.

"I remember the night I went to visit Landon's grave. It wasn't too long after they put the headstone on his grave." My voice sounds hoarse. "It was my mom that suggested we go visit—'Maybe we can go with the Evanses'—like it was a great idea or something."

I stare at my eyes, begging them to show me what I'm feeling on the inside. "It'd been a couple of months since he was buried, and I'd barely made it through his funeral... well, *barely* might be exaggerating. I'd puked my guts out in the bathroom afterward. I think deep down I knew I wasn't ready to go to his grave, but I couldn't admit it to my mother... or maybe to myself. Going and staring at a stone that marked the date he was born and the day he decided to go..." I suck in a breath. "Yet, I'd agreed, because that's what I always did, I agree and go along with things because I could never think of an excuse."

My hand trembles as a tear rolls down my cheek. "So we went with the Evanses, and his mom cried the entire time, and so did my mom. I probably should have said something—or done something—to make it easier for everyone, but all I could do was stand there." More tears flood my eyes, but I don't move, capturing the realness of the moment. "I felt disconnected, like it wasn't real, like someone had made a mistake and put the wrong name on the headstone and that really Landon was at home sketching the mountains or maybe the trees outside while he smoked weed and lost track of time, because that seemed more plausible than him deciding he'd rather be underneath the ground than up here with me."

I pause as my emotions become too uncontrollable and I begin to chatter. "After the visit was over, I went home and... I don't know..." My eyebrows knit. "I just wanted to understand what he felt like right at the end... what the hell he was thinking that made him go through with it. So I went into the bathroom and started cutting my wrist open. It's not like I wanted to die... at least I don't think so. Honestly, I have no idea what I wanted or want. An explanation? A way to travel back through time? A way to do everything differently? Or maybe I'd just lost myself with Landon—"

The sound of the door zipper moving causes me to drop my phone. I quickly sit up, wiping my eyes with the back of my hand right as Quinton sticks his head in. My teeth are still clattering together and there are a few stray tears on my face.

"I think I..." His voice trails off as he takes in the sight of me. "Nova, are you okay? What the hell happened?"

I shake my head, stretching the bottom of my tank top up to my cheeks to clean off my face. "It's nothing."

He crawls into the tent, zips the door up, and kneels down in front of me, appearing regretful. "I'm sorry I kind of yelled at you...I just...I don't even know why I did it."

"It's fine," I assure him, pulling the bottom of my shirt back down over my stomach. "That's not why I'm crying."

"I know," he replies, releasing an uneven breath. "But I needed to say it...I feel bad yelling. I should have never raised my voice at you."

It feels like I need to say a lot of things, because I didn't say so much when I was with Landon. "It's okay. I promise... But..." I struggle for the right words that can maybe get him to open up to me, but my mind is exhausted from the alcohol last night and thoughts of Landon just now, so no words ever come. "Nothing. Never mind."

"Are you sure?" he asks. "You can...you can talk to me if you want to, Nova."

I force a smile. "I'm fine. I promise."

He smiles back, but it's a sad smile. He starts to scoot back toward the door, taking hold of my hand, and his palms feel a little sweaty. "Now, come on. I just found out that there's this little diner place like three miles up the road, so we can actually have real food instead of granola bars and that shit we ate last night."

"I think it was hot dogs. That's why we put them on the hot dog forks."

"They may have been hot dogs, but they sure as hell didn't taste like it."

"I think Delilah burnt them," I say. "She sucks at cooking."

"So do I," he states. "I once burned a Hot Pocket in the microwave."

"How do you burn a Hot Pocket in the microwave?"

"By leaving it in there for over ten minutes," he says with an amused grin. "I was high, and instead of trying to set the time, I just pushed a bunch of buttons, figuring it'd work. I still ate it, though."

We smile at each other, on the verge of laughing, but I'm not sure if it's real or if it's just something we know we're supposed to do, and as quickly as it ascends, we're sinking back into the desolation again.

He stops in front of the door and traces the folds between my fingers. "Nova, I really like you…but there are things… stuff that I can't talk about. I'm not sure if I can be with you like I was last night."

An elongated pause passes between us. He continues to trace the folds in my fingers with his head tucked down, and I analyze his demeanor, sad and broken, and God, I hate to think it, what if he's suicidal? What if below the surface, there's even more pain eating away at him, and I'm the only one who sees it because I've seen it before but didn't recognize it until it was too late? I'm about to ask him why he's so sad, even if it means getting yelled out or hated or completely jumping out of my comfort zone.

"I have to ask you something," he says, before I get a chance. "And as much as I hate to ask it, because I hate being nosy, it's going to bug me if I don't." He peers up at me.

My chest tightens in anticipation. "Okay…"

"Were you… were you just talking to yourself in here?" he asks and then quickly adds, "I mean, it's cool and everything… we all do it… but you were crying so…"

So he thinks I'm crazy. "Yes and no."

"Care to elaborate?" he asks with an oh-shit-please-don't-let-her-be-insane look.

Not really. "I just…" I try to think of a lie, because telling him about my video-making endeavor feels too private. But he has my hand in his and it's comforting and familiar, and all I want to do is tell him the truth, like I used to do with Landon. "I'm making this video…" I trail off as his expression abruptly alters from confused to amused.

Balling his hand into a fist, he covers his mouth with his hand, hiding a smile. "Like a sex video?"

"What… no!" I swat his arm, shaking my head. "Why the hell would you ask that? I was in here by myself."

He lowers his hand from his mouth, humor lacing his voice. "Oh, you can make a sex video by yourself."

My cheeks flush and I grab the pillow beside me, hugging it with one arm, as I bury my face into it to hide my mortification. "Well, that's not what I was doing."

"What kind of video then?" he asks with interest, and I peek up at him. His hand is on his lap and his fingers are softly stroking my wrist.

"It's just a video about me," I say, shivering when his finger grazes a sensitive area on my arm. "Or my thoughts. I guess kind of like a documentary."

"Or like a Novamentary," he says. The moment is so real, so raw and fresh, that I can't help but want to find a way to capture it and keep it forever, because soon it will be replaced by alcohol and weed or numbers and order. Tossing the pillow aside, I pick up my phone. "How about you say something for my Novamentary?"

"You want to record me?" he questions warily, and I nod. "Well, I'm not that great on video."

"Neither am I." I aim the phone camera at him, and I have to admit he looks stunningly beautiful on it; clear honey-brown eyes, long lashes, short, soft hair, and very kissable lips. "Delilah did it, but you don't have to if you don't want to." I keep the camera aimed at him for a little bit longer and then start to lower it when he doesn't say anything.

"Wait." He compresses my wrist between his fingers. "I'll say something." He pauses. "Do you want honesty?"

I'm taken aback by his question, but nod. "If you're comfortable with it."

He releases my wrist from between his fingers and scoots away from me. I think he's going to leave, but then he criss-crosses his legs and supports his elbows on his knees. "Once upon a time there was this guy."

"I thought you were going to tell something honest," I interrupt. "Not a fairy tale."

He holds up a finger. "Give me a minute... I promise it's not a fairy tale."

I relax, watching him through the screen as he cracks his knuckles and pops his neck, then stirs in his own silence. His neck muscles are rigid and his skin has gone pale.

"Once upon a time there was this guy," he starts over. "And he was a good guy. The kind that girls could take back to their parents and who held open doors and who fell in love with the girl he knew he was going to marry." His forehead furrows and he gazes over my shoulder. "Or at least that's what he believed... but shit happened and the guy ended up dying, only somehow he made it back, but the good in him remained dead and all that was left was this really bad guy who fucks up shit and who really, really wishes he'd stayed dead."

He stops and blinks, and for a moment it looks like he's forgotten where he is, who I am, and who the hell he is. We stare at each other, and I'm trying to figure out what to say to him because he's openly talking to me—or the camera, anyway—and the pain I've seen inside him is slipping out through his words. I want to ask him how the guy died, what happened to the girl, and why the guy thinks he's such a bad person.

I lower the camera. "Why do you think you're a bad guy?"

"Because I am," he says it so simply as if it's factual, but from what I've seen—from what I'm seeing right now—he's not.

"No, you're not," I say. "Not even close."

He shakes his head. "You don't even know me, Nova, so you can't say that about me."

"I know some things about you," I tell him. "You make me smile, and no one's done that in a very long time."

He offers me a halfhearted smile. "Just because I can make you smile doesn't mean I deserve to smile."

"Why? Because you do drugs? Or...or is it because of something else?"

"It's everything." He almost sounds frustrated, as if he wants me to stop telling him he's good. "Everything I do—have done—is bad."

"That's not true," I tell him and set the camera down on the floor. "What we do doesn't define us, although I think some people would probably disagree with me." I scoot forward and only stop moving when our knees touch—when I make a connection with him. "I think that sometimes things just get confusing and we get lost, and sometimes you can't figure out which path is the right path...which is the right decision." *Quit or move forward. Heal or break. Fight or die. I'm still figuring that out.*

His eyes crinkle around the corners as his expression softens. "Are you confused and lost, Nova?"

I nod and I feel something break inside as my confession hovers between us. "All the damn time."

He swallows hard. "I completely understand where you're coming from." He sucks in a breath, and then the mood shifts as he rubs his hands together. "So how about some breakfast?"

"Breakfast sounds good," I tell him, which seems extremely

ordinary after the conversation we just had. But sometimes ordinary is a good break from complexity, I guess. Or maybe there's just nothing left to say.

He uncrosses his legs, kneels up, and unzips the tent door. "Now, is there anything you don't like to eat, besides melted ice cream?" He crawls out of the tent into the sunlight.

"Burnt hot dogs," I joke as I crawl out of the tent behind him. "Or how about Hot Pockets?"

"Yeah, no more burnt hot dogs. Or Hot Pockets," he says, offering me one hand as he brushes the dirt off his knees with the other.

I place my hand in his, and he interlaces our fingers, then lifts me to my feet. I breathe in the fresh air and tip my face up to the sun. It's a nice day, with only a few clouds spotting the sky. The stage is empty and the field is fairly vacant.

"Where's everyone?" I ask, stretching like a cat in the sunshine.

He smiles, amused at something. "I think they wandered off to the lake."

"The lake?" I tug at the bottom of my tank top, covering my stomach back up.

He nods and then walks around the tent, towing me along with him. "Yeah, they went to get clean, I think."

"By taking a bath in a *lake*?" I ask, maneuvering around coolers and fold-up chairs.

He shrugs, kicking a bottle out of our path. "Yeah, it's not that big of a deal. I think they have their clothes on."

"You *think*?" I ask and then realize how immature I sound.

He shakes his head, wrapping his arm around my shoulder, and then he surprises me by kissing my forehead. "Actually, I don't think. I went down there a little earlier, and for some reason everyone seems to think this is a nudist colony. Or they all might be tripping on something that gives them that whole I'm-free vibe."

"Why were you down there?" I scoot to the side out of the way of a tent.

He glances down at me inquisitively, and his eyes look lighter in the sunlight. "Is that your way of asking if I was down there joining in the nakedness, too?"

"Kind of," I admit, even though my cheeks heat. I chew on my nails, letting my hair fall down to the side of my face. "I don't know a lot about you, and it would be nice to know if you're into stripping down in front of a bunch of people."

"Why? Would you hate me if I said yes?" he asks seriously.

I shake my head. "No, I just want to know more about you."

He gazes at me quizzically as we veer around a dropped tailgate that's littered with beer boxes and cigarette butts. "Well, the answer is no. I actually hate being naked in front of people."

I tuck my hair behind my ear and gaze up at the clear sky. When I look back at him I find him staring at me. "What?" I ask.

"I'm waiting for *your* answer," he says, slowing us down as we reach Tristan's rusted old Cadillac.

"My answer for..."

He takes the keys out of his pocket. "On whether or not you're the kind of person who likes to get naked in front of other people."

I bite down on my lip and shake my head. "No, not really."

He smiles as he unlocks the car door. "Good, now we have something in common."

"Is that the only thing we have in common?" I catch the keys as he tosses them to me.

He stares into my eyes, and I wonder what the hell he can see in them. "No, I think we share a lot more." He scratches at his head as he considers something. "Can you drive? I don't think I should."

I wonder if it has to do with being under the influence or if it's related to what Tristan said. I wonder a lot of things about him, about me, about him and me together, and why I seem like a different person around him, like I get lost in him instead of numbers, control, and order. My thoughts drift off as something strikes the inside of my head like a lightning bolt. Is that how I was with Landon? Lost? Different? I'd been so consumed by him when he was alive. Have I ever really known who I was?

I climb in and turn the engine on while Quinton rounds the front of the car and climbs in. I start to back up when he says, "Stop."

I tap on the brakes, panicking, thinking I'm about to run over someone or something. "What's wrong?" I ask, glancing in the rearview mirror, but the dirt road behind me is empty.

His eyes are slightly wide as he leans over the console, stretching his arm across the front of my chest. Then he grabs the seat belt, pulls it over my chest, and buckles me in. I wait for him to buckle his own, but he relaxes back in his seat, and remains still.

"Aren't you going to put yours on, too?" I ask, letting the car slowly roll backward.

He shakes his head stubbornly. "I'm good."

"Quinton, I . . ." I trail off as he turns his head toward the window and folds his arms.

"I said I'm good," he says in a tight voice, gesturing at the shifter. "Now let's go get some breakfast."

I want to argue with him, but how the hell am I supposed to force someone to do something they obviously are dead set on not doing. Sighing, I press on the gas, maneuvering the car around potholes. The closer I get to the main road, the more pissed off I get, because he won't put his seat belt on, and I know he's probably done a ton of other things that put his life at risk, but this makes it seem like he doesn't value his life at all, which makes me even more agitated.

Finally, I stomp on the brake a little too hard and it sends us both forward. My seat belt locks, but because he doesn't have one on, he ends up hitting his head on the dashboard.

"Shit," he curses, rubbing his head, and then stares at me coldly. "Why the fuck did you do that?"

My foot that's holding down the brake is shaking as I stare straight ahead. "Because I want you to put your seat belt on."

He pauses. "Nova, it's really my decision whether I want to wear one or not."

I shake my head, my jaw set tight. "No it's not. Regardless of your fucking reason for not putting one on, if anything happens then everyone who ever cared about you will be left hurting and missing you and probably pissed off because you chose not to put your seat belt on."

There's a long pause as my words and sharp tone startle both of us.

"No one cares about me, so it's fine," he states with indifference. "And I never wear one."

"*I care about you*," I insist, and my chest compresses as I realize that it's the truth. The painful, inconceivable, unplanned truth. I care about him. My breath shakes as I say, "So, if not for you, will you please put it on for me?"

He's quiet for a while, and I think he's going to refuse. I get ready to drive forward, back to the field, and skip out on breakfast, when he sighs and straps his belt on.

"There, are you happy?" he mutters, slumping back in the seat.

"Yes." I shove the car into drive, feeling a little bit lighter, like I might have just done something right.

Quinton

She's still pissed off about the seat belt even when we arrive at the restaurant. I don't really think it has to do with me not putting on my seat belt and more with the fact that I'm not cherishing my life. I'm still trying to process the fact that she cares about me enough to want me to put on my seat belt. Part of me is angry with myself for allowing things to get this complicated between us, for letting her in enough that she actually cares about my life. She shouldn't be caring about it. It's worthless. I'm worthless. I may be walking around, breathing, heart beating, blood running through my veins, but my existence, my soul, everything that made me who I was is dead. At least I thought it was. But there's another part of me, one that's been repressed for a very long time, that relishes in the fact that she cares about my life—about me.

I was torn with putting the seat belt on, because I really don't care what happens to me, and I sometimes secretly hope that something bad will happen and I'll finally be able to be buried with everyone else, beneath the ground, right where I'm supposed to be. But in the end I give in to Nova, because I remember what happened to her boyfriend and how it probably has something to do with that. But I know that by giving in to her, I'm admitting that I'm developing feelings for her, so I try to mentally picture Lexi during the drive. It becomes harder with each movement Nova makes, though, like when she fiddles with the keys and adjusts the mirror, because it makes her real, and the images of Lexi just memories.

She doesn't talk to me the entire drive, only nodding when I give her directions. It takes a few minutes to get up to the restaurant because the road is rocky and bumpy and made more for four-wheel-drive vehicles.

Finally we pull up to a small log cabin in the center of the trees. There are flashing neon signs on the windows and twinkle lights trimming the roof, along with a few around the doorway. Plants and flowers and trees surround the path that leads to the entrance, and the sun shines down through the branches above, making everything fun and cheerful on the outside.

She turns off the engine, removes the keys, and opens the door to climb out.

"Nova, wait," I say, unclicking my seat belt, and mentally screaming at myself to keep my mouth shut and let her remain angry with me.

She pauses with her legs out of the car and her back turned to me as she adjusts one of her fallen straps on her red shirt back over her shoulder. "Yeah."

Just let her be. "I'm . . . I'm sorry."

She glances over her shoulder at me and locks of her hair fall across her bare shoulders. "For what?"

"For being an ass," I tell her, letting the seat belt slide up into the wall.

"It's fine." She gets out of the car and stuffs the keys into the pocket of her short denim shorts.

I climb out of the car and meet her at the front of the car. She doesn't say a word as we walk into the restaurant, where it seems the entire concert has flocked to. We manage to find a small booth at the back, squished between the back door and the kitchen. It's noisy, but our table is agonizingly quiet because Nova's not talking to me. The waitress comes and takes our orders. Nova starts fiddling with the salt shaker, twirling it around in her hand. I'm searching my mind for something to say, but nothing seems right, and I'm beginning to think I should just let her stay upset with me when she just starts talking.

"You just seemed like you didn't want to wear it because you were..." She spills a little salt and sweeps it off the table and onto the floor with her hand. "Because you were sad."

"It wasn't because of that," I lie, unrolling the silverware from the napkin.

"But that's what it seemed like." She's still staring at the table and it looks like her eyes are getting watery. "And I had someone... close to me... a friend who stopped... doing stuff because of the sadness." She bites on her trembling lip so hard she draws blood.

"Nova, I..." I have no fucking idea what to say to her.

"It was my boyfriend," she whispers, and tears stream down her cheek. "And he was sad and then he stopped doing everything." Her voice is quivering, and she's sniffling as she wipes the tears away from her eyes. But more tears escape her eyes and drip all over her skin, and the tabletop beneath her ends up soaked with her grief.

I'm the last person she should be talking to this about, because I think about it all the time. I think about stopping

260

everything because of the sadness. But she's crying, and it hurts to watch, so I end up climbing out of my side of the booth and sliding into hers. She starts to sob as soon as my shoulder touches hers and then she buries her face into my chest, drenching it with her tears. I place my hand on the back of her hand and hold her, because it's all I can do, because I know death hurts, death breaks, death consumes, and there's no magic cure to making it go away.

I let her cry for as long as she needs with my arm around her shoulder. Even when she stops sobbing, she keeps her face pressed against my chest. The waitress drops off our food, giving us a strange look, but I shrug it off and wait. Finally, when the food's getting cold, Nova pulls back.

Her cheeks are stained red and her eyes are swollen. "I'm sorry...I have no idea why I just did that."

I brush my finger up her cheek to wipe away the tears, but her skin is sensitive and she winces, so I lean forward and softly place a kiss to each of her cheeks instead. Shutting my eyes, I allow myself one second to enjoy the moment. Then I move back and look her in the eye. "Are you okay?"

She nods and opens her mouth, but her stomach decides to rumble really loud and it makes me smile and her laugh. "I think maybe I should eat, though."

She starts to unroll her silverware, her mouth turned downward. "Quinton?"

I pick up my fork, ready to devour the food. "Yeah?"

"Thank you," she says quietly in a hoarse voice.

It's amazing how two words can mean so much. I nod with my eyes on my food, and we dig into our eggs, pancakes, and toast, keeping the conversation light. By the time we head back to the car, we've got full bellies and are feeling content with one another. When we climb into the car, I put my seat belt on without her asking, even though I don't want to—I do it for her. She doesn't say anything, but it makes her smile, and for a brief moment I smile, too.

Nova

I feel bad for crying in front of him, but at the same time I don't think I could have helped it. I was too overwhelmed and, honestly, I'm just exhausted. Of being who I am. Of not knowing who I am. And of always being confused. I'm starting to wonder what it would be like to move on past the numbers and finally start to breathe again. Although it doesn't seem entirely possible, the idea of doing it seems less tiring. Perhaps I could stop, but then what? What would become of me? Would the past crush me?

Later that evening we're sitting in front of a fire, and the night sky looks like a blanket sprinkled with stars above us. Dylan surrounded a small area with rocks so we could cook dinner on a fire, even though he never ate dinner himself. Then we all sat around the fire, laughing and drinking beers. One of my favorite bands is playing, and I'm sitting on Quinton's lap singing along with the lyrics.

"Hey, I have an idea," Delilah announces as she picks at the overly cooked marshmallow on the end of her stick. "Let's play truth or dare."

Dylan shoots her a dirty look as he stirs the fire, the logs inside it hissing and smoldering. "I already made it pretty clear that I fucking hate games."

She rolls her eyes as she puts a blob of marshmallow into her mouth, and then wipes her sticky fingers on the side of her shorts. "Then you can watch."

Shaking his head, Dylan returns back to his chair by the cooler. "Do whatever the hell you want as long as I'm not a part of it."

"I'll play," I tell her, sticking the hot dog fork into the fire. I have three marshmallows on it and they instantly start to bubble against the flame. "I like games."

Quinton smiles up at me, squeezing my hips. "I know you do," he says with honesty, and it's strange because he does know that part of me, which means he's getting to know me. He looks over at Delilah, who's sitting on a log beside Tristan. "I'm game."

The three of us stare at Tristan and he looks hesitant, but shrugs. "Whatever."

Delilah slaps her hand against her knee and shoves the rest of her burned marshmallow into her mouth. "Okay, who wants to go first?" When no one offers, she adds, "Okay, I will then." She balances the stick on the rocks in front of her feet and then swallows the mouth full of marshmallows. "Okay, mine's for Nova, and if you turn down the question or the dare you have to take a shot."

Nodding, I gulp down the rest of my beer. "All right, I choose truth."

She sticks out her tongue at me. "I so knew you would."

"What the hell does that mean?" I ask, offended.

"It means you're predictable," she says, kind of being a bitch.

I'd say more to her, but everyone is watching, so all I say is, "What's your question?"

She wavers, staring up at the sky thoughtfully. "Have you ever made out with a guy just because you were drunk?"

"You know I have," I answer in a tight voice, glaring at her, wondering what the hell her problem is. Is she just being a bitch because she's mad at me for something, or is she on something? Out of the corner of my eye I catch Tristan looking at me, and it makes me extremely uncomfortable. "So I don't know why you're asking it."

"Because truth or dare is all about causing drama, and I thought that one would," Delilah replies, then waits for a soap opera scene to unfold. But it never happens. Yes, there's awkwardness between Tristan and me, and Quinton seems to be a little uncomfortable, too, but thankfully no one says anything. Looking disappointed, Delilah leans back on the log, resting her weight on her palms. "Quinton, truth or dare?"

He shrugs and I feel his chest rise and fall as he lets out a tired sigh. "Dare, I guess."

A devious grin creeps across Delilah's face and she looks evil in the firelight. "I dare you to kiss me."

I tense, knowing I shouldn't, because he's not my boyfriend or anything, and I'm not even sure what I want from him. All I know is that I don't want to share him. I glance over at Dylan, who simply shrugs and pops the top off another beer.

"I don't care what she fucking does," he says and throws his head back, guzzling the beer.

Everyone kind of glances around uncomfortably, then Quinton shifts his weight. "Nova, can you get up?"

I nod, quickly stand up, and shuffle to the side. I consider running out into the crowd, instead of watching, but I can't determine which one is more painful to endure. So I stand there next to the fire, trying not to cry as he makes his way around the fire toward Delilah. I can feel Tristan watching me, and Delilah wets her lips with her tongue in anticipation. I'm not sure why she's doing it. Is this just a side of her I've never seen or is it the drugs, because I'm beginning to understand that they can make a person act completely different from the ordinary character. Happier. Sadder. Angrier. Bitchier.

Quinton gets to his feet and heads in Delilah's direction. Right as he's about to reach her, he veers to the left toward the box of alcohol bottles nestled up next to the tent. He selects a bottle of cheap vodka, and twists off the cap. Putting the bottle to his lips, he bends his head back and knocks back a shot. "I'm declining on this one," he says, his muscles twitching as the burn of the alcohol gets to him.

Delilah shrugs as he sets the bottle back into the box. "Your loss."

She grins at me and I don't know why, because I really want to hit her. And then I realize that the fact that I want to hit her means I might be feeling something for Quinton, and I'm not sure how to handle that. I'm about to get up and knock back my own shot, when Quinton walks up to me and holds out his hand.

"How about we ditch the game and go for a walk?" Quinton asks me with his hand extended out.

I nod and lace my fingers through his, the contact instantly giving me a sense of familiarity. "Okay."

"Hey," Delilah protests, sitting up straight like she's about to stand up. "We have to finish the game first."

"I think I'm done with the game," I say, letting Quinton pull me to my feet. We hike toward the field, holding hands, and the inside of me feels momentarily peaceful.

"Wait," Tristan calls out, as he retrieves his pipe from his pocket. "Don't you guys want to smoke a bowl first?"

I start to say yes, but Quinton shakes his head. "We're good."

I get a little annoyed that he says "we're" as if he's my spokesman. But he's holding my hand and it feels warm against mine, not cold, which means he's here. With me. Not ready to leave. Without me.

We walk away from the fire and the silly little game, heading out into the quiet field behind the tents, the one just in front of the forest. He finds a rock for us to sit on, and then we climb up on it, sitting by each other but not touching.

"I'm not sure what to think of her," he states, gazing at the fiery glow of the stage lights gleaming in the distance.

I draw a pattern in a patch of dirt beside my leg on the rock. "Who, Delilah?"

He nods, his gaze sliding to me, his honey-brown eyes a shadow against the darkness and the trickle of light from the full moon. "You two are so different. How did you become friends with her?"

"I went through some stuff..." I trail off and shrug. "She was there for me when no one else was."

"That's kind of hard to believe."

"Well, it's true." I mull over the question in my head and then finally just say it. "Is that why you didn't kiss her? Because you're not sure about her?"

"No. I'm not sure about a lot of things, and that's why I didn't kiss her." He stares down at the section of rock between us where our fingers are only inches away from each other's. "I know one thing, though."

"Oh yeah, what's that?" I stare down at our hands, too, so close, yet they still seem so far away.

He glances up at me the same time I glance up at him, and the intensity in his expression thrusts my equilibrium off balance, and I feel dizzy. "That I really want to kiss you," he utters softly.

"Okay." I blame my eager response on the alcohol in my system, or perhaps it's just really what I want at the moment.

"Are you sure?" he questions, eyeing my mouth. "Because I don't want to... that thing at the restaurant—"

I crash my lips into his, because I'm caught up in the moment and I want to taste him again and I want to avoid taking a detour down memory lane again. I've never really instigated a kiss before, and it makes my adrenaline skyrocket and I shiver from the rush and the high. But soon my emotions calm as we settle on the rock with his body positioned over mine. His tongue moves slowly, but deliberately as he explores my mouth, while my fingers slide underneath his shirt. He has his knee between my legs, and with each movement our mouths make, his knee matches the smooth motion, rubbing between my legs. When he hits the right spot, a tingling sensation erupts all over my body, and it makes me moan as my fingertips press down against his abs. I feel like I'm flying yet falling at the same time, spinning out of control like I'm stuck on a carnival ride and I'm not sure how the hell to get off it. Then my head starts to spin as his fingers sneak up the bottom of my shorts, gradually and softly dousing my skin in heat. I tense, wanting to tell him to stop, yet my lips stay sealed to his, because I can't seem to find the willpower or desire to break the kiss.

He slips a finger inside me but then he pauses, propping up on his elbows to look me in the eyes. "Is this okay?"

No. I nod. "Yeah."

A deliberate exhale releases from his lips, like he's nervous and was hoping I'd say no. Then he's kissing me and feeling me from the inside, as our bodies move in harmony like the song playing onstage, and for the briefest of seconds, in the darkness and scarred world that surrounds us, there is a split moment of perfection. The cluster of emotions swarming in my head and body make me feel like I'm going to explode, and I cling to his arms as I move my mouth away from his, tipping my head back, falling deeper into the perfection. When it's all over, he lays us back on the rock and holds me, combing his fingers through my hair, as I slowly return to the scarred world around us.

I have a weird sense of déjà vu as we stare at the stars and exhaustion attempts to take us over, my mind and body becoming heavier and groggier with images of the last time I lay under the stars at night. I don't want to go to sleep, because I'm afraid of what I'll wake up to. Or what I won't wake up to.

"Do you ever think about the future?" I ask him, breaking the silence.

"Not really," he replies, tensing, his fingers tangled in my hair. "Do you?"

"Sometimes, but I never really see anything."

"Nothing at all?"

I trace a long line up and down his chest with my finger, right where I know the scar is hidden under the fabric. "I used to. A lot. But in the end, it's pretty much pointless, because it doesn't matter what you want or plan. You never end up getting it."

At first he doesn't respond, and I think it's because he

agrees with me. Then he transfers his weight to the side and scoots down so he's at eye level with me. He places a hand on each of my cheeks and looks me in the eyes.

"You know what I think," he says, vining his legs around mine. "I think you're going to have a really amazing future, full of drumsticks, and songs and videos, and anything else you want, because one day you're going to wake up from all of this and realize that you're too good to be here."

His words slam against my chest because he doesn't mean them. Not really. He doesn't even know me. My lips part to tell him that. "I think that—"

His lips collide with mine and it's the final thing we say to each other. We kiss until the stars begin to dwindle, and then we hold on to each other, clutching at something I'm not sure really exists. It could all be just an illusion. Like Landon and I were. Maybe I'm feeling things for him and he's feeling things for me, but maybe not. Maybe what's on the outside isn't necessarily what's on the inside.

Chapter Sixteen

July 30, Day 72 of Summer Break

Nova

"What the hell is with the rain?" Delilah frowns at the muddy mess that has become the field. "This sucks."

She and I are sitting in the tent with the door open, watching the sky drizzle against the ground, as she smokes from the pipe and I occasionally take a few hits. People are out in the field, though, as the band plays without their amps, the music muffled by the vibration of the thunder and the lightning and the raindrops colliding with the ground. Quinton, Tristan, and Dylan took off a little while ago, being very vague about where they were going.

"If it keeps up"—Delilah hugs her knees to her chest, props the pipe on her kneecaps, and flicks the lighter—"then we won't even be able to set off fireworks." She sucks in a breath with her mouth wrapped around the end, then she holds it in before letting it out, and smoke envelops the tent.

"Were we going to anyway?" I ask as I brush the tangles from my hair. I'm trying my best to clean up, since I haven't had a shower since we got here. My hair is gross and tangled, my skin feels really grimy, like each of my pores is stuffed with dirt, and I stink.

She gapes at me as she hands me the pipe. "Uh, yeah." She lets her auburn hair out of the clip and her hair falls to her shoulders. She snatches the brush from my hand, grinning, and starts to brush her own hair.

"Hey," I protest, snatching the brush from her. "I was using that."

"Yeah, but what were we always saying back at college?" she asks and waggles her eyebrows at me. "What's yours is mine and what's mine is mine."

I stick out my tongue as I robotically position the pipe to my mouth. It's becoming a routine that I'm still trying to figure out if I need. "Only because you're greedy."

She rolls her eyes, laughing. "Whatever, bitch. I'm so nice and that's why you love me."

I can't help but smile as I light the weed, and once it's kindling I suck in a toxic hit. I wince as it hits the back of my throat and then cough, letting it out. I hand her the pipe and reach for my bag to take out my deodorant. "Yep, you caught me."

She drops the brush on my lap, sets the pipe down by her feet, and starts making a braid at the back of her head. "I have to say this and I don't want you to get mad or anything, but you . . . you look happy."

"Why would I get mad at that?" I ask, putting the deodorant on. "It's not like you're calling me a bitch or anything... Well, I guess you kind of did, but so what? I'm happy. That's not bad, is it?"

She shakes her head and slides the elastic off her wrist. "No, it's good, but like I've said a couple of times, sometimes it feels like you're trying to be sad."

I take in what she said as I put the cap back on the deodorant. "Well, I'm not now, so..."

She secures the elastic around the end of her braid. "So, is the reason why you're not trying to be sad, because of this?" She points a finger at the pipe. "Or because of a certain someone who likes to draw and who has a freaking hot-as-hell body? Because if it is, I have to say again that I don't think you should act on it. He's not boyfriend material."

"I never said I was looking for a boyfriend." I take my perfume out from my bag and flick the cap off. "And when did you see his body?"

She giggles under her breath. "I kind of accidentally walked in on him while he was changing."

"Why were you walking into his tent at all?"

"Um..." She tenses. "Because I was confused."

"About what?"

"I don't know..." She drifts off, letting the braid fall down her back, then she straightens her legs out and slaps her hands on top of her thighs. "Hey, you know what I should do?"

"Tell me why you were in Quinton's tent?" I say in a sarcastic tone. "Was it to try and get him to kiss you again?"

"No, silly." She slaps the top of my leg. "That's not even important. I was only messing around when I did that."

I spritz myself with perfume, trying to cover up the stench I know has to be flowing from me. "Then what should you do?"

Her eyes stray to the veil of rain outside and the mud splattering the ground like wet paint. "Actually, it's a *we* thing. *We* should go out and play." A lazy grin spreads across her face as she glances at me.

I drop my bottle of perfume in my bag. "Are you crazy? I'm already filthy."

"Then what does it matter if you get a little bit dirtier?" she asks, collecting her pipe from off the tent floor. She takes a few more hits and then pushes it at me.

I take it because it's there and I don't really want to say no. I take a few more inhales of it, and the more the smoke enters my lungs, the more warmed up I get to the idea of what she said.

My eyes start to water as I think about what my dad would say if he were here, besides the fact that he'd probably be disappointed in me. He always loved to play in the rain.

"It's good to play in the rain," he said once when I was younger.

"Why, Daddy?" I'd asked, looking up at him. "Won't we get all muddy?"

He nodded and took my hand as he headed for the door. It was pouring down outside, making a muddy mess of the grass. "That's the point, Nova. To let go and have fun." He opened the door, and raindrops fluttered into the house. "Besides, it's more peaceful when it's raining. It means everyone else is inside and you get the whole world to yourself." He winked at me and I'd laughed, then we'd sprinted out into the rainstorm, dancing and jumping in puddles until our clothes were soaked and our cheeks hurt from laughing.

God, how simple life used to be. I want it to be simple again.

"Okay," I say to Delilah. "Let's go play in the rain."

Her smile broadens. We take a few more turns with the pipe, because it's there and it makes the idea of running out into the rain easier. By the time she snatches my hand, my thoughts and feet are moving really slow. She laughs as she jumps out and runs out of the tent, dragging me along with her. The first contact of rain against my skin sends an icy shiver through my body, but as the mud splashes up on my bare legs I bask in the freeness.

We sprint out of the tent area and dive into the madness going on in the field, where people are covered in mud, sitting in it, dancing in it, throwing it at each other. As I sink into the mud up to my ankles, I slip my fingers from Delilah's hand and span my hands out to my sides. Laughing, I tip my head back and shut my eyes, whirling in a circle, pretending that no one else is here with me, that I'm completely sober and calm, and that the whole world is mine.

For a moment, life feels perfect.

Rain trickles across my face and my hair gets drenched, along with my shirt, but it's worth it because it's been a long time since I've felt this free: free from worrying, counting, trying to keep things together and fix things that I know I can't fix.

"What the hell are you two doing?" I hear Quinton's voice and I lift my eyelids open.

He's standing at the edge of the field with Tristan and Dylan behind him, their hair and clothes soaked from the rain. Dylan looks annoyed, arms crossed, jaw set tight, Tristan is distracted with his phone, and Quinton appears utterly fascinated with the scene.

Delilah stumbles up beside me and her fingers wrap around my arm. "Playing," she calls out to them and then shoves me back.

I trip over my own feet and fall into the mud right on my ass. They laugh at me and so does Delilah, so I grab her leg and jerk on it, causing her to fall down, too. She lands on her hands and knees and laughs so hard she gasps for air. I laugh, too, then wipe some mud on the side of her face.

"You're a terrible friend," I say, as we slide around in the mud.

She rolls her eyes trying to wipe the mud off her face, but she only makes a bigger mess. "Oh yeah, the worst."

She smiles at me and I smile back. We start to laugh, then throw mud at each other. After we stop, she springs to her feet, doing a little twirl before sprinting across the field. She runs right at Dylan, who shakes his head, glaring at her.

"Don't you fucking dare," he warns, backing away.

But she keeps running at him, and when she reaches him, she wraps her arms around him, getting mud all over his shirt and jeans.

"What the fuck, Delilah," he curses and shoves her back, kind of roughly, and just like that the rain and the moment of magic it brought disappears as she lands on the ground hard.

I start to hike through the mud toward her as Dylan rushes off, cussing. Delilah jumps to her feet, and she's crying as she chases after him. I want to scream at her for being an idiot and to leave him alone, but I can barely get my legs to move, so all I do is stand there.

Tristan roams off toward the truck area. Quinton waits for me at the border of the field where it shifts to grass, making it less muddy. He has shorts on and his shirt off, and his skin is wet and gorgeous and all I want to do is touch him.

When I reach the edge of the mud, he extends his hand out to me. "God, I leave you alone for ten minutes and all hell breaks loose."

"You've been gone for more than ten minutes," I say, taking his hand. He helps me out of the mud, trying not to laugh at my appearance. "I got bored."

"That's a nice look for you," he comments, and I can tell he's trying really hard not to laugh at me. The rain is slowing down and the mud on my skin, clothes, and hair is starting to dry out and become crusty. He runs his eyes over me, stopping on my eyes. "Are you high?" he asks, and when I don't answer, he frowns. "Nova, you're too good—"

I cover his mouth with my hand, because I don't want to hear it, just like I never wanted to hear it from Landon. Not only because the similarity of their words makes my heart feel like it's rupturing open, but because right now I'm not *too good* for anything, stuck in the subdued state of being high. I'm just me. Nova. Good and bad. "Don't say it."

He keeps frowning as I lower my hand and I start running my fingers through my hair, plucking out the chunks of mud. Quinton begins wiping off my legs, but we only cause the mud to smear everywhere, and by the time I'm done I look like the monster from *Swamp Thing*.

Finally, he pulls his hands away and stands up straight, letting out a sigh. "I think you're shit out of luck, Nova. It's not coming off."

I frown as I pick a large chunk of mud out of my leather bands. "It *has* to come off."

He snorts a laugh and I stick out my tongue, tossing the chunk of mud at him. It hits him square in the forehead and he picks it off, frowning. I pull a *whoops* face, and I start to back away as fake aggravation crosses his face.

"You're so going to pay for that," he says, matching my steps as I speed for the mud pit, because I know I'm safe there.

I reel around to run, but he snags the back of my shirt and pulls me toward him. I thrust my hands out, putting all my weight forward, trying to get away, as my shirt stretches. But he maintains his hold on me until I get close enough to him, then he encloses me in his arms, picks me up, and heads toward the field.

"Quinton, don't," I halfheartedly protest, because I'm already muddy and it doesn't really matter if he throws me back in it.

"No way," he says, constricting his hold. "You don't get away with throwing mud on me." He wades a little into the mud, then drops me on the ground right on my butt.

I roll onto my back, and mud oozes all over my skin, hair, and clothes as I sink into the ground. "You're mean."

He grins at me, placing his hands on his hips as he stares down at me, looking pleased with himself. "And you're a mess."

I stick out my tongue and then spit when I get a mouthful of mud. He laughs, hunching over and clutching at his gut, like he thinks I'm a freaking comedian, and suddenly lying in the dirt becomes worth it.

I stick out my hand. "This is getting gross. Can you help me up?"

Shaking his head, he smiles and slips his fingers through mine. I give him no time to react as I tug down hard on his arm. His knees give out, and he collapses into the mud right on top of me. His hands spring out and he catches himself before he squishes me. Mud covers him as he hovers over me, supporting his weight with his arms.

"I can't believe you fell for that," I say, smearing my muddy hand across his forehead just because I can.

He brings one of his hands up and rubs it all over my face while I squirm and laugh. "I blame it on those beautiful eyes of yours. They make you look like a trusting person."

I hold my breath inside my chest, part of me wanting to fully hear, see, and feel the moment and fight against the high, yet part of me wants to embrace it and not feel anything at all. The rain softly trickles down on us, and my skin is wet and muddy. In the distance the band is playing an acoustic song. There are people everywhere, and mud flies through the air. My heart beats in my chest like a tiny drum that wants to play a song so goddamn badly it hurts, and maybe I finally will. Maybe I'll really make good on my promise and pick up a set of drumsticks again and play for Quinton like I told him I would.

Quinton's beautiful honey-brown eyes are on me, the ones that first drew me to him, as rain beads his skin, lips, jawline. I want to kiss him, and he must want to kiss me, too, because he starts to lean down as I sit up and we meet halfway, colliding together at the precise moment that lightning snaps and thunder booms.

The rain picks up again as our bodies and tongues melt together and water soaks through our clothes. Everything seems to move in slow motion as I trail my fingers up his bare, lean chest, while he runs a hand through my hair, tugging softly at the roots. Heat flows off us, and mud is getting everywhere. He traces his tongue along the roof of my mouth, and when he slips it out I bite down on my lip. He lets out a groan as his weight lowers and my arms get pinned between our chests. I wiggle them out as our mouths stay attached, our breaths mingling together, and I circle them around his neck and pull him even closer, despite the fact that we're sinking into the mud. I sketch lines up and down his spine, feeling the smoothness of his skin, and I hold on to him, because I don't want to lose him.

I begin to kiss him frantically the more time goes on because my thoughts are getting mixed together and nothing makes sense at the moment. I can't see any kind of future, and I have no idea what's going to happen in the next thirty seconds. I try to count to calm myself down, but I'm too far gone to make it past five and the idea is frightening me. The silence the weed has been instilling in me has suddenly become too silent.

"Nova," he groans against my mouth as I dig my fingers into his back. "Nova, slow down."

I start gasping for air, my nails plunging deeper into his skin, and my lungs feel like they're burning. Then he's pulling away and I think he's going to leave, but instead he grabs my hand and helps me stand up.

He leads us across the field and through the tent area and I think he's going to stop at our tent, but instead he curves to the right and continues walking, heading toward the line of trees.

"Where are we going?" I say through the chattering of my

teeth. My hair and clothes are drenched, and my skin is covered with flaky mud that makes my skin feel tight. I have no idea where he's taking me, and it feels like I should be counting my steps and trying to turn back to the tent, but I can't seem to find the pattern of the steps I'm taking, or the willpower to let go of his hand, so I keep following him helplessly through the tall grass.

"I'm taking you somewhere where you can wash off," he says, staring ahead as he walks determinedly through the tall grass. "And to give you a break so that maybe you can get your mind in the right place."

"Wait, you're not taking me to the nudist colony place, are you?" I start to pull back, but then I stop because it doesn't seem as scary anymore.

He shakes his head. "No, I'm not." His shorts are covered in mud and his hair has flecks in it. On his back are muddy handprints and streaks of mud from where I touched him, along with small crescent cuts on his shoulder blade.

"I'm sorry I stabbed you with my nails," I say as we wind around a rock and dip into the trees. The thick branches above our heads block out the remaining rain and gray clouds but there's a current falling off them so we still get wet.

"Don't worry about it." He reaches around to his back, touching the scratches. "But Nova... how much did you smoke?"

I shrug, because I surprisingly lost count, and he sighs, letting his hand fall to the side. We don't say anything else until we reach a river flowing among the lofty pine trees. We pause at the edge, and Quinton glances around for a way across it.

"What is this place?" I ask, glancing up at the gray sky peeking through the branches.

"I found it while I was wandering around trying to find a place to clean off without giving everyone a show," he says, winding around me and hiking toward a large rock near the edge of the stream.

The water gently flows over it, but it acts as a stepping stone, and without warning Quinton grips my waist and lifts me onto it. Once my feet are planted on the rock, he lets me go and then jumps onto the rock himself. He stands up straight and takes my hand, then leads me over to the other side of the rock. There's a little bit of a gap between the rock and the shoreline, and Quinton hops down, landing in the river, his shoes getting wet. He stands in the water and reaches for me. When I crouch down, his fingers spread around my hips, and he carefully lowers me to him. Then he wades over to the shore, pretty much carrying me in his arms so my feet don't get wet.

Once we're both on the shore, he threads his fingers through mine, and I let him guide me deeper into the trees as rain drips down on my head and down my arms. We keep hiking through the forest, and the farther we go the more I start to calm down. By the time we reach an area where the trees open up, I'm mad at myself because I'm so tired of doing things and having no direction and being confused all the time. I just want to be Nova, or at least find out who the real Nova is.

When we stop, we're standing on a rocky shore that stretches out to a glistening pond. The river flows into it over the towering rocks in front of us, and the entire area is almost completely encompassed by enormous, jagged rocks, and flourishing trees. "I give you a private place to clean off." He smiles, motioning at the water.

I remove my fingers from his grip and walk up to the water peering down in. "You just found this by accident?"

He nods, stepping up beside me with his head tipped down so he can examine my eyes. "How are you feeling?"

I rub my eyes. "A lot better, actually, but a little tired."

"You look a lot better," he says. "I figured the walk here would calm you down and then you could clean off. And when we're done, I'll take you back and you can get some sleep."

I rub my eyes again. "Thank you."

He starts to unbutton his shorts. "You're welcome."

I don't think he gets my whole meaning. I'm not just saying thanks for pulling me away; I'm saying thanks for letting me calm down, for letting me breathe, and for telling me that I shouldn't be doing the things that I do.

He slips his shorts off and my gaze instantly goes to his boxers, my heart beating deafeningly inside my chest. Even though I'm a little out of it, I can feel my cheeks heating, because I'm pretty much staring at his manly parts.

But he gives me no time to get too embarrassed as he takes off toward a section of cliffy rocks at the side of the pond and he climbs up to the top of the highest one of them. "What do you think?" he calls out as he stands on the edge, staring down at the water. "Cannonball or swan dive?"

"Belly flop," I say, and he shakes his head.

"No fucking way. Do you know how bad that would hurt?" He turns around and does a backflip right off the edge, his head coming so close to hitting the edge of the rock that I gasp.

He makes it into the water, though, and launches a splash into the air. Seconds later, he bursts through the surface again, running his hand over his head, slicking his hair back. "Your turn," he says, paddling his arms as he floats farther out into the water.

I glance down at my muddy clothes, nervous about stripping down in front of him. When I glance up at him again, though, he has his back turned to me, staring up at the rocky cliffs at the far side of the pool.

I seize the opportunity to drop my shorts and pull my shirt off. My bra and panties are covered with mud, too, but I can rinse them off in the water. I walk up to the shoreline and stick my toe in, shivering from the cold temperature.

"What? You're not going to jump in?" he asks. When I look up at him he's looking at me, and I mean really looking at me, his honey-brown eyes skimming my body. I think about ducking behind a bush, but then what'd be the point? He's already seen me, and I can't erase that from his head.

I hike up to the rocks and hoist myself up on the tallest one. I stand on the edge and then shut my eyes. Summoning a deep breath, I jump up and cannonball off the side, falling and falling and falling. When I hit the water, a chill disperses through my body, and I quickly paddle my way to the top, breaking through the surface. I take a deep breath, wiping my eyes off and blinking against the water droplets dripping down my forehead.

"It's pretty fucking cold, right?" Quinton asks, floating over to me as I smooth my hair out of my eyes.

I nod, tipping my head back into the water. "A little warning would have been nice."

"Yeah, but then you would have probably backed out and not jumped in."

"Yeah, you're probably right. It's probably a good thing you didn't tell me."

We grow quiet as we float around in the water with our arms out to the side, listening to the river water falling off the rocks. The clouds start to break apart in the sky and I detect a tiny bit of sunlight streaming in.

"I seriously want to draw this place," Quinton divulges, looking around at the rocks and the trees.

"You could, still," I say. "We still have a couple more days left here."

"Yeah…maybe." He tears his eyes off the rocks and focuses on me. "Nova…I have to know, do you really want to be with me, because sometimes it seems like you do and sometimes it seems like you don't, and I don't want to add to your confusion." He moves his arms in a circular motion, swimming backward and putting space between us. "In fact, I think I should probably back off...I like you and everything, but I think I should back off." He repeats himself at the end like he's trying to convince himself more than me.

I use my arms to turn in a circle, gazing up at the clearing sky. "I'm confused...," I mutter. I'm not sure if he hears me, but it's the realest thing I've ever said. I stop spinning and float in front of him. "About everything. Not just you, but life. And I want you to back off, but I don't at the same time."

His breathing becomes ragged as he stares at me and his pupils shrink as I tilt my head back and smooth my hair down with my hands again, my chest and bra rising up over the water. When I sink back down under the water, he starts to swim at me and seconds later his lips crash against mine as his arms encircle my waist. My arms link around his neck in response and my mouth opens up to his tongue as he slips it inside, devouring me with a deep wet kiss. Our bodies crush together, and it feels odd because the cold water masks our body heat, almost like neither of us really exists, and this moment isn't really happening, which makes it easier to do things.

As if my legs have a mind of their own, I wrap them around his waist, and he's supporting both of our weight as he swims one-handed, moving us toward the shore until my back collides with the sandpaper edges of the rock. I feel a little of my skin scrape off, but I don't care. I press at his back, trying to pull him closer, even though there's no more room left between us. His mouth consumes mine as he braces a hand on the rock next to my head and his other hand moves across my back. Then with a flick of his fingers, he unhooks my bra. I have no time to react as he jerks it off and tosses it up onto the rocks above our heads. The sensation of my nipples against his chest sends a quiver through my body, and suddenly I'm shivering from his touch and the cold water, desperately seeking heat.

His hand starts to travel down my back, and I arch into him when he reaches the top of my panties, then he pauses. I know I should tell him to stop—that I'm not in the right state of mind—but not being in the right state of mind makes it harder to say no. And what if I do and then he leaves me and I never see him again? What if I miss the moment *again*?

I don't say anything and he continues to slide my panties down my legs and works to get them off my ankles underneath the water. Somehow he manages to do it without losing them in the current swirling around us and then he's throwing that piece of fabric up there too. Within seconds he takes off his boxers and I have no time to react because everything is happening so quickly. I'm suddenly naked for the first time in front of a guy.

"Nova," he breathes against my mouth as he cups my cheek with his forehead resting against mine. His eyes are squeezed shut and then he opens them up, and for a fleeting moment he looks like he doesn't want to do this, like he's torn on what's right and wrong, real and fake, and I understand completely.

I don't say anything as he presses his mouth to mine again,

slips his tongue out and parts my lips with it. He groans, shuddering, and I shiver in response. My legs open up to him, and he positions himself between them as he strokes one of my nipples with his finger. When our bodies connect in every place, I can feel the tip of him pressed up between my legs. Part of me wants him to slip inside me, so I can feel what it's like before I miss my chance again. But the other part of me thinks it's wrong because we're in the middle of a pond, with no protection, and I have no idea what I want or who I want. *I should know what I want, shouldn't I? I need to figure stuff out.*

But I can't seem to get the words to come out because the regret and what-ifs own me, so I let him slip his tip inside me. I immediately wince from the pain, sucking in a sharp breath as every one of my muscles seizes into knots. I feel wrong, along with a million other things, because I'm not sure I want this. In fact, I don't think I do. Not like this. The truth in my thoughts suddenly opens my eyes and I figure out what to do next. *What do I do next?*

Quinton freezes, goes dead still with the tip of him barely inside me. My chest is heaving from the pain and fear and my thoughts are a blurry stream or numbers, emotions, and distorted thoughts as I try to figure out what to do. Keep going. Stop.

"Nova," he says in a strained, almost pained voice. "Is this...is this..." He opens his eyes, which are filled with more guilt then I've ever seen. He sucks in a deep breath. "Have you never done this before?"

My body is shaking and my teeth are chattering and I can't seem to get control of my nerves or voice, so I shake my head instead. His whole body goes rigid, and I can feel the beat of his pulse pounding between my legs. He starts breathing so loudly it covers the sound of the water falling from the rocks, but I can't hear myself breathing at all.

"I can't do this," he whispers, and it looks like he's going to cry as he pulls out of me. He starts to swim away, but I grab him, panicking, fearing I'm going to lose him. Or maybe it's Landon. I'm so confused. Lost. Always lost.

"Please don't go," I say, but it sounds unreal, just words disconnected from my emotions.

He shakes his head, looking horrified. "You don't want this, Nova...want me. You're better than that."

"No, I'm not!" I scream. Actually scream. My eyes go wide, shocked at the anger in my voice, so real and raw. "I'm not better than you. Him. Anyone!" My voice echoes for miles and the water ripples around me as I try to stay afloat. "I don't even know who I am..."

He shakes his head again, moving his arms in the water, backing away from me. "No, you are better. You're just confused right now for whatever reason. But soon you're going to open your eyes and see who you really are and that you don't belong with a bunch of fucking loser drug addicts." Pain laces his eyes and I can see something inside him, something heavy that I can't even begin to understand. "You don't belong in a pond about ready to screw some guy while you're fucking high, headed down a road of self-destruction. Because that's where you're going to go if you keep going down this road. Trust me. I know."

My lips tremble as tears threaten to spill down my cheeks. My head falls down and I stare at my distorted reflection. "I belong here." But my voice is just a whisper as memories of my past overwhelm me, ones of who I used to be—with Landon. "I belong somewhere..."

He reaches up over the rock above us and grabs his boxers before swimming to the shore and I don't try to stop him. I can't. I'm losing focus on the present as the memories that I try to block take over my mind.

He gets dressed and then hurries for the trees, leaving me alone in the water, alone. Alone. Alone. Alone. I try to backtrack how I got here, to this lonely place, but I can barely remember the journey and all I want to do is go back to a time in my life when everything felt right and made sense. I want stuff to make sense again. I don't want to feel so wrong inside.

I cover my chest with my arms and start to count the beats of my heart, but it doesn't do anything for me. I try to count the tree branches, the clouds, the stars as they peek out of the sky. But nothing is helping, and as my emotions start to emerge and chip down the wall I built around that night—around myself—I can no longer shut it down. It rams me in the chest, like a wrecking ball, and nearly drags me under the water. But somehow I manage to heave myself up onto the rocks. Staring at the stars, I grab onto my wrist, pressing my finger to the scar that's over my erratic pulse, feeling myself falling to that place again. The one where nothing makes sense and the past overtakes me.

Then I break to pieces, losing control over my thoughts and actions. I can barely understand what's going on as I try to grasp reality. But panic, sorrow, anger, and remorse take me over and pull me down. I try to count something—the stars, the trees, my heartbeats—but nothing is helping. And in the end, the past catches up with me.

And I remember. Everything.

Are you sure you don't just want to stay over?" Landon asks, as I put my shirt on and sit up on the bed. "We could just cuddle or something?"

"Cuddle?" I question, glancing over my shoulder at him, pretending everything's okay, when really I'm a mess inside. "Really?"

He shrugs innocently. "What? I could be a cuddler."

I roll my eyes, stand up, and slip my sandals on. "Yeah, yeah." I start to head to the door. "Besides, what if your parents walk in and catch us?" That's actually not the real reason I won't have sex with him. I'm secretly afraid that it'll hurt too badly or that he won't like how I look completely naked. Or that I'll be so bad he'll never want to touch me again. But I know that soon my excuses are going to run out, and either I'm going to just go through with it or he'll leave me. And then what? What will be left of me?

He stands up, slipping his shirt on with a faint smile on his lips. "They never come in my room after I go to bed, so we can cuddle all we want."

Sighing, I quietly open the door and lower my voice. "I should probably get home."

Nodding, he walks up to me and kisses me on the head. "I love you, no matter what," he whispers.

"I love you, too," I say, on the verge of crying because I really don't know if he means it. Sometimes it seems like he does and sometimes it doesn't. "And I'm sorry."

He pulls back a little, looking confused. "For what?"

"For not..." I trail off, glancing at his bed. "For disappointing you again."

Shaking his head, he takes my face in his hands and bends down to look me in the eyes. "Nova, you have never once disappointed me. I'll love you no matter what, even if we never have sex."

I resisted the urge to roll my eyes at him, because even though I know he may mean it now, there will be a point where he'll get tired. "I love you," I whisper and brush my lips across his softly, clutching the bottom of his shirt, afraid to let him go, afraid to admit my fears. Always afraid.

When I draw back, he gives me a small smile and laces his fingers through mine. "Come on," he says and heads out of the room, tugging me along with him.

"Where are we going?" I ask, rushing to keep up with him as he trots up the steps.

"It's a surprise," he says and we take lighter, nearly soundless steps as we reach the main floor so his parents won't hear us.

We tiptoe across the kitchen, laughing under our breaths when he runs into the kitchen table. Finally we make it to the door, and when we're both outside and off the porch we start laughing again. But our laughter quiets down as he leads me down the hill in his backyard. When we near the bottom, he stops and glances around at the damp grass below us and the starry sky above our heads. Then he sinks down to the ground, still holding on to my hand, and I sink down next to him.

"What are we doing?" I ask, as he lays down on his back.

"This way we can sleep together without worrying about getting caught," he says, letting go of my hand so he can tuck his below his head.

"You're seriously going to sleep out in the backyard with me?" I ask, lying down beside him.

"For a little while," he says. "But eventually I'll have to go back inside."

Chapter Seventeen

Quinton

I leave her in the pond, naked and chattering, and run back through the trees toward the tent. I'm stunned. Horrified. Hitting a full-on panic attack. She was about to hand me her fucking virginity. Me. A fucking loser, who she'll probably regret knowing when she moves on from this lost period in her life. And to me, it'll probably mean something to me— she means something. *She means something.* The truth stabs at my chest like a chunk of shrapnel lodged in my heart, right where the scar is. Things aren't supposed to mean anything. I'm dead. I gave up. I'm not supposed to be here. With Nova. With anyone.

The closer I get to the tent, the worse I feel. I know I shouldn't have left her like that, and it's one of the hardest fucking things I've had to do. Nova is beautiful, interesting, a good person, and she makes me feel things I thought I'd never feel again. On some level I think she understands me, even though I haven't told her anything about me. She gets pain and loss, and that's pretty much what exists inside me. I think in a different life I probably could have loved her, been with her, made her happy. But this is this life, and I can't love anyone or be loved. And that's the way it will always be—should be.

Right after the accident happened, some people tried to tell me that it would get easier and that I wouldn't always feel this way. That time would heal the pain, the guilt, everything that I'm feeling. They'd say it's not my fault. That I was just in the wrong place at the wrong time and just happened to be behind the wheel. Some people said otherwise, like Ryder's parents, who insisted that it was my fault and that I should have been driving more safely. They said that I ruined their family, killed their daughter. Lexi's parents wouldn't even talk to me or look at me anymore. Some people pretended I didn't exist, like my father.

In the end, it all comes down to one thing: I was driving too fast. I knew that. And I wasn't watching the road when I should have been. Lexi saw it first. That the turn was too sharp and I was going too fast. She screamed. I swerved. There was a crunch as we collided with another car. And then just like that, everything that once existed, lives, breaths, heartbeats, were gone. And I was left with blood on my hands.

Finally, after what seems like hours, I make back to the tent. The muddy field is drying in the sun, shriveling and cracking. I search for Dylan, and when I can't find him, I look for Tristan. I find him smoking on a tailgate with a group of guys and girls who I've never met but he seems to know. When he sees me approaching, he hops off the tailgate, his forehead immediately creasing as he takes in the reckless state I'm in, my eyes bulging, my clothes and hair soaked with water and sweat, shuddering from head to toe with fear, desire, and need.

"What the fuck's wrong?" he says with a joint pinched in his finger.

"I need something hard," I say.

"Why?" he asks. "What's wrong? Why do you look so upset?"

"Nothing's wrong, and I won't look upset once I get something hard." It's all I need to say. There's only one thing that matters to druggies, and that's getting high. Tristan may dither consciously for a second, but when it all comes down to it, drugs always conquer.

He nods his head at one of the larger tents near the edge of the tent area. "Come on." He hands the joint to some girl with long, wavy black hair and crooked teeth. Her breasts are popping out of her black sleeveless dress and she's looking me over, her mouth salivating to get a taste. I think *later*, when I'm numb. But Nova's blue eyes and freckled face overlap the thought, and guilt creeps inside me. I tell my guilt to shut the fuck up. Because I'm already guilty of a lot of other terrible things, worse than hooking up with some random girl.

"Hurry," I tell Tristan, my mind wanting, seeking, needing solitude. Now.

He nods, and I practically make him run toward the tent.

When we reach it, we duck right in as if we both belong there. And we do. I do.

There are these greasy, cracked-out-looking guys inside and a girl with her top off, smoking what looks like a joint in the corner. But I know it's not a joint by the dazed look on her face. She's gone. Hollowed out by the toxic smoke. Whoever she was before all of this only exists in a locked box inside her head, and she probably can't even remember how to get it open. This place doesn't even exist to her, and I want to be where she is because I don't want to feel it anymore, everything that comes with living after everything is lost. I want to leave. I want to escape.

Really, what I want to do is die.

"We need a hit," Tristan tells a guy with a ponytail sitting in the middle of the tent with his shirt unbuttoned and his shoes off. He hands him some money and I keep staring at the girl, watching her drift farther and farther away from reality, right where I want to be. Gone. Gone. Gone.

Nonexistent.

When she turns her head in my direction, she smiles, but there's nothing behind it and I'm envious of her. I want what she has. I want.

Nothing.

The guy takes the money from Tristan and then takes the joint from the girl, who groggily rolls on her side, her arms flopped out in front of her. She keeps blinking her eyes, until there's nothing left but large massive pupils that are glazed over and bare.

Empty.

"It's the best around," the guy says, handing it to Tristan, like it matters, like if it wasn't we'd take our money back and go somewhere else.

Tristan nods and puts the joint to his lips. Taking a long hit, his pupils instantly dilate, his breathing quiets and evens out, and he relaxes back on his elbows, handing the joint to me. I don't give myself time to think, because thinking leads me to places I don't belong. And where I belong is here.

My hands shake uncontrollably as I put it up to my lips, suck in a breath, as everyone in the tent lies down on the floor, some moving their hands above their hands and others not moving at all. Then smoke crashes into my lungs, saturates, and completely sucks out the good in me, and suddenly everything stops.

Dies.

Chapter Eighteen

Nova

I cry until my eyes are swollen shut, remaining there for hours, and then somehow I manage to get my clothes on and climb down the rocks. Nighttime has arrived, the sky pitch-black, and the only thing I have to lead the way is the sound of the music and shouting and the small amount of stage light making it through the trees. I try not to think about how he left me like that, but it's all I can think about. He left me. Landon left me. Quinton left me. My dad left me. Even I left me, in a sense.

It feels like I'm never going to make it through the trees, and I'm not even sure if I want to. Maybe I'll just lay down in the dark and stay perfectly still. When I stumble over a rock and fall to the ground, I can't seem to get up. I lie in the dirt, staring up at the night sky, counting the stars that form the constellation Cassiopeia, trying to settle myself down. But nothing is helping. Nothing. And I feel the memory prickling up against my mind, like rusty, bent, and crooked nails.

His skin looks like snow and his eyes are open, like he's looking at something, like he's still there, but the lights have turned off inside his eyes. I fall to the ground, wanting to forget everything, wanting to forget that Landon is hanging from the ceiling and that he's written the word good-bye on the wall and that I don't even know who he was writing to. I want to forget this moment, but how can I forget it? It's not real. How could it be? Because he can't be dead. It's impossible. He wouldn't leave me. He loved me.

Knowing that what I'm seeing has to be wrong, I get to my feet and my foot is bleeding and my heart is thrashing in my chest. I'm losing control and my thoughts pile up in my head like bricks upon bricks upon bricks like they're building a wall around my mind, only the wall is crooked and split...

I get up from the ground and run, trying to get away from the memory, the bushes and branches slicing my palms open, and I try to keep track of my footsteps, how many I'm taking, where I'm going, but the memory catches up with me anyway...

I climb onto his bed, my hands shaking as I reach for the rope, because I know that if I can get him down, he'll be okay. He has to be okay. Because I can't picture my life without him. Without him I am nothing. I have no one. Nothing. Everything that makes me me belongs to

Landon, and without him I'm nothing but a shadow of a person with no substance. And I can't be a shadow.

I lean over the side, extending my arm as far as it will go until my fingers brush the coarse rope, and dig my nails into the knot, trying to loosen it. My fingers are trembling and my heart is as unsteady as my thoughts, like nothing inside me will connect. My arm keeps brushing his skin, and he feels so cold and unreal, and it doesn't make any sense because the Landon I know is warm and thriving, breathing, has a pulse. This isn't him. It can't be.

I've lost all control, and I can barely acknowledge what I'm doing. What I'm seeing. And this stupid song is playing in the background over and over again and the lyrics and sound are embedding into my head. I want it out. Because I don't need to remember this. It's not real. It can't be.

It can't be.

The knot is too tight, and my fingers scrape open and bleed all over the threads of the rope, my hands, some even drips down my arm. But I keep trying, refusing to give up, because he's not gone. He just needs help. He wouldn't leave me. He loves me…

I stumble into the field and run across it, the dewy grass hissing at my legs and my bare feet scuff up dirt. I forgot to put on my shoes. I need to go back. No, I need to keep going forward. I need to keep running, moving, breathing.

I need to keep holding on to Landon.

I keep working on the rope until my arms grow tired and I can't feel my fingers or my heart—or anything. I lose track of time and where I am, and suddenly the sun is blinding and I realize that time is still moving, catching up with me as Landon's mom walks in and starts crying and screaming hysterically. Moments later his body comes down, and more hysteria builds. She manages to call an ambulance, and eventually the paramedics and police show up. They start asking me all these questions, and everyone is crying and watching as they examine me and dope me up on sedatives. But I can't say anything, because I can't remember—won't remember. How could I when I don't even know who I am anymore? The Nova I was is dead.

I stumble onto the tent area, dodging around the people, and pushing my way through the crowd. Everyone is staring at me and there are so many people. Some laugh at me, others step away. There are a few guys that grab at me, telling me profane things while they cop a feel. I hit at them, shout, but this only seems to encourage them, and for a second I can feel them dragging me down and I realize how alone I really am. That no one around here cares. That I'm just another lost soul that's lost her way, only I'm suddenly wanting to find my way back.

"Nova, no matter what happens, you'll never be alone in this world," my dad had said to me once. I'd gone through a weird phase where I wore different-colored socks and refused to comb my hair and no one wanted to be my friend. "You'll always have your mother and me."

But I'm alone now. By choice.

A guy grabs my ass and prods his fingers into my arm, saying, "Hey, sweetheart, slow down and try to relax. Don't be in such a hurry. Have some fun. I can show you some fun." He starts to jerk me forward, toward the people flocking to the stage, and so many people look out of it that I doubt that anyone will hear me if I scream. He keeps dragging me farther into the darkness and I know if I keep going, things are going to end up bad. I knee him in the thigh and then stab my nails into his skin.

"Let me go!" I scream. He staggers back, his feet scuffing the dirt as he comes back at me, looking pissed off, and he slaps me across the face hard. I choke on the impact and the blinding pain radiating across my cheek as I cup my face with my hand.

The guy swings his arm around to hit me again, but I run. I run and run and run, even when my legs feel like they're disconnecting from my body. Then I spot the purple tent. Delilah and Dylan are in front of it and they say something to me, but I have no idea what and I don't care. I run straight for my tent and collapse onto the sleeping bag, clutching my head as tears burn my eyes and streak my cheeks.

I want it out of my head. This moment. Every moment. I want it gone. I want to be gone. From the life I fell into. This place. But how the hell can I escape it when I can't even remember getting here? It's like I've lost track of the last year or maybe all the years. I want to go back when skipping in the rain was fun and all it took was ice cream to make me happy.

I just want simplicity. Direction. Understanding.

I want...I don't even know what I want. My head starts to race as I realize the painful truth of the revelation. I am lost. Broken. Searching for something that doesn't exist. What Landon did may never make sense because he's the only one who truly understands why he did it.

And he's gone. He's really, really gone. The rope was around his neck and he put it there and I couldn't save him. No matter what I do, nothing will change that. Not counting. Not making videos. Not getting high. Not wandering meaninglessly through life.

He's gone.

My mind continues to race until the anger, rage, pain, confusion, love, heartbreak—every piece of him and me builds up inside my chest like shards of jagged glass, cutting me from the inside. When I can't take the pain anymore, I open my mouth and let out an uncontrollable scream as I reach for my phone.

My fingers tremble as I turn it on and unlock the screen. Loud voices blare around outside along with the unbearably deafening sound of the music. My heart is thrashing inside my chest as my mind searches for numbers and control, but there's so much noise and I can't think straight. Everything around me and inside me is a mess, unstable, erratic like my pulse and my breathing. I can't think straight.

Then I click open the file, and with a faltering breath I hit Play. Seconds later the video clicks on and then everything becomes silent.

Chapter Nineteen

Nova

The song plays in the background, the one he had playing when I found him that day. The camera is angled crookedly, so his honey-brown eyes look like shadows; his inky black hair hangs over his forehead and only conceals his eyes more. I can barely note the pain in them, but it's there and it's radiating in his voice, more than I've ever heard.

The moonlight trickles through the window in the background, his skin hauntingly white, but in the most amazing way. He's beautiful sitting in front of the screen, like he sketched it himself, his final portrait. The heart-wrenching lyrics playing through the speakers only amplify the finality in the scene.

I hold my breath as I wait for him to say or do something, speak, or move, but he's still as a statue, staring at the screen, like he's trying to decipher me instead of me deciphering him. He's eerily calm, like he's sedated, and maybe he is. It's too dark to see if his eyes are bloodshot, and I'm not there to smell him. I wish I was, though. God, I wish I was.

Finally, he takes a breath. "I'm not sure who will watch this...whether anyone will or if it will be put away with the rest of my things...boxed up...shuffled away...forgotten." He shifts his weight in the chair, crossing his arms on the desk. "I'm not sure if I actually want anyone to watch it, either. I'm conflicted, like I am with everything else in my life." He pauses, and I can hear him breathing. I almost expect him to cry with how much repressed sadness is flowing out of him, but his eyes look dry. "I really did try. I promise I did...but I just couldn't do it anymore. The days...they just became too hard...waking up became too hard...I couldn't even numb the heaviness in me anymore...Not even with drugs..." He rakes his fingers through his hair, his breath trembling. "Life's just too heavy. Walking around, breathing, functioning, when I can't even find a point of doing it." He drops his hand on the desk. "There's just no point."

He drags his hand down his face, glancing around at his room, then he reaches over and turns the music down, but I can still hear it quietly haunting the background. "It feels like I'm living in this hole...this dark hole in the ground, and all I can do is stare at the same damn dirt walls every single day. And there's no point to it, but I have to do it because there's nothing else I can do." He inhales and then stridently exhales. "And then there's all this pain inside of me and I can't figure out how to turn it off. I keep waiting for it to turn off, but it just keeps getting worse...Everything does...God, I can't even remember the last time I fucking smiled for real." He shakes his head, muttering under his breath. "And Mom, if you do watch this, I know what you're thinking. You're blaming yourself because that's the kind of person that you are, but it's not your fault. My head is just seriously fucked up."

He taps his fingers nervously on the desk, studying the screen. "I really don't want to be here. I think about it every single day, the idea that maybe something will happen and I won't wake up and have to deal with the same goddamn weighted routine of my life, but it just never happens and I just keep walking around, lost. All the fucking time. There's nothing there inside me. And I just feel like I'm dragging everything—everyone—down around me, because I can't get past it. I can't find the will to smile and walk through life, pretending to be content with the heaviness on my shoulder, living in the same dark, goddamn hole forever."

He sucks in a deep breath and his voice drops to a soft, barely audible whisper. "Nova...beautiful, amazingly...wonderful...Nova. The one thing that was good in my life...I know you're going to watch this eventually, because that's the kind of person you are. You're strong...your dad died and you moved on, and me...I haven't even gone through anything that tragic and I've barely been hanging on for years." He pauses, his voice dropping even softer. "I love you. I really fucking do, even though I didn't want to. I didn't want to drag you into this mess, but I wasn't strong enough to stay away from you…I got too caught up in your smile, your kindness, the sound of your voice and your passion about life. Everything you did…" A small, distorted smile fleetingly reveals at his lips. "From playing the drums to knowing who you are…knowing what you want…It was amazing to watch everything you did with some freedom…You just did stuff and never overthought it. There's so much good in you…and it was the one thing that made living life just a little bit easier…"

He trails off and stares at the camera for the longest time. The song ends and then starts up again, playing on Repeat, and I can feel it in my heart, the moment where he's going to say his final words and then click off the camera. Leaving. Going. Dying. Giving up. He takes a deep breath and another, then reaches for the screen.

"Please just forgive me," he says. "I know you can…stay strong…move on…Please, please, forgive me."

Then the screen goes black.

Chapter Twenty

July 31, Day 73 of Summer Break

Nova

I'm not even sure how long I cry for. It feels like forever, but when I finally close my eyes, it's still dark outside. I surprisingly don't dream, at least nothing that I can remember, and I wake up in the morning with a splitting headache, puffy eyes, and swollen cheeks. But strangely the weight on my chest, the one I've been carrying since Landon left me, feels a tiny bit lighter. His last words echo in my head. *Please forgive me.* I hadn't even thought about it before. Not in those terms. Forgiving him. And how can I? How can I forgive him for leaving me? I'm not sure, but the Nova he described in the video sounded like she would. The good one, the one that smiled and was able to hang on even after her dad died. But this one, the Nova I am right now, can't hang on to anything.

An overwhelming homesick feeling wells up in the pit of my stomach, not just for my mom but also for my dad. He'd be so disappointed if he saw me now, and honestly, I feel kind of ashamed of myself. And so would Landon. Nothing about this place is making me happy, not even the music playing outside or the people I came here with.

I slept alone in the tent last night and I was angry, because Quinton just left me and I haven't seen him since. But I'm also relieved, because it allowed me time to cry alone. Not just over Landon, or the video, but over what I've become. I've been so afraid of everything. Afraid of living life without Landon. Afraid of moving on. Afraid to lose control, ever since that night, that I've made my whole life about controlling things and counting, yet I never had control, just an illusion of it. I'd used numbers and order to cover up everything in life, give myself a fake sense of stability, and not fully accept that Landon is gone and I'm going to have to move on without him. And not admitting the real problems out loud has broken me into fragments of a person that once use to be a good person, but now she's scattered all over the place. I'm sitting in a place that I don't understand and I don't think I ever really wanted to be here. I just fell into it and it only took me 73 days, 1,752 hours, 105,120 minutes to get here.

I smell like a Dumpster, my clothes are still muddy and stiff, and I shake dry dirt to the floor every time I shift my weight. I need a shower. I need a good meal. I need everything that this place can't offer.

I climb out of the sleeping bag, slip on a clean red tank top, a pair of shorts, and pull up my hair into a messy bun.

I rub some black stuff off my arm, and then douse myself with perfume before I exit the tent.

The sun seems really vivid today and stings at my eyes and my thoughts. There's a guy playing his guitar solo, his melodious voice carrying across the field, and the sound of it brings me a little bit of peace. But the people who surround me look rough and broken, muddy, wearing very little clothing; some have cuts and bruises on them like they got into a fight. *This isn't where I want to be.*

I open the cooler and take out a bottle of water. I twist the cap off and devour half of it in one gulp, letting out a sigh as I put the cap on. The chairs in front of the tent are empty, and when I tap my fingers on Dylan's and Delilah's tent no one responds.

I'm not really sure what my plans are. Who I should be. How I should move forward. Where I should go. But it seems like I should be doing anything else but standing in this exact spot. With the bottle of water in my hand, I start wandering around the outskirts of the field, zigzagging around the tents, searching for a familiar face but wondering if it's even possible to find one. I keep replaying what happened in the pond and the memory that's opened up inside me, even though I fought so hard to keep it hidden for the last year. I'd always been so afraid of the memory, fearing my reaction when I finally remembered that awful night. I feared almost everything about that night because I lost so much and I didn't want to accept it. But after watching the video, hearing his last words, the blunt truth is I'll have to finally accept that Landon is gone. He left this world forever. And now I need to find a way to forgive him and figure out my place in this world. Somehow. Do I want what's around me? The fake silence? Do I want to keep aimlessly searching for where to go next or finally figure it out?

The people around me are smoking and drinking, laughing and talking. They make it look so easy. Like just one drink or hit will take it all away. And it does. For a moment. But what about after? Then what?

I'm considering backtracking to the tent when I round the tailgate of a truck and there they all are. Quinton, Dylan, and Tristan all have their backs to me and on the other side of them are three guys; two that look really tall and one that looks shorter than me and has a bald head like Dylan, only his has tattoos all over it. Delilah's standing in the middle of them and she has her T-shirt knotted at the bottom so her stomach is showing and her shorts rolled up so high her ass is pretty much hanging out.

She's chatting to one of the taller guys who has dark brown hair, oily skin, and yellow-stained teeth, along with a goatee that stretches to his chest. She keeps laughing and smiling, throwing back her head in a flirty way, and I keep waiting for Dylan to get pissed and intervene, but he never does. Then she hands him something, a plastic bag, and the dots connect inside my head. They're dealing. I'm about to back away, when the shorter, rounder of the three guys notices me. His gaze sweeps across me, and anger masks his sore-covered face.

"Who the fuck is she?" he asks with a nod of his chin as he cracks his knuckles.

Suddenly they're all looking at me and I start to step back, wondering if I should walk or run away when Quinton's honey-brown eyes lock on me and I think of what he said to me at the pond. It's almost like he can see the old me, the part of me that I lost. I wonder how, though? How can he see the good?

I'm backing away, running away, when I stop in my tracks near the corner of the tent. I stare at the pain in his eyes, the dazed look that lets me know he's not himself, and the pure and utter torture that I still don't truly understand and I wonder if I ever will. *Did I ever really know him? Did he ever really know me? Will we ever really know each other? I'm not sure, but I think I need to find myself first.*

My feet long to go to him, but my mind has the upper hand this time, because it's as clear as the sky and suddenly I understand. At this moment in my life I can't help him, even though I want to so badly that it consumes my body and mind. I want to take his pain away, save him like I couldn't save Landon, but I'm not strong enough right now. I'm not the strong girl Landon talked about in the video. I wish I was, but I can barely hang on myself, let alone hold someone up with me. I'm understanding this now. I'm suddenly understanding a lot of things. It hurts to realize it and makes it hard to breathe, like my lungs are shrinking or maybe they're expanding and there's no more room left in my rib cage. Either way, I'm hyperventilating. I massage my hand over my chest, my heart aching as he stares at me, mystified. I look at the blue sky above us, the dirt below our feet, and a sea of people walking around, a sea we could easy get swept away into.

I'm sorry, I mouth.

He stares at me for a moment longer and I can't tell if he gets what I mean or not, but he nods once before turning away, and I think that maybe, just maybe, he knows what I mean.

"Hey, Nova," Tristan says, taking a step toward me. He nods his head to the side, indicating for me to walk away. "You should go."

I gladly turn around and walk off toward the tent. *One... two... three...*

"Nova, wait," Tristan says and moments later he grabs my arm, jerking me to a stop.

I slowly turn around to face him. He looks a little different, his pupils larger, his hair disheveled, and there are bags underneath his eyes. "I'm sorry," I say, wiggling my arm out of his grip. "I didn't know you guys were busy."

He shakes his head and then rakes his fingers through his blond locks. "You don't need to be sorry... it's just... it's just better if you weren't around... that." His voice sounds subdued and it seems like he's really struggling to move his lips.

"It's fine," I say. But it's not. Nothing is fine. *I don't want to be here anymore.*

"Yeah..." He bites on his lip, glancing over his shoulder, and then he ushers me forward, motioning his hands at me.

"Look, I remember you in high school and you weren't . . . you weren't like us . . ."

Us. Like we're two different breeds. But we're not. We're all just living a different path and seeing life differently—I'm seeing life differently. "I know, but it doesn't mean I was sheltered. I saw stuff." I turn my shoulder inward to squeeze through a truck and a tent. "I saw stuff all the time." *Where do I go from here?*

"Yeah, I know," he says, kicking a cooler out of his path and spilling a beer that was on top of it. "You were always hanging out with that guy that . . . died."

He did die. A while ago. But he's gone now. "His name was Landon," I say, pressing my hand to my chest. "Landon Evans." The world starts to spin, but it's a good spin. A natural spin and I let it be. *Please, forgive me.*

When we reach the tent, I sit down in one of the chairs, watching the crowds, and listening to the music as it flows over the field. At one point I shut my eyes and bask in the freeness of the vocals, tapping my foot to the beat of the drum, remembering what it was like to play, when Landon would watch me with almost a smile on his face and I felt happy inside. I let the sound own me, take me over, and pull me back in a direction I was running away from.

Tristan sits down beside me, and he instantly starts smoking something that smells strange and makes the air just a little bit hotter. The longer it goes on, the more droopy his eyes get, and the more he looks like he's going to sink into the ground and vanish from the world.

I don't want to watch him. I don't want to be here. *I want to go home.*

I sit there, listening to the song, remembering what it was like when I would sit and listen to music with Landon and we'd talk about life and what we'd do when we got older, where we'd go, who we'd become. But that's gone now, and I need to accept that.

Please, forgive me.

"If you could be anything in the world," Landon had once asked me, "what would you be?"

"A drummer," I'd replied easily. "How about you?" I'd thought I'd known his answer. An artist. How could he say anything else?

He'd thought about it forever and finally sighed. "I have no idea. Maybe I wouldn't be anything. Maybe I'd just follow you around to concerts and carry your drumsticks."

I'd laughed at the time, because it seemed so silly, but thinking about it now, I start to cry. We could have been great together. Perfect. We could have been a lot of things, but now we can't be anything other than memories.

"Here," Tristan says, urging the burning cigarette at me as he watches the tears freely rolling down my cheeks. "You want a hit? It'll calm you down."

I stare at the joint and then back at him. Do I want a hit? Do I want this life? Is this the road I'm choosing to go down?

I shake my head, and then get to my feet. "No thanks." I start to back around the chair toward the tent.

"Where are you going?" he asks, with the joint positioned between his lips and smoke masking his face.

I shake my head, backing up to the tent. "I'm not sure." I duck into the tent, grab my phone, and then climb back out. Tristan's heading into the crowd, and I think about chasing him down and saying good-bye. I think about telling Delilah that I'm going. I think about telling Quinton I'm sorry.

But instead I head toward the road, the sun blazing at my back, the clear sky above me, focusing only on myself and the path ahead. I take it step by step, letting myself count, because that's what I need to do for the moment, but telling myself that I'll work on breaking the habit when I can. It's the first time I've admitted aloud that it's a habit, and it's liberating and gives me a sense of peace, and in the end, I run.

I run all the way to the restaurant where Quinton and I had breakfast and he let me cry on his chest. By the time I reach the front door, I'm dripping in sweat and I have no idea how long it took me to get here. But I'm still breathing and my heart's still beating.

When I enter, it's pretty much empty. I sit down and order a coffee, and the waitress looks at me like I've just climbed out of a Dumpster. But she's polite and brings me a coffee along with a piece of pie and says it's on the house, and I wonder if she thinks I'm a homeless person.

Eating the pie, I take out my phone and call the one person I know will always be there for me. It rings three times and then she answers.

"Nova, what's wrong?" she says, worried, and I can tell she's been crying. "I've been trying to call you for the last few days, and you haven't answered your phone." She starts going off on a rant, but I stop her in the middle of it.

"Mom, I'm sorry," I say, wiping the tears from my eyes. "And I want to come home."

She asks me a billion questions when I tell her where I am, but in the end she tells me she's coming right now and that she loves me. We hang up and I sit in the booth staring at the trees outside, and sipping the coffee. Eventually, I take my phone out again. At first I just stare at my reflection in the screen. I look terrible. Plain and simple. Pale skin. Big, bloodshot eyes. My brown hair is matted, and there are scratches on my forehead from when I fell in the trees and a bruise on my cheek. It's like I've altered into this monster over the last few months, and I'm just now noticing the change.

I flip the camera on and clear my throat, preparing to make my final video. "I'm not really sure when I look back at these clips if they'll mean anything to me or if I'll even remember anything of what happened, just like I'll probably look back to this day and wonder why I decided to leave, other than I finally watched the video and Landon's words spoke to me. I woke up and finally saw what things really were. I could close down all I wanted, lock who I am out, shut down all the things that happened with Landon…the good and the bad… but in the end they did happen. Just like this moment. Just like this breath I'm taking. Stuff happens. We get lost. We try to control what will happen. We give up. We do things that don't make sense. We search for things in the wrongest of ways. We lose our way, but sometimes, if we're really, really strong, we manage to find our way back."

I summon a deep breath and put the phone away. Then I rest my head onto the table and quickly fall asleep as the last two months smash down on me.

Chapter Twenty~One

Aug 20, Day 103 of Summer Break

Nova

I've heard about revelations before, when people's eyes open up, and suddenly everything becomes crystal clear. I wouldn't necessarily call what I had a revelation because everything isn't crystal clear, but I do see things in a different light, or maybe it's just that I see the light, like the darkness I've kept inside me is dissolving. Looking back, it was Landon's video that finally opened my eyes. It was painful and heartbreaking to watch, but it made me realize so many things, like how he saw me and how he wanted my forgiveness. I'd never thought to forgive him—I hadn't even realized I was angry with him, not really, anyway. I kept holding on to him, not accepting the whole-hearted truth, knowing he was gone but letting go and moving on. I was so lost and unsure of who I was, because I didn't want to be anything without him. But watching him talk about me like that, saying I was strong, made me want to be strong. Be the person that he was talking about.

The first week at home was pure and utter hell. Everything everyone said annoyed the shit out of me, and I felt like jabbing their eyes out. I yelled at my mom. I yelled at Daniel. I yelled at the mailman because he rang the doorbell and it woke me up from my nap.

Then came the tears. There were a lot. In fact, I was pretty sure they'd never turn off. I'm not even sure why, other than it felt like I was a vampire stepping into the light for the first time, and my skin and brain were on fire and nothing seemed to take away the pain.

But then my mom and I started to talk. We talked about my dad. We talked about Landon. We talked about me. We talked about what I did. We talked and talked and talked. She got angry and I cried. She cried and I cried.

"Nova," she said through tears. "I feel like this is all my fault. I knew when your father died...how he died...that you saw it, that it had to be hard for you, but I never forced you to talk about it with me. I only suggested it."

"But I couldn't talk about it with you," I'd replied, hugging a pillow against my chest, balled up on the bed. "You were sad yourself."

"I'm your mother," she said, smoothing my hair away from my forehead, like I was still a little kid, and maybe at the moment to her I was. Maybe we were going back in time and

323

doing what we should have done to begin with. "It's my job to make sure you're okay, even if I'm hurting."

"I didn't want to make you hurt more."

"That's not how it works. If anything we should have hurt together."

We started to cry again, and it seemed like we were never going to stop, but finally, like almost everything always eventually does, our tears faded.

It's been over a month since I ran away from the concert, and my head is a lot clearer than it's been in a very long time, maybe even since my dad died. It's strange, but it took all this time for me to realize just how hazy things had gotten. Somehow, through Landon's death, through wrangling the mourning, through life, I lost my way. I'm still working my way back from it, one baby step at a time, trying to heal myself correctly this time.

I managed to take out the sketches Landon's parents gave to me and let myself cry without running away from them. They really were beautiful sketches, and it hurts to think that his talent doesn't exist anymore, but I have a piece of his talent still—a piece of him—and I'll always hold on to it. I've finally accepted his death, and it's good to remember him in healthy doses. I'm learning that it's okay. It's okay to hurt. It's okay to cry. It's okay to admit when we need help. It's okay to let go.

Not everything is easy and perfect, though. I still need my anxiety medication. I still find myself counting sometimes. I still get lost in memories of Landon. The key is letting it pass instead of searching for a quick Off switch. I feel it, I move with it, and then I move past it.

And I don't have to move past it alone. I've been going to a group where people can talk about loss, specifically related to suicide. It helps to hear stories, to know I'm not the only one to wonder so much that it nearly cracked my head open. I plan on going to one when I'm back at school. I've also finally picked a major. Film. I'm still not one hundred percent sure if I want to stick with it, but it's a start to working on some of my goals or at least setting them. I also might do a minor in music, but I'm taking it one step at a time now. I'm focusing on moving forward and slowly accepting the past, getting better, and trying to create a future. And I know I'll be able to because I want to. And just like my dad told me once: if you want something bad enough, anything's possible.

I haven't talked to Quinton since I left. Delilah stopped by my house a few times, but we're no longer on the same page, and I'm not strong enough to bring her up with me, nor can I fall with her. She's not going back to school, something she disclosed during her third visit.

"I'm happy here," she'd said while we sat on the living room couch. My mom wouldn't let us go into my room, afraid of what we'd do behind closed doors, and I was okay with that. I'm afraid of closed doors, too.

"I don't think you should stay," I'd said, noting how thin she was starting to look. "There's nothing here, really."

"There's Dylan. And my life," she replied snippily. "And that matters to me."

Her pupils were wide and shiny, and she had this funny smell to her. She's also chopped her hair off and her skin was a little pallid. I could tell she was on something, and that the person sitting in front of me was not the Delilah I met back in high school. This was her alter ego. A darker side of her. A reflection in a cracked mirror.

"Okay," I said, knowing I had to let her go, but it was hard. "But if you change your mind, I leave on Friday and you can come with me."

"I won't." She got up from the couch, left my house, and I haven't seen her since.

"Are you sure you just don't want to stay home for a semester?" my mom asks, carrying out the last of the boxes, the one that carries my drumsticks. I'm taking the pink drums back to school with me, even though I haven't played them again yet. I'm planning on it, though, when it feels right.

"Are you seriously trying to talk me into dropping out of school?" I joke, tossing a section of my drums onto the leather backseat of the cherry-red Nova. I'm driving it back to school, which is scary, but it's one of my goals. Besides, it's what my dad wanted.

She sighs, pushing the trunk closed. "No, but I worry." She walks up to me, with her arms crossed, like she's resisting the urge to grab me and haul me back into the house. "I feel like I just got you back and now you're leaving me again."

I hug her, and I mean really hug her, without fear or restraint. "I know, but it's a good thing, Mom. It's...it's my way of moving on."

"I know, Nova," she hugs me tightly to the point that I can barely breathe. "And I'm proud of you for admitting everything to me. Whether you think so or not, you're a brave person." She pulls back and looks me in the eyes. "Not many people can admit they're heading down the wrong path."

"But doesn't it kind of make me weak for even going down the path?" I ask, blinking against the bright sunlight, refusing to shield my eyes from it.

She shakes her head. "We all do stuff that isn't great. You've been through a lot...a lot more than most. And the important thing is you pulled yourself out of it." Tears start to bubble up in the corners of her blue eyes. "I'm just glad to have my daughter back."

Not completely, but I'm working on it, and that's the impor-tant part. "I love you too, Mom."

She embraces me in a hug, and it's hard to get her to let me go, but ultimately she does and I get into the car, and she heads into the house. I take a deep breath, buckle my seat belt, and then reach for my phone in my pocket.

I hold the phone up to my eye level and then hit Record.

"In a sense it kind of seems like I'm starting over, like it's freshman year again." I roll my eyes, but then smile, and it's a real smile, not the fake, plastic ones I've been using for the last year. "Because I was so out of it last year, I could barely comprehend what was going on. But now I'm ready to embrace what lies ahead of me instead of drifting through it. I don't want to drift. That broken, lost, wandering, searching-for-something-that-will-never-exist-again Nova is not who I want to be. And while I don't know exactly who I am, the important part is that I'm focusing on discovering it in a healthy way."

I smile, and it brightens up the whole screen. "Hopefully the next video I make, I'll have more." I pause, taking a deep breath. "Now I just need to make one more stop, because if I've learned anything, good-byes are important, even if they're scary and awkward. Always, always, say good-bye."

I click off the camera and put it away, heading down the driveway with one thought in my mind.

Time to let go and move forward.

༄

When I pull up to the trailer park, it takes me a moment to gather myself together and find the strength to get out of the car. My first instinct is to start counting all the cracks in the house, the buckets in front of the fence, the broken windows. But I calm myself down and remind myself that I need to do this; otherwise I'll regret it.

I get out, walk through the gate, and trot up the steps to the front door. I smooth down my hair, tug the bottom of my shorts down, and adjust one of the fallen straps on my shirt. Then I raise my hand and knock on the door.

There's a lot of banging going on inside the house, along with laughter, and I can also hear music. I knock again, louder, and a few moments later the door swings open.

"What the fuck are you doing here?" Dylan asks. He looks different, thinner, paler, grungier, with sunken eyes, and sores all over his face, and his shaved head almost looks wrinkly. "Do you want to talk to Delilah or something?"

I shake my head, crossing my arms over my chest, telling myself that I'm okay. *Everything is okay.* "No, I want to talk to Quinton."

He rolls his eyes, annoyed, and then opens the door wider. Smoke spills out like poison vapor and I'm not sure whether I hate the scent or miss it. "He's in his room."

I take a step back toward the stairs, knowing that until I can hate the scent, I need to stay away. "Can you go get him?" I ask as politely as I can.

He cusses under his breath, his face reddening, and I think he's going to slam the door in my face. But then he says, "Hang on."

He leaves the door open, and I catch a glimpse of the people inside, doing things that want to pull me in. I take another step back, continuing until I reach the bottom of the stairs. Then I sit down on the step and wait for him. The music keeps bumping, vibrating against the ground, and I hear someone shout something about everyone taking their clothes off and it's echoed by cheering. I want to leave, but I need to do this.

Wait for him.

Seconds later, I hear his voice, and it makes my heart leap inside my chest. "Nova, what are you doing here?"

I turn around, preparing myself to see him again, but it still impacts me more than I hoped. He looks different, too, thinner, paler, and his jawline is scruffy and unshaven. His hair has grown out a little and is sticking up all over his head. But his eyes are still the same honey-brown-tinted red and overflowing with sorrow.

I get to my feet and brush off the dirt from the backs of my legs. "I came to say good-bye."

He smashes his lips together as he hesitates at the top of the steps. He doesn't have a shirt on, and his jeans hang loose at his waist. I can see his muscles are diminishing and not as firm as the last time I saw him, and the tattoos on his arms: *Lexi, Ryder,* and *no one,* along with the scar he never told me about, either. One day, if I ever see him again, I'll have to get him to tell me what they mean and where the scar came from, when we're both in a different place and can handle it. I want to be there for him, and help him with whatever he's going through, but I have to heal myself first before I can be a good support system.

"Look," he starts, taking a step onto the stairs. "About what happened—"

I shake my head, holding my hand up, and cutting him off. "We don't need to talk about that right now. I'm just headed back to school and I wanted to say good-bye and to make sure that you understood something."

His forehead creases as he steps down another stair. "Okay..."

I've been preparing what I was going to say to him for a couple of weeks, when I realized what I needed—wanted. But standing here in front of him, it's hard. But I'm going to do it.

"I know I've been kind of screwed up," I say, tipping my chin up to meet his eyes. "And I still am kind of screwed up and trying to figure out everything that happened over the summer...It feels kind of like a daze, you know." I pause. "But I'm glad I met you...you kind of made me realize a lot of stuff."

He scratches his head, glancing around like he has no idea what the hell is going on. "Nova, I don't get what you're saying."

"I'm not really saying anything," I explain the best way I know how. But in the end, I don't know if it makes sense, because nothing about us made sense, except for the fact that we were falling together. "Other than good-bye."

His expression softens and he steps in front of me. He looks me over, from head to toe, like he's trying to decipher who I am. "You look good," he finally says. "Different, but good."

"I feel good," I say, and for once it feels like the truth. "And different."

He sighs and I release a breath, then suddenly we're hugging each other. He's a little resistant, his muscles stiff, but I help him out, wrapping my arms firmly around him. Closing

331

my eyes, I breathe him in, unsure if I'll ever see him again, but hoping. Maybe. One day. When I'm in a different place.

"I'm sorry," he whispers in my ear. "For everything."

I shake my head with my cheek pressed against his chest. "You don't need to be sorry. Everything I did was my choice."

"Still—"

"Still nothing," I say. "Nothing was your fault."

He stills, his pulse thudding inside his chest. We hold on to each other, until my arms grow heavy and then I know it's time to go, otherwise I might not. I pull back first and offer a smile as I back away to the car.

"If you're ever in Idaho, look me up," I say, waving as I reach the gate.

He nods, but it doesn't look like he thinks he'll see me again. "Okay, I will."

"And take care of yourself," I tell him, which seems like a really silly, cliché thing to say, but it's all I can say right now. If I said meaningful things, like that I care for him, loved kissing him, that my heart aches that I'm leaving him, that I wish it were another time in our lives when we met so we could be together, then it'd be harder to leave. Because even though it's hard, I need to go and heal.

He smiles, but it's forced, unreal, sad, and I want to cry for him. "Yeah, you too." He watches me all the way to the car and when I'm about to climb in, he calls out, "So you finally decided to drive the car."

I swallow hard, nod, and open the gate. "Yeah, it seemed like it was time."

Nodding, he lets out a breath, and starts toward the door. "Take care of yourself, Nova, like the car." A touch of a smile appears on his face.

"I will," I return his smile, and then I climb into the car and back away, gripping the steering wheel as I watch him slip farther away.

He watches me until I'm just about out of sight, then he turns around and walks into the house. And I keep driving. I'm ready. Moving forward, I'm ready to start moving on.

Quinton

I'm happy for her. She looks good. More than good. She looks happy. It's amazing to see, and it makes me wonder how she got to that place after everything, but I don't want to ask her, fearing I'll ruin it for her.

After she took off from the concert, I knew we'd never be anything. It was good she ran away, and I made sure to keep my distance, even though it hurt not to see her. I miss the sound of her rare laugh, her smile, her random thoughts, her love for music, her smell, the way she feels. But she's better off without me.

I watch her drive away, knowing I'll never see her again. I wish I could have kissed her one last time, a real kiss, one that wasn't diluted by drugs and guilt. But I know it's not possible, and when she drives out of my sight, I head back to the reality of my life.

Dylan has a bunch of customers over, although only half of them end up paying, the others pretending like they're just sampling his stuff. It's part of my life now. He makes the arrangements, Tristan and I deliver for him, and then we get high, pass out, and start the whole process of falling all over again. The vicious, repetitive circle of my life. But I don't deserve anything more.

"Are you going to fucking go with us?" Dylan asks, as I head back toward the curtain. He's sitting on the couch with Delilah, but she's passed out on his lap, and he's flirting with another girl.

I nod, drawing the curtain back. "Yeah, I just got to put a shirt on."

"You should keep it off," some girl yells from the kitchen. She's smoking a joint, and I think her name is Candy or Kitty or something. Honestly, it could be Brenda. I really don't remember her other than I slept with her a few times and we shared a few lines, then talked about shit that doesn't matter, even though we pretended it did.

I ignore her and go back to my pathetic little room that reminds me of what I've become. I put a shirt on and slip on some shoes. Then I pick up my sketchbook, glancing at the last picture I'll ever draw. It was created from memory, images I hate but needed to get out. Each line is heavy, like I was trying to cut through the paper with my pencil. It's of Lexi and me lying side by side in the field beside the accident. We're holding hands and bleeding out together—dying together. It's perfect. It's real. And it's where I'll always belong.

I let out a deep breath, shut the sketchbook, and tuck it away in a box next to the dresser. I'm about to walk out of my room, when Tristan walks in carrying a mirror with a white line of powder running across it and a razor in his hand. My hands instantly itch to hold it, my mouth salivating to taste it.

"You're going to need this," he says, urging it at me. His eyes are pretty much popping out of his head, and his nose is a little red and running. "We have a long night ahead of us."

I snatch the mirror and immediately take what he offers me, not because I need to stay awake, but because I want it. Need it. It's embedded into my skin, my blood, my veins, my thoughts, my dreams. It's my life.

It owns me now.

Once it hits the back of my throat, all the doors in my head slam shut and any good left in me is locked behind them.

Epilogue

Nine months later...

May 9, 7 days before Summer Break

Nova

I'm supposed to be packing up the last of my stuff in my apartment, getting ready to head home for summer, while I work on the last of my finals, but I've taken a break to pound on my drums. I do it almost every day now, and I'm finding it therapeutic.

"Do you mind! The neighbors are going to call the landlord again if you keep it up!" my friend and roommate, Lea, calls out. I bang on the drums a little harder, teasing her, and she rolls her eyes and laughs. "Fine, be a bitch."

I laugh, hitting one more note, and then set the drumsticks down. I'm sweating and panting, but I feel so alive inside. Catching my breath, I climb off the stool and head over to a half-packed box on my bed. It's strange to be going back home, since the last time I was there I was in such a different place than I am now. But it'll be good to see my mom again and even Daniel, granola bars and all.

"Are you sure you don't want to take this with you?" my friend Lea asks as she holds up an old band poster of Chevelle.

I nod, tucking the last of my CDs away into a box on my bed. "Yeah, it's all torn and ripped."

She rolls her heavily lined eyes and drops it into the trash can next to the shelf. "Okay, if that's what you want."

"It's what I want," I tell her, clicking my computer on as I sit down on the floor in front of it.

I met Lea at one of the meetings I'd been attending for people who have lost loved ones to suicide. Lea lost her dad when she was about twelve, strangely around the same time as I lost my dad. That was our initial conversation starter, but we hit it off really quickly, and it's nice to have someone I can openly talk to about my feelings of Landon's suicide; the hurt, the anger, the guilt, the feeling of being lost and confused. She's felt the same things too, only she handled it in a different, healthier way.

In the beginning stages of our friendship, she gave me hope that I could move on, and now she's just there for me. We've been friends for about six months now, and it's a good friendship, one not based on drunken outings, heavy drugs, drifting. We share a lot of things in common, like a love for music and a good documentary. She plays guitar and her boyfriend sings. They're fun to hang out with, and we all volunteer to help out at the local suicide hotline. It's nice to do something good. Help people. We also laugh. A lot.

I've even been on a few dates, but haven't really felt the spark or connection with anyone. That's okay, though. I have time. And it's nice to know that I do.

Not everything is always easy, though. There are dark moments, when I get overwhelmed, and I start to count and crave the silent solitude that I experienced last summer. But it always passes. And it's happening less frequently. I know what I want in life. I want happiness. I want hope. I want a life. And that's important. I consider myself lucky for being able to get where I am. It's not easy and not everyone makes it. Some people stay in the dark and some people leave it a different, more permanent way, while I managed to step into the light again.

"Are you still working on that?" she asks, gathering her long black hair into a side ponytail. She's wearing an old T-shirt with "Music Rocks my World" written on the back, and a pair of denim shorts. She's tall and has a few tattoos. Each one means something to her, and every time I see one of them, it always makes me wonder about Quinton's tattoos. "You know it's due in four days."

"I know." I move the cursor to the videos folder on the home screen. I've watched the videos time and time again, and it's scary watching how much I changed over the course of two and a half months. In the end, I barely looked like me, and I never want to go back to that place again. "I think I might end up taking a zero on it, though."

I really want to use the clips for the final, even if it means showing the world what I was once because I feel like it's important for people to see. And there's one video I really want to use; the one I made of Quinton. I watch it all the time, wondering what he's doing, thinking. It feels like I'm finally in a point in my life where I can talk to him again.

Lea sits down on the floor beside me, crisscrossing her legs, and resting back on her palms. "If you take the zero, you're going to fail the class."

I sigh, clicking the folder. "I know, but I can't use the video without a signed release form. Professor's rules."

"Then get his permission," she answers, reaching for her purse. She takes out a pack of gum and pops a piece into her mouth.

"I've tried." I reach for the computer's Off button. "I have tried. A lot. But I never did get his number, and I've yet to be able to track his phone number down. I've tried to call Delilah a few times, but it always sends me straight to voice mail. I even sent my mom over to the trailer, but she said it was vacant, so apparently they moved somewhere else. It's like that whole part of my life didn't even exist, like it never really happened. But it did, and I remind myself every day that it did, because it's important to remember how easy it is to lose track of myself and just how lucky I am that I made it out. But I can't find him anywhere. It's like he's disappeared off the face of the earth."

"He didn't disappear off the face of the earth," she says. "You could try calling that...old friend of yours again." Lea knows all about Delilah and she's not a fan. I think she blames some of the stuff that I went through on her, but I don't blame

Delilah for anything. Everything I did was my own choice. No one forced me.

Sighing, I scoop my phone off my bed. "Yeah, I guess I can, even though I've left her a ton of voice mails already."

She shrugs. "It can't hurt to try."

"No, it can't." I press Delilah's number on my phone and then hold it up to my ear. I wait and wait and I'm about to hang up, when suddenly there's a click.

"Hello," Delilah says from the other side. There's loud music playing in the background and a lot of banging and yelling.

"Hey, it's me," I tell her. "Nova."

"Who!" she shouts. "Hold on! Let me go somewhere quiet." There's a pause and then I try to wait patiently. The noise gradually fades and finally it goes quiet. "There we go," she says and I can tell by the slur in her speech that she's high or drunk. "Now who the hell is this?"

"It's Nova," I tell her, shaking my head. Lea is watching me with worry and I hold up my finger, stepping out of the room. I head to the sliding glass door and step out onto the back deck and into the sunlight. "Nova, the girl you used to be friends with."

"Oh." She lets out a giggle. "I'm sorry, I'm a little out of it, but now I remember."

I take a deep breath, reminding myself that I've been in that place where nothing matters. "Hey, I just wanted to see if you knew where Quinton was," I tell her, leaning my elbows onto the railing, praying she can remember who he is.

"Yeah, he's with me," she replies, and I hear the flick of a lighter. I wonder what she's smoking or where she even is. "Well, he's actually in the house right now. Not outside with me."

"But he lives with you." I'm shocked. "Are you...are you guys dating?"

"No...we just share an apartment...with Dylan. You remember him, right?" She inhales and then releases a strong exhale, coughing at the end.

"Yeah, I remember," I say, disappointed that she's still with him. I shift my weight, rotating my back to the railing, and inclining against it. "Look, can you put him on the phone. I really need to talk to him."

"I can't right now," she says, coughing again. "He's passed out in his room. He's totally crashing right now."

I press my hand against my chest, telling myself to take deep breaths. Nothing changes. Oh my God, my heart hurts so much. "Can you please just go try and wake him up? It's important."

"He won't wake up," she assures me. "Not after being up for like three days."

"Why? What was he on?" I hold my breath, scared, nervous, and I don't even know what else. So many emotions are racing through me simultaneously at the moment, and I need to get control again, but not with numbers. I take a deep breath and then another.

"Some really fucking good crystal," she says with envy in her tone, letting out a euphoric grunt at the end.

"*Crystal meth.*" I'm stunned. Horrified. I struggle for air. "Why would he do that?"

"Why do we all do it?" she asks and then starts to chatter on, the speed of her voice picking up with each word. "Because we're running away from stuff. Me, my mom…and Dylan, well there's so much with him. Although, Quinton has it the worst, you know. Killing his girlfriend and cousin like that in that fucking car accident." She sucks in a sharp breath, talking so quickly I can barely interpret what she's saying. "Plus he died himself. Jesus, to die and then live after that with all those deaths on your hands…Crystal is his sanctuary."

A lump the size of a baseball forms inside my throat as I recollect Quinton's tattoos. *Lexi* and *Ryder. No one.* Is that what it meant? Is *no one* Quinton? I'm choking. I stop breathing. I can't remember how to get air into my lungs. I grip onto the railing, feeling like I'm going to fall over.

"Oh my God," I say, breathless as memories of Quinton rapidly flip through my head. "All that time I spent with him and I didn't know."

Everything is starting to make sense. All the anguish and guilt in his eyes…how he always looked so depressed. The scar on his chest and how Tristan threw the driving thing in his face. He was carrying this all inside of him, the deaths, his own death. Even with everything I've been through, I couldn't even imagine.

"That's because you didn't care enough to know," Delilah

says venomously. "You know he broke even more when you left him—left us."

"I left for a reason." For a moment I feel guilty, but then I remember that there was nothing I could have done at the time. I was in my own dark place, falling myself, and trying to stop myself from crashing along with someone else wasn't impossible. It takes strength to rise back up, strength in yourself and from those around you. I didn't have that at the time. But now I do. Now it feels like I could try to help him climb back up instead of fall with him. But I know better than to try to do it alone.

"Delilah, where are you?" I ask. "You're not still living in Maple Grove, are you?"

"No, we moved . . . had to get away from that stupid, judging town, you know," she says simply, and then I hear someone's voice in the background. "Look, I gotta go. It was nice talking to you."

"Delilah, please don't hang up," I say, but it's too late. The line goes dead. I try to call her back multiple times, but each time it goes to voice mail. "Shit." I slide the glass door open and hurry back to my room.

"I need your help," I tell Lea as I rush in, trying not to panic, but it's difficult. "With something really important."

She nods without question. "You know I'm always here for you."

"Thank you." I take a deep breath, knowing she means it. And I'm glad. It's going to help me through this because I'm going to find Quinton and help him, like I wish I had been able to a year ago.

I just hope that I'm not too late. That the small glimpses of the caring, good, thriving Quinton that I saw still exist. The one that made me smile when I thought it was impossible. The one that tried to talk me out of drugs because he thought I was too good. I hope that the sadness in his eyes hasn't entirely taken over.

I hope he's not lost completely.

Nova Reed can't forget him — Quinton Carter, the boy who made her realize she deserved more than an empty life. But Quinton is out there somewhere, sinking deeper. She's determined to find him and help him . . . . before it's too late.

See the next page for a preview of the next book in the Breaking Nova series,

Saving Quinton

Quinton

I wake up every morning feeling content. Blissfully, numbingly content, without worry or being haunted by my fucked-up past. At least after I take my first hit. Once I get the taste of that bitterly sweet, toxic, white powder, I'm good to go for days. The guilt that I carry around in me briefly dies with each drip of the white, poisonous powder, along with a part of me.

And I'm glad.

I want to be dead.

And I'm working on getting there, one tiny, wonderful, mind-numbing line at a time.

After a night of struggling to shut my eyes, seeking sleep, but never getting there, I finally climb out of bed. I've been going for days, strung out on line after line, my eyes bulging out of my head, my body and mind so tense and worn out from the energy overload.

I grab a pair of ripped, faded jeans from off the chipped linoleum floor of my bedroom that's the size of a closet. None of the apartment has carpet or painted walls or a ceiling without stains on it. My bedroom consists of a shitty mattress on the floor, a box with stuff of my past that I never look at anymore, a lamp, and a mirror and razor that's always within reach.

I pick up the mirror from off the floor and then the empty plastic bag next to it. I must have finished it off last night... although I can barely remember doing it.

"Shit," I mutter, wiping my finger along the mirror's nearly dry surface, and then lick my finger clean. It doesn't do anything for the hungry monster waking up inside of me, and I toss the mirror across the room, watching it shatter. "Dammit." I snatch a shirt from off the floor and pull it on as I hurry out into the hall, tripping over a few people sleeping on the floor, none of whom I know, but they always seem to be around.

I reach the door at the end of the hall, and try to open it but it's locked, so I hammer my fist against it. "Tristan, open up the fucking door... I need some now."

There's no response, and I bang on the door harder until the weak wood starts to cave beneath my fist. Finally, I can't take it anymore. The need to feed the starving, irrational, unstable monster becomes too much, and I ram my shoulder into the door. With each force, I see the images of the people I lost; Lexi, Ryder, my mom I never met. And then at the end of it, I always see Nova's eyes that look blue at first unless you look close enough to see the green hidden in them. I don't know why I see her. It's not like I lost her. She's still alive and out there somewhere in the world, hopefully happy. But for some reason I can't stop thinking about her. Well, at least until I get my dose of fake bliss, then all I'll be thinking about is where to channel the burst of energy.

Finally, the door caves and I stumble into the room. Tristan's passed out on the mattress, a girl lying beside him with her arm draped over his chest. Beside the mattress is a spoon and a needle, but I don't go for it. It's not my thing, not what I want. No, what I want is in his top dresser drawer.

I rush over to it, the faces of everyone I lost surrounding me, the memories of them pounding at my skull. I see Lexi dying on the side of the road, soaked in her own blood, because of me. I see the life I never had with my mother, the look in Tristan's eyes whenever he mentions Ryder. Then I see Nova in that goddamn pond, where I ultimately left her. I see her face at the concert when see sees me dealing and then when she's getting in her car, ready to drive away and leave me forever.

The last time I saw her.

And that's how it should be. She should be away from me and this mess that's supposed to be a life, when really it's just me being too much of a pussy to fully give up.

I jerk open the dresser drawer and take out the plastic bag, my hands shaking as I open it. I don't even bother looking for a mirror. I need it now, and so I dump a thin line out on top of the dresser. My heart is thrashing in my chest, noisy and obnoxious, and I wish it would shut the hell up, because I don't want it making any noise at all.

Taking an unsteady deep breath, I lean down, suck in, and allow the white powder to fill up my nose and drip down my throat. My heart speeds up, but somehow it becomes quieter— everything does—as it coats my body with its poison and instantly kills all thoughts of Lexi, Ryder, my mom, and Nova. It kills everything.

sphere

To buy any of our books and to find out
more about Sphere and Little, Brown Book Group,
our authors and titles, as well as events and
book clubs, visit our website

www.littlebrown.co.uk

and follow us on Twitter

@LittleBrownUK
@LittleBookCafe
@TheCrimeVault

To order any Sphere titles p & p free in the UK,
please contact our mail order supplier on:

+ 44 (0)1832 737525

Customers not based in the UK should contact
the same number for appropriate postage
and packing costs.

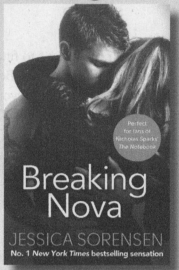
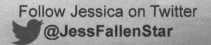